Bring me back! he shouted with all his might, straining until he felt something nearly snap within him.

Noel hit the ground with a thump. Lightning ripped the sky overhead, and with a start he came fully conscious, finding himself in the darkness of the night with a rainstorm lashing about him, wind howling in his ears, thunder crashing overhead, lightning illuminating a stark, unknown world of boulder and crag. He was cold, drenched to the skin, and the earth beneath him was shaking.

Out of the night came a group of horsemen. Flashes of lightning strobed off upraised swords and metal helmets. He had one split-second glimpse of a horse coming at him before it knocked him aside. Sheer instinct made Noel grab the reins to save himself from being trampled.

The rider swung at him with his sword. Noel could not dodge it, and only luck and perhaps the darkness put the flat of the sword to him instead of the edge. He felt a sickening drop beneath him. He slid on his back, scooping ice-cold mud down the neck of his tunic. He had time to realize he wasn't in Constantinople . . .

TIME∞TRAP

Ace Books by Sean Dalton

TIME∞TRAP

Operation StarHawks Series

TIME TRAP

SEAN DALTON

ACE BOOKS, NEW YORK

TIME∞TRAP

An Ace Book / published by arrangement with
the author

PRINTING HISTORY
Ace edition / March 1992

ISBN: 0-441-81256-2

Ace Books are published by The Berkley Publishing Group,
200 Madison Avenue, New York, New York 10016.
The name "ACE" and the "A" logo
are trademarks belonging to Charter Communications, Inc.

PRINTED IN THE UNITED STATES OF AMERICA

10 9 8 7 6 5 4 3 2 1

This book is dedicated
to Jack Catlin,
and the rest of the gang
who stood with me
on the ramparts.

PROLOGUE

"You're late," said the traitor.

"What is the code phrase?"

"We won't have enough time to accomplish everything."

"What is the code phrase?"

Feeling slightly ridiculous, the traitor sucked in a breath and replied, "Freedom or death."

The shadow vaguely outlined in the darkness gave the countersign: "Unless we are willing to squander lives, there can be no freedom."

The traitor frowned. The propaganda these anarchists spouted made him uneasy. But they had offered him more money than he could refuse. His debts, his *needs,* made him vulnerable.

"Very well," he whispered. He took off his identity badge and inserted it into the first set of security doors locking the Time Institute. As he led the shadow down a silent corridor, his own heartbeat thumping in his ears, he told himself that had the Institute remained strictly concerned with historical research according to its original specifications, he would never have betrayed it. But when the Institute used its resources to influence modern politics, to dare impose past structures upon today's society, to mold the way people thought . . . that was wrong.

The traitor unlocked three sets of security doors in swift succession. Only then did he brush his hand over the photocell to manually activate the lights.

He saw the anarchist revealed as a thin young man wrapped in a hooded cloak. The anarchist's eyes burned with the fervor of a fanaticist.

"Quickly!" he said. "Show me the records. Show me the lab and equipment."

A band constricted the traitor's throat. He thought of the travelers, all eminent historians in their specialized fields, all human beings of worth and creativity. Some of them were his friends; others he merely knew as colleagues. After today, at least half of them would be dead, cast adrift forever within the time streams. Were political ideals worth murder?

"Hurry, I said!" The anarchist plucked at his sleeve. "There is less than an hour before the first work shift arrives."

The traitor roused himself from his moral paralysis. "You're the one who came late."

"Never mind. I am here now. Show me the equipment."

The traitor took him to Laboratory 14, a gleaming white expanse of assembly tracks, motionless manufacture robots, coiled sheets of alloy, and delicate optic filaments kept sealed from dust in clear acrylic boxes.

Eight small objects stood in a row upon a polished steel table. Each was the size of a wide bracelet. Each held state-of-the-art components designed to interface with the main time computer. Each contained an advanced data retrieval and storage system miniaturized to the size of a thumbnail. Most wondrous of all, each possessed the capability of molecular shift. This allowed the bracelet to assume the shape and appearance of any object that would fit into the particular location and time visited by the wearer.

"The Light Operated Computer," whispered the traitor with reverence. "The best we've ever devised. Refinements in these models took seven months of round-the-clock work. They've been tested and modified to—"

"Never mind the lecture," broke in the anarchist. He seized one and held it up so that the light shone through its clear sides. "You may have refined the LOCs, but essentially they still operate on the same old light transmission theory."

He drew forth a fold of waterproof cloth and unrolled it to reveal a set of highly specialized tools, some of them with points no larger than the head of a pin. From among them he picked up a slim black tube, finger narrow, and handed it to the traitor.

"These are the limiter components. Install them quickly."

The traitor sucked in his breath as he accepted the tube. He felt the urge to take them to his microscope and check them for precise alignment of compatibility codes, but he quelled the impulse. It was not necessary.

Sweat broke out upon his forehead. "You have the money?"

"We will settle up later, old man."

"We'll settle now!"

For a moment there was only silence, with the traitor's shout echoing faintly. Then the anarchist bowed his head.

He produced a slim card and handed it to the traitor. "Already credited to your account."

The thin card felt slick and cold beneath the traitor's fingers. He checked the credit line, and felt himself breathe easier. It was worth it, he told himself. Calm returned to him.

Securing the card within his smock pocket, he clamped on a set of goggle scanners designed to magnify the microscopic-sized circuitry within the light fibers.

"Which ones?" he asked.

The anarchist smiled. He had discolored teeth, and his smile showed no amusement. "You choose."

Although the LOCs were theoretically identical, each one contained an organic coding that linked it to its wearer. Thus, one LOC could not be substituted for another. If the wrong person attempted to use a LOC it would not activate. Because each historian on the team had a different personality and research style, the LOCs tended to reflect the idiosyncrasies of their owners.

One LOC, for example, always looked slightly more ornate than the others. Another tended to have a pink tint. Yet another resisted internal code changes and upgrade implants.

Hesitating, the traitor reached out and finally selected one. Selecting a tiny laser probe, he used it to open the casing.

"What is this one's destination?" asked the anarchist.

"I—I don't remember."

The anarchist seized his smock and twisted it about his throat. "Yes, you do. Tell me!"

The twisted cloth cut cruelly into the traitor's neck. Gasping, he stared up into the mad eyes of his coconspirator and dropped the laser probe.

It clattered upon the polished floor, and the anarchist released his grasp. Coughing, the traitor sagged forward over the table.

The anarchist picked up the laser probe and handed it to him. "Tell me."

"Why don't you just have me set the LOC to destruct within the time stream," gasped the traitor, wiping his eyes.

"We are not that crude," said the anarchist with a quick glance at the wall chronometer. "Just make minor adjustments to skew the destinations."

"It's not that easy," said the traitor. "If we tamper with history in any way, we could erase our existence altogether—"

"Shut up, old man. I know the primary rule of time travel. Despite our more inflammatory rhetoric, I realize that sometimes it is better to cripple a thing than to kill it. With their best historians trapped within time loops, the officers of the Time Institute will have to mark this project a failure. It will be shut down, and our purpose will advance."

The traitor thought he heard a sound in the distance. He clutched the anarchist's arm. "Someone's coming!"

"Quiet!" The anarchist ran silently to the door and listened there while the traitor felt his heartbeat thundering. It was almost time for the first shift to come in.

"Nothing," said the anarchist, returning. "Don't try that trick again. Get to work, and make sure they do not detect any problems with these LOCs until it is too late."

Biting his lip in worry, the traitor began the adjustments. Tampering with destination was difficult. He needed the LOC activated and tuned to the main time computer to make a precise adjustment. As it was, all he could accomplish was a minimal shift. He finished, uncertain that he had achieved anything.

"This is very dangerous," he said worriedly, selecting another probe. "If I don't adjust it correctly, he could be thrown from the time stream completely, or—"

"Or what?"

"Or trapped in an incomplete time loop, or duplicated, or just killed." The traitor swallowed with difficulty. "I don't want murder on my—"

"Just get on with it. Install the limiter. It is the only guarantee we have of creating a broken time loop. We do not want them entering the Industrial Revolution or any moment of history past that. They might be able to repair the LOC."

"There were no fiber optics in the Victorian era," said the traitor harshly. "As long as the twentieth century is avoided—"

"Do not argue. Set the limiter, and hurry! You are taking too long with this first one."

"It's done." The traitor laid down his tools. He felt slightly sick.

The anarchist smiled. "Whose is it?"

"Does it matter who dies first?" said the traitor wearily.

"Yes."

"We'll have to call up the records. Read the serial number off the LOC and find the destination—"

"No! You know them by heart, old man. Tell me now!"

The traitor envisioned a face in his mind, a lean, tanned face with clearly etched features, hooded gray eyes, a mouth more sensitive than the sardonic curl at the corners might suggest. He wanted to weep, yet it was too late.

He whispered, "Destination was . . . sixth century Byzantium. The last bastion of the once mighty Roman empire. It alone stood against the crumbling of civilization, holding the last dim years before the first Dark Ages. It might almost be considered an exact parallel of our current political situation. Our best traveler is assigned to go there."

The anarchist picked up the tampered LOC and laughed. "Not anymore. Wrong century. Wrong location. Wrong everything. When did you send him? To the Ice Age? I like that. Let him play with the Neanderthals."

"No," said the traitor. "It will be the fourteenth century. I—I'm not exactly sure where."

"Good enough. Maybe he will die of the plague."

"He'll probably die from the anomalies in the time stream. We don't know all the possible effects yet. We have tested and researched most carefully, but our parameters remain narrow. We can't predict what this tampering will do."

"Good." Still grinning, the anarchist put the sabotaged LOC on the table and picked up the next one. He handed it to the traitor. "Do this one faster."

A sound in the distance made the traitor glance up. This time the anarchist heard it too. For an instant they stood frozen. Then the anarchist snatched up the tube containing the remaining limiters and swore.

"You told me we had an hour, old man."

Fear paralyzed the traitor. He stared at the door, half expecting people to come bursting through it at any moment.

"They—they must be excited, unable to wait," he said. His voice was faint. He couldn't draw enough breath to strengthen it. "I didn't anticipate early . . ."

"Come on! Show me a way out!"

The anarchist seized him roughly by the arm and slung him around. Somehow the traitor found his wits.

"There is another way out. Don't panic," he said.

The anarchist glared at him. "Old fool. In a few seconds I could set enough explosives to completely destroy this lab and all your precious research."

"No—"

The anarchist gave him a violent push. "Show me then. Damn, damn, damn! All this effort for just one. My coordinator will blame you for this."

The emergency exit door opened beneath the swift touch of the traitor's fingers upon the lock keypad. "You got the *best* one," he said, and could not keep his own grief from his voice. "He's dedicated to bringing back the ancient values of courage, valor, sacrifice, and achievement. He thinks our way of life is too soft, too self-indulgent. He travels more than the others. Don't worry. What we've done will set the project back years."

"That is what you say." The anarchist shoved him through into a cramped access tunnel and closed the door after them. Just before the light from the lab was clipped off, he leaned close to the traitor with a snarl. "We do not want to set back the project. We want to *stop* it."

Regret welled up within the traitor, but it was too late. He could not undo what he had set into motion. "We'll come again," he said. "When this travel phase is finished, we'll sabotage more LOCs."

Something hit him in the back. For an instant he thought the anarchist had struck him with his fist. Then there was a burst of sharp pain within his chest, a pain so great that his cry died in his throat from lack of air. His lung was filling up. He could feel a swelling, a hot bubbling inside. He couldn't breathe. Crumpling to the floor, he gazed up at his cloaked attacker in the shadows.

For a moment his mind focused in absolute clarity. He saw the fatal flaws in the anarchists' position. He realized that as long as they moved on the sheer impulse to destroy, they could not be ordered enough to create serious damage. Yet once they found discipline, they would no longer be anarchists. They stood trapped in a loop of their own.

He almost laughed. Yet at the same time he wanted to weep. The heat in his chest grew into fire, warning him that he was drowning in his own blood. A clawing desperation to live went through him. He gripped the forearm of his attacker.

"Go back," he gasped. "Tell them what you've done. It's not worth this—"

"Go to hell, old man," said the anarchist and pulled out the knife.

It was a tearing agony that wiped him in a clammy sheet of sweat. A great gout of his blood rushed forth as the knife scraped free. In that moment he knew that he had been a fool. He had destroyed a historian, a man he had known and loved as a son, and all for *nothing*.

Whiteness burst in his brain, wiping away all thought and feeling.

It was over.

CHAPTER 1

Soft background noise imitating ocean waves filtered through the speakers of Chicago Work Complex 7. Citizens glided on escalators and moving sidewalks through a spacious vista of glass and gleaming bronze. Although it was morning rush hour, with hundreds of people streaming into the complex for work, there was little noise beyond the soft chime of glass-enclosed lifts, the recorded ocean music, and the rush of real water from the half-story waterfall in the main reception lobby.

Despite the crowds upon the escalators or gathered at each lift station, there was no shoving, no insults, no sense of urgency. Most people wore bland, dreamy-eyed expressions. They moved slowly as though underwater, sufficiently aware of their physical surroundings to get off at the proper station, but focused primarily on the inward fantasy world created by the hologram chips implanted in their brains.

Noel Kedran, however, did not wear a head chip. He was not locked into a fantasy world, but remained firmly lodged in reality. Right now reality said that he was late.

"Hold that lift!" he called, shoving past a woman and sprinting for the elevator ahead. "Please! Hold the lift!"

The passengers already inside the lift stood like cattle. One, however, reached out and dreamily caught the closing lift doors.

Noel jumped aboard, and the doors glided closed behind him. Huffing in relief, he wiped the gloss of perspiration and blood from his forehead and shifted position so the scanner beam could read his security badge. A chime marked registration of his identity. The lift started up. It would stop automatically at his floor. He dabbed at the cut above his eyebrow with a wince. It would not stop bleeding, and it had begun to hurt.

"You should start earlier, man," said the youth who had held the doors for him. The youth's voice was soft and helpful. "Try a time monitor. Cheap at twenty-five creds, you know? Then you always get up on time. Guaranteed not to let you run late."

"Yeah, thanks," said Noel shortly and glanced away to stop the conversation. He would rather be deaf, blind, and senile than have any Life-design implants. There were chips to put you to sleep, chips to get you up, chips to boost your memory, chips to keep you from getting drunk, chips to make you feel drunk without suffering physical side effects, chips to arouse your passions, chips to depress your passions, chips to manipulate and control you just about any damned way you wanted. Life by design was not for him, not in a million years.

The lift stopped at the fifth floor, and he stepped off alone, veering right toward the security lock. A beam scanned him, registered clearance, and opened the first set of doors. He passed through the entire lock system quickly, but it wasn't quickly enough to offset his gnawing sense of urgency.

He'd wanted to be the first one in this morning. He'd wanted to get at the new assignment list before anyone else. For seven months there had been a hiatus in all time travel while the bugs were worked out of the new LOCs. Noel had hated every boring, idle minute of it. He hated the increasing softness of the twenty-sixth century, with its technology that babied mankind into becoming a race of increasingly helpless morons. The gulf between the technocrats and the laborers—who droned their way through their jobs, then went home and fantasized in the sensory-rich worlds provided for them—grew wider all the time.

Back in the twentieth century, men had worried that their future meant being controlled by a vast, impersonal government. Instead, men had become controlled by their own dream states.

"The ultimate vegetable," muttered Noel aloud.

"What's that?" said a voice from behind him. "Talking to yourself? That's a sure sign of—"

Noel flung up his hand without bothering to look over his shoulder. "Don't say it!"

"—a worn head chip," said the voice cheerfully.

Noel sighed in mock exasperation and swung around to confront his best friend. "Only you could get away with old jokes this early in the morning."

Trojan Heitz, a burly giant with a head of frizzy red hair and a full beard, grinned broadly. Like Noel, he was dressed in conservative street clothes: trousers and a high-throated jacket in soft blue knit. His security badge provided the only ornamentation.

As always, Trojan looked sloppy and unkempt in modern clothing. The tailoring line was wrong for him. But put him in a Tartan kilt, wide leather belt with an axe or short sword hanging from it, and sandals laced to his hairy knees, and his rugged, muscular build looked absolutely right.

"You're bleeding," he said. "Or is that something I'm not supposed to notice?"

"It's nothing," said Noel quickly. Dabbing again at the cut, he looked at his bloodstained fingers. "The bleeding's slowed down. I'll swing by the infirmary later."

"In the meantime you're dripping on the floor."

Noel glanced down, but there weren't any splatters of crimson on the white, polished floor.

Trojan chuckled.

"Very funny," said Noel.

They started down the hall together.

"You're seriously late," Trojan said. "Want coffee?"

Noel swore to himself. "I missed the whole meeting?"

"Every last word." Trojan sipped from his cup. "Rugle was at her boring best. Practically recited the whole time traveler's creed to us. Gave us a list of admonitions and a pep talk that put Bruthe to sleep. Treated us like raw recruits." Trojan snorted. "As though we'd forget anything in seven months. The only exciting part of the meeting was the fact that old Tchielskov didn't show. He hasn't missed a meeting in ten years."

Noel stood frozen, not listening to Trojan, aware instead of his heart thumping loud and hard against his rib cage. "How many assignments?"

Trojan sniffed the bottom of his cup as though it had something growing in it. "Promised us eight at the last meeting."

"I *know* that." Noel could have throttled him. He knew Trojan was enjoying this. But if he didn't go along with the baiting, Trojan wouldn't tell him anything. "We already figured out that the whole advanced team wouldn't travel this time."

"Yep." Trojan's gaze came up slowly to meet Noel's. His blue eyes twinkled. "Four assignments."

"Half! Only half? They *are* being cautious."

"Can't overload the time stream—"

"Bunk!" said Noel forcefully. He saw an official coming toward them and shifted to one side of the corridor to keep his bloody face averted. "The new LOCs are supposed to handle that little—"

"Gossiping in corridors?" said the official snidely. "What's your rank and grade?"

Officials were always poking their noses about, trying to pretend that they understood a fraction of the research being conducted within the Time Institute, and feeling justified in checking on how they spent taxpayers' money.

Noel had little use for officials. Trying to mask his attitude, however, he faced the woman and replied, "Security grade two. Rank, historian."

"Same," said Trojan.

"Oh," said the official with a blink. "You're travelers."

"That's right."

"Well," she said, impressed but trying not to show it. "Uh, why are you bleeding? Were you in this morning's riots?"

"Momentarily," said Noel. He caught Trojan's eye on him and scowled. "I missed the last shuttle flight over Lake Michigan and had to take—"

"Never mind," said Trojan. "I can imagine the sordid details. You saw a defenseless woman and child struggling against anarchists and you just had to step in."

"Well—"

Trojan held up his hand. "Such modesty. No doubt when you pulled her to safety, the child clinging to your shoulder, she sobbed out her gratitude on her knees while the child lifted your credit card. Am I right?"

Noel couldn't meet his eyes. "You're right."

"Disgraceful," said the official. "But how typical of the lower orders. Well, carry on."

She walked on toward the security lock. Noel glared after her, making faces until Trojan's massive hand closed on his shoulder and pushed him in the opposite direction.

"Don't say it," he warned Noel. "Don't say anything."

As soon as the official stepped into the lock, out of hearing, Noel hooted loudly. "Did you hear her? Carry on. As though she has any idea of what we're trying to do here. She even believed I met a kid pickpocket this morning. You could tell her anything about the so-called oppressed rabble, and she'd believe it. I'll bet she's never seen anyone below a grade three rank. These official parasites are—"

"Be serious," said Trojan in rebuke. "Did you play the knight errant?"

Noel snorted. "Not my period of history. You're the chivalrous one, remember? It was just a basic traffic riot, started by some anarchist punks for general reasons. I caught a piece of brick in the face."

"Oh, very heroic," said Trojan.

Noel put his hand over his heart and bowed sardonically. That started his cut bleeding again. He swore.

"Blame yourself for it," said Trojan. "If you must live on the wrong side of town—"

"Drop it," said Noel. "We're not all independently wealthy like you and the parasite."

Trojan frowned. "Don't call her that. She's a new representative. Came in for the meeting. And she's pro-Institute, which is more than can be said for the last one who came by."

"Who, the anarchist?"

"Don't *say* that," said Trojan, glancing overhead. "Your mouth is going to get you chopped one day."

"I tried to call in," said Noel. "Did you know that the comm booths at the shuttle terminal no longer reach this section of Chicago? Overloaded lines. I ask you, how long can this—"

"Blood pressure," said Trojan. His blue eyes grew dim and stared into the distance. It was his way of tuning out, and it warned Noel to control his temper.

"Hell," he muttered. "You're right. It's just that I *want* this assignment. I can't stand modern life. It's ruining my nerves."

Trojan's chuckle was a rumble deep in his throat. "We all know that. Here's the infirmary corridor. Why don't you get that cut fixed?"

"No time—"

"There's time." Trojan clapped him on the shoulder and grinned. "After all, you don't want to be scratched from your new assignment just because you flunked your physical."

Noel stared at him a moment, drinking in his words, letting the knowledge, the relief, the *triumph* sink deep into his brain. Then he gripped Trojan's arms and let out a muffled whoop.

"Really? You too?"

Trojan nodded, his grin spreading from ear to ear. Gripping each other, they began an impromptu jig in the middle of the corridor. A couple of smocked scientists stepped around them, disinterested, and used to the aberrations of historians. Down the hall, a door opened and a gray-haired woman with a face like a mountain crag looked out.

"Heitz! Kedran! Stop making that noise and report to your stations at once. Kedran, if you bleed on the floor I'll have you mop this entire area."

They stopped dancing at once and stood shoulder to shoulder at attention, like schoolboys caught in a misdemeanor.

"Yes, ma'am," said Trojan.

"Yes, Dr. Rugle," said Noel.

"One would think, Mr. Kedran," said Rugle, "that you aren't interested in traveling after all, since you didn't bother to attend this morning's orientation meeting."

Noel pulled in his chin and tried to keep his dislike of the old harridan off his face. "I'm very interested, Dr. Rugle," he said. "I got caught in a riot on the way to work."

"A riot?" She frowned. "Can't you think of a less mundane excuse? Get to your stations. Tchielskov has decided to take the day off, for some inexplicable reason, leaving us short of prep technicians. Processing is going to take at least two hours longer than usual. Your cooperation will help that procedure go more smoothly. Thank you."

She vanished, her door closing. Noel and Trojan passed her office in silence, not daring to meet each other's gaze. As soon as they turned the corner and entered the archives section, they glanced at each other and snickered.

"What an old bag," said Noel. "Our cooperation will assist the proccdurc of processing to proceed in an ongoing direction. I'm glad I did miss the meeting."

Trojan veered off to a coffee machine and got another cup. "Want some?"

"No. You know I hate the stuff." Noel eyed him critically. "At the rate you're swilling it—"

"Coffee drinking didn't come into practice in Europe until the late eighteenth century," said Trojan, slurping. "No coffee where I'm going."

"You mean *when* you're going."

"That too." Finishing his cup, Trojan refilled it again.

"You're getting Agincourt," said Noel, unable to hold off asking any longer. "The first modern battle in Europe. One of the finest examples of courage and achievement against impossible odds. Well? If you know we both got assignments, you must know what they are. Tell me!"

Trojan chuckled. "I thought you'd never ask."

"Did you get Agincourt?"

"You know I wanted Malta."

"That's just because you like the Mediterranean climate. Tell!"

Trojan let out a mighty sigh. "Yes, I got Agincourt."

Noel grinned, his expectations wired tight. "And? Oh, hell, Troj, stop playing this out."

"You got Constantinople."

Excitement burst in Noel. He threw his arms in the air like a marathon winner and crowed.

Three people instantly appeared in the lobby of the archives: the librarian and two other historians.

The librarian shook his head indulgently and retreated without a reprimand. One historian grinned and shook Noel's and Trojan's hands. The other scowled.

Noel made himself sober quickly, although the excitement beating inside him was stronger than his own heartbeat. "Sorry, Rupeet. No go for you?"

Rupeet's dark face scowled harder. He made no reply. His tall, fair-haired companion, however, shot Noel a rueful smile.

"Nor for me, I'm afraid," he said in a soft, singsong voice. "We're to wait until your lot returns."

"We'll only be gone about an hour, this time," said Noel.

"Slack," said Rupeet angrily. "Slack thinker. Slack planner. Slack in everything you do. You're never properly prepared. You don't read the manuals. You even missed this morning's meeting—"

"Easy, Rupeet," said Trojan.

"Damn it all! It's forty-nine minutes," said Rupeet. "Not sixty."

Noel shrugged. "So?"

"You see? *You see?* It's a crucial variation in the time streams. With the previous model LOCs we had only a thirty-six-minute return lap. It's *significant,* Kedran. If you ever did half your job, you'd know that."

Noel's temper, ever quick to fly, was barely held in check. His eyes narrowed. "I know it indicates we can stay in the time stream longer with fewer adverse effects. I know it indicates a forty-nine to one ratio, with forty-nine of their minutes equal to one of ours. That gives us roughly two days in past time—"

"Exactly 1.667 days. More than enough time for you to make a mistake that could seriously alter—"

"Oh, give it up, Rupeet," said Noel rudely and walked away.

Trojan fell into step with him. "You're making an enemy there."

Noel shrugged.

"Office politics are sticky. It's not wise to have enemies within the Institute. We have enough outside it."

"I *hate* politics," said Noel irritably. "We each have our jobs to do. There's no competition. Why should he care who goes first?"

"Why did you?"

Noel glared at him, but Trojan was staring into the bottom of his cup.

After a moment Noel sighed. "Yeah, okay. You made your point. But Rupeet doesn't love the past. He doesn't have a feel for it, an understanding of its richness, of its texture. He doesn't see the interweaving of the time streams as a poetry of the universe. He—"

Trojan's quizzical look made Noel realize he was getting carried away. His face flamed hot and he cleared his throat.

"Uh, well, he just plods through and makes his recordings. We might as well send a pack mule on his assignments, for all the joy they bring him. He sees each assignment as another step to his promotion into the administration. It's like a profanity. The whole experience is *wasted* on him."

"It's just fun for me," said Trojan mildly, finishing his coffee and tossing away the cup. "When it stops being fun, I shall stop traveling. You always want to turn it into a religious experience—"

"Cute, Troj. Very cute."

"Poetry of the universe," said Trojan and snorted. "That wallop you took this morning must have addled your brain. Come on."

Four hours later Noel strapped on his LOC, feeling it turn warm and settle around his wrist like an old friend. He walked through the sterile Laboratory 14, now filled with row after row of technicians, each sitting at a terminal, each linked into the data-retrieval-run system that supported the massive time computer.

He wore a knee-length tunic of thin, natural-colored wool and a cloak of bright blue. The leather belt around his lean waist held a dagger and a heavy purse of coins bearing the imperial seal of Rome. He kept muttering Latin phrases to himself, testing the heavy syllables on his tongue to regain the natural rhythm of the language. Although he was implanted with a universal translator, he liked to be able to *think* in the old tongues.

At the last minute before they parted, Trojan had pressed a small pouch into his hand. "Salt," he said. "For luck . . . and good eating."

The worst thing about the past was the food. No matter how much they trained, none of the historians could acquire a taste for the bland, boiled, slightly gamey muck that passed for stews and pottages.

Noel had forgotten to provide himself with a supply of salt. Gratefully he took the pouch and gave Trojan a quick hug.

"Thanks, friend," he said. "Watch out for arrows."

"I'll be on the English side of the battle," said Trojan in mock exasperation. "The French didn't use the longbow then, remember? Really, Noel, you are pretty ignorant for a historian."

"Focused," retorted Noel. "Specialized. Not ignorant."

"Ignorant," said Trojan, but with gentleness. "Fly by the seat of your pants."

"Intuitive," retorted Noel. "You should play your hunches more and depend on your experience less."

"Don't catch the pox," said Trojan.

They grinned at each other.

"Get on with it," muttered the technician Bruthe.

They always had this little ritual of swapping insults and advice before they traveled. Stepping back, Noel watched his friend enter the portal.

It was like watching a man walk away from you down a long hallway into the mist, becoming increasingly indistinct until the mist curled across his shadow and he was gone. The first time Noel had ever seen the time portal, he had been disappointed at the tameness of the effect. He had wanted to see lightning flash, or hear great cracks of thunder as time was rent to let them enter its stream. But no dazzling pyrotechnics happened in time travel. Only the mist and a gentle sense of being sucked away into a fuzzy nothingness that lasted a few short seconds before arrival.

"Your turn, Kedran," said Bruthe.

Normally Tchielskov performed the portal duties. Noel was fond of the old man, who had taught him how to avoid the slight nausea that crossing the portal could cause, who had taught him to go in thinking in the language he was to shortly be surrounded by so that the actual transition was less of a shock. He had never known the old man to miss travel, but Bruthe—or anyone else in the room—could handle the portal controls. It was just a matter of monitoring; the time computer did all the real work.

Adrenaline built in Noel's veins. The center of his palms grew moist. He sucked in a deep breath and entered the portal ramp, bouncing just once on his toes and making sure he started on his left foot. It was a mindless, meaningless superstition of his, a way to distract himself as he entered the mist.

Although it appeared to be mist to those watching in the laboratory behind him, in reality it wasn't a ground cloud of moisture at all. In reality, it was nonreality. Tendrils of gray nothingness dissolved his tangible surroundings. The deeper he walked into it, the more he dissolved. He kept his gaze ahead, knowing better than to watch himself fade.

A frisson of energy rippled through him, making his black hair stand on end. He could hear the pulse of the time wave, and felt it washing over him in an immense, sucking tide.

Normally about now he should be nothing more visible than a vague outline. He was crossing the actual portal, the most dangerous moment of travel, when he was in neither dimension but only *between*.

His LOC was getting warmer, too warm, uncomfortably hot on his arm. The pain of it grew sharp, piercing enough to make him gasp, although by now he shouldn't be feeling any physical sensations.

He should be through by now. But instead of clearing, the misty grayness around him grew suddenly black, as though he'd been dropped down a hole. He had the dizzying, terrifying sensation of falling.

This had never happened before. For an instant he panicked, then he clung desperately to his training and tried to project his mind *back* to the laboratory. With fear curling around the edges of his thoughts, warping his ability to control himself, he envisioned the lab with its whiteness, its rows of terminals, the hush of the air, the men and women going about their jobs, *faces*.

He was still falling. The pain in his arm had spread to his chest. He felt as though he were being halved by a saw, slicing its way in steady strokes through the center of him. He wanted to scream, and couldn't.

What was happening? Why couldn't he go back?

No hearing, no sight, no feeling of anything solid around him. Complete sensory shut down. He shuddered, feeling the panic blank him again.

He sought to rebuild the lab in his mind, but he was too scared. It wasn't working. All those drills, all that training to equip him to deal with any difficulty in traveling . . . nothing *worked*.

In desperation, he focused on an image of Tchielskov's face, making it real to him, pretending he could hear the old man's patient voice talking him through this, talking him *back*.

What *was* this? wondered Noel frantically. Time loop? Vortex? Aberration? Anomaly? This close to the portal, it should have registered on the monitors. Hadn't Bruthe been paying attention? Was it sabotage?

The pain intensified, and there was only the inside of his own skull to scream in. He stopped falling and felt himself jolted, then bumped through a series of ripples like being caught in the wake of a ferry upon Lake Michigan.

He heard a voice. Hope swelled through him. He called out, certain now that he was being pulled back. The voice echoed to him, not heard exactly, but somehow sensed within his mind. He could not understand its words. Everything was gibberish, like listening to a recording played backward. He shouted in response, but it gibbered on for a while, then stopped.

The silence was even worse.

He felt as though he were spinning, end over end, eddying down, looping nowhere, like a child's kite falling when the string is severed.

How long? he wondered.

Infinity perhaps, whispered a corner of his mind.

This then was death. And there was no end to it, no place of beginning, no point of reference. This was to be nothing, yet *aware.*

This was hell.

And damnation.

He had never believed in such things before. Now, sobbing in his own fear and the agony that ripped him into pieces, he was forced to believe. He had never considered death beyond a casual ending, preferably in action, hopefully quick. How little he had known, or even guessed.

He would be the first traveler to die in the time streams. They would give him a memorial service. They might even close the Institute for a day, although he doubted it. Trojan would grieve for him, if Trojan himself was not dead too. The project would probably be closed.

Bring me back! he shouted with all his might, straining until he felt something nearly snap within him.

There came a jolt, hard and tangible, as though he had struck something. Energy waved through him, scraping his nerve endings. He felt a rush of wind, and then he heard a churning babble of noise, a din that grew into a crescendo of mindless, deafening, horrible cacophony. Grayness spread before him in an arc, changing to a rainbow of colors too vivid to bear. They seared into him with their brightness. If he had eyes, he tried to shut them, but it did not keep away the colors that branded themselves upon his brain. Images hurled themselves at him, shapes without meaning, alien, confusing.

He heard a crack of sound as though the universe itself had broken apart. It spread out into deafening, numbing thunder that crashed and grumbled forever, echoing in upon itself before finally fading away.

Noel hit the ground with a thump. He had no warning—no return of vision, no smells, no sense at all that he was back in corporeal existence—until he landed. It knocked the breath from him, and at first he could but lie there limp and dazed, unable to comprehend his surroundings.

Lightning ripped the sky overhead, and with a start he came fully conscious, finding himself in the darkness of night with a rainstorm lashing about him, wind howling in his ears, thunder crashing overhead, lightning flashes illuminating a stark, unknown world of boulder and crag. He was cold, drenched to the skin, and the earth beneath him was shaking.

Noel looked up, half scrambling to his feet on instinct more than anything else. Out of the night came a group of horsemen, on top of him before he really saw them. Crying out, Noel threw himself to one side and rolled frantically to avoid the galloping slash of hooves.

One struck him a glancing blow anyway, and the pain was like a shock, numbing him all over again. More horsemen were coming, with yells that rent the night in furious counterpoint to the storm. Noel dodged and scrambled among the riders who were oblivious to his existence. Flashes of lightning in strobe action played upon upraised swords and metal helmets. The sounds of thunder, screaming horses, yelling men, and metal clanging upon metal were deafening.

Rain lashed into his eyes, half blinding him. He had one split-second glimpse of a horse coming at him before it knocked him aside with its chest, hooves digging, nostrils distended, white gleaming around its eye. Sheer instinct made Noel grab the reins to save himself from being trampled. The horse's impetus slung him around hard enough to wrench his shoulders. He cried out and let go, stumbling to keep his balance. The rider swung at him with his sword.

Noel could not dodge it, and only luck and perhaps the darkness put the flat of the sword to him instead of the edge. Still, being struck by a yard long piece of iron packed a wallop that tumbled him down the slope.

Winded and gasping for air from his flattened lungs, he felt a sickening drop beneath him.

Fear came back, like hot bile in his throat, and he thought he had slipped back into the time stream. But it was only a short fall before he thudded onto solid ground again, and went rolling down the hillside with too much impetus to stop himself, lost in the darkness and the rain and the howling night while the battle raged on in a thunder of hooves, swords, and jingling harness, oblivious to his existence.

His shoulder hit something solid, like a boulder, and he slewed sideways, his wild progress slowed. He slid on his back several more feet down, scooping ice-cold mud down the neck of his tunic. He had time to realize that he wasn't in Constantinople. He wasn't in a city at all.

That realization brought a new brand of fear all its own. Then his head bumped against a stone, and the stars themselves fell upon him. He knew nothing more.

CHAPTER 2

"Poke 'em first ere ye cut their purses."

"Aye, I'm doing it, ain't I?"

"Well, poke 'em harder than that, ye dolt. The first one playing as he's dead will put a dagger in yer throat."

"Then you do it!"

"Nay, get on with ye and stop dawdling. We've not got much time."

"Look at this one. Not a mark on him. He must have looked up to call on God for mercy and drowned himself in last eve's storm."

"Blasphemous dolt! Hold tongue or it'll be cut from ye."

"All right, all right. It was only a joke."

"A poor joke, and at God's expense. If yer not careful, Thaddeus, ye'll end up with a worm eatin' out yer soft parts."

"Don't say to me about worms, not and you half-poxed."

"I'll pox ye—"

The arguing voices buzzed in Noel's head like angry bees. His comprehension came and faded, along with his hearing. A dim sense of curiosity enticed him to open his eyes, but they were glued shut and too heavy to bother.

"Ooh, look at this one. A fine ring on his finger, with a diamond even."

"Let me see."

" 'Tis mine. I saw it first!"

"Let go, ye dolt. All we find today be goin' to the treasury."

"No fair, I say," said Thaddeus, his voice a whine. "You don't have to say all we found. It's pretty. I want to keep it."

"And how will ye wear it if all yer fingers be cut off yer hand, eh?"

Noel managed to drag open his eyes. He found himself staring into a man's dead face, covered with blood dried black from the side of it that had been hewn away. A single brown eye stared sightlessly back at him.

Shock and nausea rose through Noel. With difficulty he held both down and closed his eyes again. Maybe, with luck, he was dead too.

A rustle told him the scavengers were coming closer.

"What's this then? A pilgrim, do ye think?"

"Aye, George, by the look of him. But pilgrims have slim purses. Go on to the next one."

"Nay," said George. "Let's steal his cloak. It be a fine blue color, and we can sell it for a good price at market. Poke him sharp now."

"I'm not poking him. You do it."

"Ye found him."

"So and I did? You poke him."

There came an oath and a rustle. Something pointed jabbed Noel hard in the ribs. In spite of his intention to play dead, his eyes jerked open.

Two dwarfs stood peering down at him, their heads looking too large for their ill-proportioned bodies. When he opened his eyes, they cried out and stumbled back. One slipped on the mud and sat down hard on his rump.

"Alive!"

"I warned ye!"

"Get away from him. He'll go for us."

"Be quiet, Thaddeus." With a thump to his companion's head, the dwarf in a green hood and homespun tunic turned back to Noel and knelt beside him. "No harm to ye, sir. No harm to ye."

Sense returned to Noel. He was lying on his stomach, with one hand beneath him. His fingers groped stealthily and closed on the hilt of his dagger. All he had to do was draw it quick.

The dwarf in the green hood reached out his hand.

"Be careful, George!"

"Quiet," said George over his shoulder. "Ye'll spook him."

"Even horses bite," muttered Thaddeus, keeping his distance.

George reached out again, and Noel pushed himself to his hands and knees, bringing out his dagger before he keeled over again. He was as weak as a wet kitten.

He tried to lift his head. It felt incredibly heavy. "Byzantium," he mumbled.

"What'd he say?" asked Thaddeus, creeping closer.

George pushed back his hood, revealing a shaggy mop of gray-grizzled hair so knotted and tangled it probably hadn't been combed all year. "I made no sense of it."

Noel raised his head higher and spat mud from his mouth. It tasted metallic and cold. He spat again. "Byzantium," he said.

"What?"

"Byzantium," said George. "Yer a stranger travelin' far then, good sir, if ye mean yer from Constantinople."

Noel frowned. "No," he said. "*Going* there. I am going there."

"Not from here you won't," muttered Thaddeus. "He's right addled, George. I'll bet he don't even know his name. Where does he think he is and who was he with, eh? Damned Byzantines all around us, ain't there?"

Noel rolled himself onto one elbow and sat up. The world spun around him for a moment, then his vision cleared. He found himself looking down a slanted mountainside. Far, far below him spread a wide, flat valley plain that looked green and fertile along a narrow river. Across it to the east, the sun was only a short distance above the horizon, still fiery orange. The sky blazed with pink and silver, and the crisp cool air he sucked into his lungs might have been champagne, so invigorating was it. He felt strength seeping back into his limbs. Twisting his head, he gazed up the rest of the mountain through the blooming branches of a tiny almond tree growing nearby. The peak towered above him, as remote as Olympus. Snow could be seen up there, although from the green tint of the coarse grass and the blooming plant life, he guessed it was spring.

Beautiful, no, breathtaking . . . if you didn't look at the twisted, bloody corpses littering the hillside between where he sat and the road above him.

Noel averted his eyes, although his instinct for survival urged him to look quick and closely, study clothing, determine *when* he was.

Ravens, or possibly buzzards, circled above him in the sky.

He swallowed, making no assessments yet, and looked to the north. Another, lesser hill shaped like a cone shouldered against the flank of the mountain range, with a narrow road scaling its terraced sides to a fortress built of stone. He could see tiled rooftops among the trees and the walls of a town perched precariously upon every available bit of ground on the hill's slopes.

Noel frowned at the narrow archways and pointed windows. He recognized the architecture as distinctly medieval. The man lying next to him wore a long surcoat split between the legs for riding, and mail armor beneath it.

He turned on the dwarfs. "Where am I?" he demanded. "Quickly. Tell me where I am."

The dwarfs exchanged troubled glances. Thaddeus, his long face twisted into a grimace, tapped his temple. "Woodly," he whispered. "Plumb queer in his reason. Let's kill him and be gone. She'll be wondering why we're not back."

George said to Noel, "This be Mt. Taygetus—"

"Taygetus!" Noel rubbed his aching head. "Impossible. I can't be *that* far off the mark."

Mt. Taygetus was located in Greece, above the plain of Sparta. Constantinople—his intended destination—was probably a good five hundred miles to the east by land, and not much closer by sea. It might as well be a million, for he definitely had landed in the wrong century.

Glancing down at himself, he took a swift inventory. His clothes were torn and muddy, still half-damp. He'd lost one of his sandals, but the rest of his belongings seemed intact. On his left wrist, his LOC had taken on the appearance of a hammered copper bracelet, very broad and heavy. His left arm still ached, with a faint, dull throbbing, reminding him of his nightmarish journey through the time stream.

He shivered. Travel wasn't supposed to be like that. Even now, just thinking about it made a cold sweat break out across him. He was grateful to be anywhere right now, anywhere but still trapped.

He hesitated, considering the dwarfs, but it had to be asked. "What year?"

Thaddeus stepped back. "Aye, see? He's mad! Come away, George, and leave him to the wolves."

George, however, stood his ground. His weathered face turned sly and calculating. "Ye've got a heavy purse at yer belt, good sir," he said. Holding his pointed stick like a spear, he said, "Hand it over with no trouble, and we'll let ye go. We don't like Latins here, but we've no quarrel with a pilgrim either."

"George!" growled Thaddeus.

George frowned, but his gaze never left Noel, who turned cold with the realization of danger, real and immediate, right here in his lap.

"Hand it over now," George said.

The purse hanging at Noel's belt was the salt Trojan had given him. His money was concealed within his clothing. Noel's gaze watched both dwarfs while he considered his chances. Although he had his dagger in his hand, to throw it at one of them was to disarm himself and still leave him with a remaining opponent. These men were small and grotesque, but they had the cold, watchful eyes of fighters. Thaddeus held his own dagger in his small hand, and George had the crude spear as well as a knife. Only twenty feet away, a mace lay upon the ground, its sharp steel spikes clotted with dried blood and brain bits. Noel swallowed. If he could create a diversion and break around the dwarfs, he could easily outrun them and reach the weapon. They'd leave him alone then.

Slowly, being careful to make no move that might be misconstrued, Noel unknotted the pouch strings and pulled the salt from his belt. He hefted it a moment in his hand, aware that as soon as he handed it over they would guess the trick. Salt was heavy enough, but it didn't sit in the hand like money.

"Now, no tricks from ye," warned George. "Hand it over easy."

With a quick motion, Noel tossed the salt between them. Both swung involuntarily toward it, and he took advantage of the moment to scramble to his feet and run for the mace, his dagger held ready just in case.

Just as he reached it and crouched down to grasp the handle, an arrow whizzed from nowhere and struck deep into the ground between his hand and the mace. George and Thaddeus howled like jackals behind him, shouting something too fast to comprehend. Noel whirled around with his heart pounding, aware that his knife was no defense against a bowman.

A figure stood on a rocky outcropping some distance away, silhouetted against the sun. Its bow was drawn in readiness, a second arrow nocked and aimed. Noel had the feeling the first shot had been a warning, not a miss. He swallowed, his mouth very dry, and stepped reluctantly away from the mace.

"Don't stand there gawping, you two dunderheads," shouted an angry voice in French. *A woman's voice.* "Come away!"

Thaddeus ducked his big head and ran obediently. George hesitated, glancing at Noel, then followed. The archer lowered her weapon and slung it across slim shoulders. Jumping down from the outcropping, she met the dwarfs halfway. Her scolding voice carried upon the thin air.

"Out all night like a pair of tomcats. And with what to show for it? A half-dozen money bags, and how many of them full? Demetrius said you were to be back by dawn. Wasn't it made clear to you?"

"Yes, Elena," said the dwarfs meekly.

"It were the dark," said Thaddeus, rolling his eyes soulfully and putting a whine into his voice. "What if their souls had still been lurking about? It be poor luck to rob dead men in the dark, Elena. What if they'd took our spirits with them to hell?"

"Hell is where you belong, all right," said Elena without softening her tone. "I might have known you would sit about and scare yourselves without someone to watch you. And what about this one? Did I not tell you to make sure they were dead before you searched—"

"We poked him!" said Thaddeus indignantly.

George wasn't making excuses. His gaze remained on Noel, who was keeping a wary distance and wondering how he could edge away without being noticed.

"He be slippin' off," said George.

Elena's head came up alertly. She stepped toward Noel with the grace of a gazelle and jumped atop a small boulder to give herself an advantage over him. Pointing an arrow at Noel, she said, "Hold your place, you shivering Byzantine dog, until we give you leave otherwise."

At least his translator implant was working perfectly. It deciphered every word of her medieval French, despite the Greek accent with which she spoke.

Automatically he rubbed his finger across a small depression on his bracelet to make sure it was recording everything.

His strongest impression of her was . . . *legs*. Slender, firm, curvaceous legs encased in dark green hose went up and up. She stood with them braced apart, boylike, her hands upon her hips. Her shoes were made of cloth, also green, and the tops flared from her slim ankles in a decidedly sexy style. A wide-sleeved shirt of linen belted at the waist and coming down to midthigh covered the rest of her. The drape of it over her breasts, which were as round and firm as apples, left him in no doubt that she wore nothing beneath it. Her low-slung belt supported a knife and a quiver full of arrows. She had hair that was a rich, lustrous auburn, curly and wild, flowing down her back in an uncombed, unbound mane to her waist. Her face looked like something from an old Byzantine portrait, oval with flat cheekbones and a narrow nose. Her lips were full, voluptuous, ripe with promise. Her eyes had a faint slant, like a cat's. At this distance he could not tell their color, but her skin had the delicate ivory tint of an old cameo.

Gazing at her, Noel almost forgot to breathe. She was gorgeous, feline, untamed. Confused, he cast his mind through dim, preconceived ideas of medieval women: cloistered, draped in narrow gowns to their ankles, locked away in towers.

Elena, however, made him think of Diana, goddess of the hunt. In his mind he reclothed her according to the style of the ancients: a softly draped chiton in purest white, bow arm and right breast bare, standing in a chariot drawn by prancing stallions. . . .

Only right now, she was hunting him. He'd better keep his mind on saving himself.

"Look," he said, spreading out his hands to indicate peaceful intent. "I'm a—a pilgrim, a traveler. I'm on my way to Constantinople, and I—"

She spat at him. "Liar! I know your Byzantine tricks. You will say anything, do anything to save your pathetic skin. Last night we showed you that we want none of you here!"

"I had no part in the battle—"

"Why not? Did you scuttle for cover at the first charge?" she asked with scorn that was like the rake of fingernails. "Are you a pilgrim, or perhaps a scribe following at Lord Theodore's heels like a trained dog to write his letters for him?"

Thaddeus barked and howled, throwing himself upon the ground and rolling about.

Hot-cheeked, Noel made no answer. She was dangerous in this mood. The wrong word from him could send an arrow flying to his chest. If he was going to get out of this situation, he'd better make them understand that he was no part of what happened last night.

"This . . . Theodore you mention," he said carefully, "is a stranger to me. I am a traveler alone. I—"

"No one is stupid enough to come through our mountains *alone*," she said with a harsh laugh. "Have you not heard of the Milengi? Do you not fear us?"

He didn't answer. He'd never heard of the Milengi. Right now his fingers were itching to access the memory store of his LOC and get some answers, but he had to wait.

"The whole Peloponnese fears our tribe!" she boasted. "And Taygetus is ours. You cannot travel here without our permission."

"Then I beg your pardon," said Noel, although it was hard to force the apology from his mouth. Own the whole mountain range indeed. "How do I get permission? It's important that I reach the city of—"

"Silence! We are not stupid. We cannot be fooled by such an obvious lie."

"I'm not lying!" he shouted back. "George tells me I'm a good month's journey off my destination. So I'm lost. That's all. I got caught in last night's mess by accident. I am *alone*."

She studied him a moment, and the contempt deepened in her gaze. "You are not only a liar, but a coward as well. And this is the kind of man that is sent to rule over us. Hah! You are as pathetic as your master. If you think you can mew about being lost and have us believe that, you must think again, Byzantine. You will be taken to our camp, where you will join your wretched companions. What will they think about your attempt to desert them, eh?"

Snapping her fingers, she said, "George, Thaddeus, quickly!"

Alarmed, Noel spun around to face the dwarfs who came at his back. Thaddeus swung at him with his dagger. Noel feinted, engaging with a swiftness that struck sparks between the two blades, and sent the dwarf's weapon spinning through the air. It was a trick Noel had learned from a seasoned Roman centurion on one of his past travels. He swung to deal with George, but from behind him Elena snatched a cloak off the nearest corpse and flung it over Noel's head. Blinded by the garment, Noel struggled to yank it off, but before he could succeed, she pinned his arms in a bear hug. She was stronger than she looked. Cursing himself for letting her get behind him, Noel thrust his foot behind Elena's and nearly succeeded in tripping the girl, who was shouting for the dwarfs to help her.

Noel whipped around, throwing Elena off balance. He broke her grip and freed one arm. Twisting sharply, he shoved her away from him and was pulling the cloak off his head when she kicked him hard in the groin.

The resultant pain was like an explosion. Choking, he doubled over and they swarmed him. While he wheezed, struggling to regain his strength, his three opponents succeeded in binding a cord about his arms and chest, leaving him semi-helpless and completely blind in the suffocating folds of his cloak.

"Now," said Elena breathlessly, her voice hard with determination. "We take him to camp and put him with the rest of the Byzantine dogs."

"No," said Noel furiously, his voice muffled within the cloak. The smell of old sweat and blood nearly choked him. "Please, you must listen to me. My uncle is a cloth merchant, a dyer. He sent me here in search of alum."

"Get him moving," said Elena, not listening. "We have a long walk ahead of us."

"Look, you don't understand," said Noel in rising desperation. "I don't belong—"

Something narrow and hard walloped him across the ribs, and he yelped. Once the agony stopped pulsing through him, and he could catch his breath again, he suspected she had hit him with her bow. His temper burned, but even as he spun clumsily around, blinded and disoriented beneath the cloak, he had no way to express it, no way to reach her. And a cautious corner of his brain warned him that she might kick him again if he tried anything. The lady played dirty.

Jeering, the dwarfs spun him around and around until he staggered with dizziness.

"You will be quiet," said Elena, "and you will give us no trouble. One quick push and you break your neck falling down the mountain. Understand?"

He was an observer, not a participant. He had no part in the events happening here. He could not afford to tamper with history, not in the slightest way. But he vowed that as soon as his hands were free he was going to put them around this little amazon's pretty neck.

"Do you understand?" she repeated.

"Go to hell."

"He understands," said George.

The dwarfs laughed merrily, and Elena laughed with them.

"Move him along," she said. "When Sir Magnin comes, we can tell him that not one whoreson got away."

She sounded far too pleased with herself. Caught by a woman and two dwarfs as easily as a greenhorn, thought Noel. Not only was his pride and body bruised, but he'd already flunked his training in how to avoid capture, arrest, and seizure.

Training class, he thought in exasperation, didn't cover female Greek bandits.

CHAPTER 3

By the time they reached the camp hidden somewhere upon the craggy sides of Mt. Taygetus, Noel was winded, hot, and furious. His muscles ached from tension, for walking blind over rough terrain made him irrationally certain that each step was going to send him plunging over a precipice to his death.

The dwarfs flanked him on either side. George tapped him or tugged at the hem of his tunic to give him guidance signals. Thaddeus's signals were all painful pinches on his thigh. Noel vowed that as soon as he got free of his bonds he was going to kick Thaddeus off the mountain.

The rocks and bracken left him bruised and scratched. Soon he was limping on his bare foot. How, he wondered desperately, had he managed to lose one sandal in the time stream?

And what the hell did it matter, considering the trouble he now found himself in? He had to get away from these people and consult his LOC's data banks. His observations so far told him he was somewhere between the eleventh and fourteenth centuries. But three hundred years of latitude wasn't precise enough. He must know exactly when he was so he could reprogram the LOC for an emergency return.

A sour bubble of fear rose to his mouth. He thought of going back through the anomaly that had cast him here, of experiencing that agony, that terrible *void*, and he broke out into a cold sweat.

There had been too many tests for him to believe the equipment at fault. That made Tchielskov's absence suddenly suspicious, although Noel hated to believe the old man capable of treachery.

But if it was sabotage and his destination had been deliberately altered, would his return capability have been tampered with also?

The thoughts raced through his mind until they half maddened him. He forced himself to calm down, to not panic yet. He had to remain stable and listen to his trained instincts. He had to wait, putting up with being a prisoner, until the moment for escape was right.

In the meantime, not being able to see through the tight weave of his cloak left him disoriented and edgy. Sounds were muffled too. He tried to walk normally, but he found that he tended to lift his feet higher, in shorter steps, groping his way although George kept a running commentary on what obstacles were ahead of him. With his arms bound to his sides, he felt off balance and clumsy.

Thaddeus pinched him hard. "Rock ahead," he said.

Noel flinched from the pain, and his temper got away from him. He whirled on the dwarf, yelling, "You damned little twerp! Leave my backside alone!" and kicked out blindly.

His foot connected with Thaddeus. Noel heard a grunt and a yell of fright accompanied by a crackling of crushed weeds as the dwarf went tumbling. George's laughter rang out through the crisp air.

"Quiet! All of you!" commanded Elena from ahead of them. Her footsteps came rustling back through the weeds and loose shale.

Noel sensed her presence as much as heard the whistling swing of her bow. He dodged blindly, and managed to escape the worst force of the blow. Still, it hurt enough to make him swear.

"Stand still, you!" said Elena. "George, stop that noise and go after your brother."

Thaddeus moaned from somewhere to Noel's left. "Kicked me, just like a mule. Broke me leg."

"Be what ye deserved," said George without a trace of sympathy. "Get up. Ye ain't hurt."

"I could have been. It's sore bruised. Could be broke."

There came the sound of a thud, and Thaddeus's quick yelp.

"I'll give ye broke. Get on with ye!" said George.

They came scrambling and panting through the scrub. Noel considered making a break for it, but Elena's hand closed upon his shoulder. "Don't do that again," she said in a low voice.

"I'll do it every time I'm provoked," said Noel hotly. "Tell him to keep his damned hands to himself."

Elena drew in a quick breath as though exasperated. "What do you expect? The rules of chivalry? We have our own laws and our own ways. We do not need the iron heel of Byzantium on our necks."

"Forget the political rhetoric," said Noel. "I'm talking about treating your prisoners decently—"

"Just havin' a bit of fun, was all," said Thaddeus. "And you bein' our prisoner means we can do as we like with you."

"Bring him on," said Elena. "And you, scribe, if you try anything else we'll slit your throat and leave you here to feed the vultures. We have enough prisoners taken already."

Noel swallowed his anger and kept silent after that. To discover that the people of this age were just as selfish, backward, petty, and vicious as any other era, including his own, was hardly surprising, but disappointing just the same. He remembered that Trojan had said once that chivalry was more often sung about in troubadour ballads than practiced by knights.

Thinking about Trojan brought a rush of homesickness that he'd never encountered before in all his years of traveling.

Then he caught himself up sharply, angry at his wallow in self-pity. He hoped with all his heart that Trojan's journey to the muddy battlefield of Agincourt had been a safe one. He hoped that none of his fellow historians had fallen into a trap like his.

Noise ahead drew him from his reflections. He lifted his head, straining to decipher the sounds of goats and horses, people talking, bursts of low laughter, moans of pain, the clank and rattle of activity.

"Hold him here," said Elena and went on.

Noel stood in place, pretending a docility he was far from feeling. To his left at a distance ran a rushing burble of water. Noel swallowed with difficulty, longing to slake his thirst in the stream. Mingled with the scents of fresh goat and horse droppings, he could smell woodsmoke and the aroma of cake and roasted meat. His stomach growled loudly. He felt hollow enough to eat a five-pound steak with all the trimmings.

"Yani! Demetrius!" Elena's voice was bugle clear. "Look what I have brought you."

Noel strained to listen to the murmur of two voices, purposely kept low although Elena's excited words ran like a mountain stream over the other's. Then the second voice lifted, revealing a man's deep tones: "Cut him free, and let us see him."

A knife cut the cord binding Noel's arms. He swept off the suffocating cloak in a fury, ruffling his hair, and felt the cool kiss of fresh air with relief. At first the bright sunlight dazzled his eyes. He squinted, putting a hand across them in protection.

By the time his vision adjusted, Elena had walked back within a few feet of him. Beside her stood a man with a bullish neck and shoulders, muscles bulging even in his wide jaws. He towered over Elena, and only the faint red cast to his dark hair and a certain similarity around the eyes spoke of any family resemblance between them. Although he wore hose over legs like tree trunks and short, ankle-high boots, his long, sleeveless jerkin was fashioned from a wolf pelt with the fur still attached to the hide. Its leather lacings strained across his broad chest with every breath he drew.

He was chewing on a haunch of what smelled like roasted kid. Every time he bit off a hunk, hot juices sizzled through the meat. Noel found his gaze locked on the man's greasy mouth, watching the powerful jaws grind methodically. He swallowed, longing for food, imagining its taste in his own mouth.

"Well?" said Elena impatiently. The breeze blew her hair across her face, and she tossed it back. "Have you nothing to say, Demetrius?"

The man drew the back of his hand across his mouth and tossed the bone to a mongrel dog cringing nearby with its tail tucked low. It snarled and snapped at the prize. Immediately two other dogs appeared. They fought viciously over the food until Demetrius uncoiled a whip from his belt and cracked it at them.

"Get out!" he shouted.

One hound snatched the bone and dashed away. The others slunk after it.

Demetrius's gaze came back to Noel. His eyes narrowed. "He's no soldier, no courtier."

"But he is Byzantine," she said in frustration. She stared at the man in plain disappointment. "We caught him and brought him in. Otherwise he'd have gone to Maina or even to Monemvasia and sounded the alarm. That is worth something, is it not?"

Demetrius ignored her; his gaze remained fastened on Noel although his mind seemed elsewhere. He belched. "Long run over to the coast. Not much to worry about from a skinny scribe like this. Should have slit his throat rather than bring him here."

Fresh alarm touched Noel. These people were all too casual about slitting throats. He took a step forward. "Just a—"

George whipped a dagger point to Noel's stomach. Without a word, he shook his head once. His eyes, weary, a touch cynical, and very serious, stared up into Noel's from his craggy, ill-proportioned face.

"Don't need another mouth," said Demetrius. "Too many to feed now. Dogs hungry."

"But—"

"Enough, Elena," he said sharply. "Bring anything for the treasury?"

She glared at him. "I dislike robbing corpses!"

"No different than robbing live ones. You—"

"Oh, you are hopeless," she said, walking back and forth with her hands on her hips. She kicked at a pebble. "Where is Sir Magnin? Has any word come yet about how he fared with the castle?"

Demetrius gave her a slow, sly grin. "Sir Magnin, eh? You talked us into this all because of your precious Sir Magnin." He gripped her arm. "What if he doesn't take the castle, eh? What if he dies with an arrow in his throat?"

She yanked free. "Why should I care?" she said loftily. "If he fails, then we have no Frank possessing Mistra. The Byzantines will send another foreign *kephale* from Constantinople, and we'll be no better off—"

"We can catch the next one too," said Demetrius, still grinning, "and ransom him like this one."

"You should wait until you have word from Sir Magnin before you send any independent ransom demands to Constantinople," she said sharply. "He planned this well, and it is to our advantage to help him."

Demetrius spat. "That *gasmoule* half-breed. Why should I take his orders?"

"Because, brother," said a youth, walking up to join Elena and Demetrius, "he is more clever than you. As long as he shares his spoils and gold, I don't mind taking his orders. What have you found today, little Elena?"

She gestured at Noel casually, as though he had ceased to matter. "Just a stray casualty on the battlefield, not dead, and ready to cause us trouble. I thought you would be grateful to me for finding him."

"Kill him," said Demetrius. He drew his dagger and tossed it to the youth, who caught the hilt deftly. "Too many mouths to feed. And that Albanian howling every minute about ransom and consequences . . . enough to drive a man mad."

"He's a scribe," said Elena. "A coward and a liar too. He did his best to talk us into letting him go, but we caught him easily."

"No talking, Yani," said Demetrius impatiently. "Just kill him. Take him over there past the rocks where the blood won't spook the horses."

Noel's heartbeat quickened. His breath came shorter. All over, he could feel his body tense, ready to fight, ready to run. Although Demetrius had tossed Yani a dagger, the boy was wearing another thrust through his belt. If Noel could seize that . . .

"Watch him," said Thaddeus in warning. "He's tricky. Damned near broke me leg."

Yani smiled, and his gaze ran briefly over the dwarf before returning to Noel. The resemblance between him and Elena was strong enough to leave no doubt they were brother and sister. He was perhaps sixteen or seventeen, built wiry and quick like the girl, with fiery red hair and a smattering of freckles across his cheekbones. There was high intelligence in his face and eyes.

"Strange," he said. "This man has not the look of a Byzantine."

"Neither does Lord Theodore," said Elena.

Demetrius shrugged. "Theodore is a damned Albanian. What does it matter? Kill this knave and be done with it. I want you to take a message to—"

"That message can wait," said Yani sharply. "We promised

Sir Magnin we'd delay until nightfall. We shall keep our word."

"Lose a whole day waiting on him," grumbled Demetrius. He pointed at Noel. "Be rid of him! Elena, get yourself in proper clothes. Thaddeus and George, take the goats out and stake them in good grass. Move!"

Now, with everyone scattering, was the time. Noel spun around to run. Only then did he see the sentry crouched atop a rocky escarpment above the narrow pass leading into the camp, which was situated at the bottom of a deep ravine. With the sheer rock walls surrounding him on three sides and a bowman at the only exit, Noel hadn't a chance.

He hesitated, his shoulders drooping. Damn. The only option left to him was to fight the boy and get one of those daggers, since his own had been taken by George. He turned his head slightly as Yani walked around to face him again. He looked at Yani, then away, not trusting himself to keep his intentions from his face.

Yani was no fool. He stood beyond reach, the borrowed dagger held ready in his hand. "No, no, my friend," he said softly. "There is no escape from here, except to your Father in heaven."

Noel swallowed hard. It didn't help. Nothing helped. He was as tense as wire.

"Elena said you are a scribe. Is that true?"

Noel looked at him and shook his head.

"Ah. I did not see a pouch to hold vellum, ink, and pens," said Yani. He paused until Noel's gaze met his. "I know how to read and write."

"Congratulations," said Noel dryly.

He said it in Latin, which he could speak on his own without the translator's assistance. His tone was clear enough to the boy. A swift tide of color spread from Yani's collar to his hairline. He frowned, his air of friendliness gone.

"You are arrogant for a prisoner. Why do you speak Latin? Are you trying to insult me?"

Noel shrugged. "Maybe. Maybe not."

"Your accent is deplorable," said Yani, showing off by switching to medieval Latin in midsentence.

"Dead men tell no tales," said Noel with a flippancy he did not really feel. He was tired of this cat-and-mouse game. If they wanted to kill him, then he was ready to get the whole business over and done with.

"I do not understand this saying," said Yani. "Is it from your country?"

"You might say that."

"What is your name?"

"What does it matter?"

"Are you trying to provoke me into killing you?"

Noel sighed. "Look, you have your orders. I—"

"I don't always do what my big brother says." Yani's lips curled into a brief, secretive smile.

Noel felt a burst of hope, but he remained suspicious. "What's the deal?" he demanded. "What do you want from me in exchange for not following your brother's orders?"

"You are a quick one."

"Let's say I'm not stupid."

"Are you Albanian?"

"No," snapped Noel, irritated with that tangent question.

"Your name is—"

"Never mind what my name is. It's irrelevant." A rule of traveling was to avoid stating names whenever possible. A traveler was supposed to blend in with the local crowds, to observe and record, *not* to participate.

Yani's hand closed on his shoulder. "You should not—"

Noel moved quicker than thought, stepping in close to the boy to force Yani's knife hand up while he grabbed the second dagger from Yani's belt. Yani shouted an alarm and swung at Noel, but Noel blocked the blow with his shoulder. Sliding one foot between Yani's, he tripped the boy and used his impetus to flip him through the air. Whirling, his gaze taking note of the sentry who was nocking an arrow to his bow, Noel ran for the pile of rocks near the mouth of the ravine.

They had spilled down from a past avalanche, leaving a sloped scar on the cliff face above. Noel thought he might be able to climb out that way, although his back would make a good target for the sentry.

Right now it didn't matter. He had to take any chance, no matter how slim. Ducking his head, he concentrated on running a fast zigzag course, ignoring the bruising pain of his bare foot upon the rocky ground.

More shouts alerted the camp. An arrow whistled past him,

missing by inches. Noel grinned to himself, sucking in air. He sprang up the rock pile, going on all fours where necessary, praying there were no snakes sunning themselves. Another arrow sliced through his cloak and bumped his side awkwardly with the fletching. Thank God for bad shots.

Noel reached the top of the rock pile and slithered over it, making sure he kept his body as low to the rocks as possible. This was not the time to stand erect.

He never heard it, never sensed it. There was no rush of air, no whisper of sound although there should have been something to warn him.

The projectile hit the back of his skull with a force that felt as though the mountain had fallen on top of him. He stumbled, feeling his body go slack in midstep, feeling his arms fly up of their own volition, feeling himself fall. Glaring sheets of red and yellow flared inside his skull, blinding him. Then the pain rushed over him in a sticky, nauseating wave. Behind it came an awful blackness, one he wasn't sure he could escape.

He fell, and never felt the ground.

CHAPTER 4

Noel awakened by degrees, gradually becoming aware of intense, uncomfortable heat and overwhelming thirst. When he finally managed to drag open his eyes, he found himself lying on the ground. Sunlight beat harshly down. Heat radiated off the dusty ground and the cliff face towering above him.

Dim noises of other voices and the sounds of activity filtered in, none of it intrusive enough to bother him. Thoughts, drifting like puff clouds in his brain, slowly came together and began to make sense.

He remembered running. He remembered being shot in the back of the head. With effort he raised his hand and groped along the base of his throbbing skull. He touched a spot soggy with clotted blood, and his head exploded with agony.

"Easy, my friend," said a voice.

A gentle hand gripped his shoulder while the clammy perspiration was wiped from his face with a cloth. Squinting, Noel fought back waves of stabbing pain, and stared up into a face silhouetted against the sun.

"Don't speak," said the man. "Are you thirsty?"

Noel's tongue had stuck to the roof of his mouth. He peeled it loose and managed to croak out, "Yes."

His friend moved away, and Noel lay limp and uncaring of what happened to him. Somewhere behind the throbbing, a corner of his mind remembered that he had an emergency injection in his LOC device. Using it would give him a pain-killer, and would also send an emergency assistance call to the main time computer. All he had to do was push it.

He rested a while longer, until the terrible pain ebbed to a bearable level.

"Here is water," said his friend, returning.

Noel dragged open his eyes. Cautiously he lifted his head.

"Wait. I want to move you to the shade. Will it hurt you too much?"

"No," he gasped. "Try."

"Very well. Have courage. I shall probably hurt you."

Strong hands scooped Noel up under the armpits and half lifted him. The pain came back with a vengeance, splitting jaggedly through his head until he had to close his eyes and grit his teeth to hold back a cry. He was dragged a short distance and propped against the rocks. The coolness of the shade, however, was a relief that made it worthwhile.

Grasping his left wrist, Noel ran his fingers over the copper bracelet until he found the proper control hidden inside its circumference. Until now, although he'd been hurt once before on a mission, he'd always prided himself on his toughness in coping with anything that came his way. But this was different. He wanted out, and he wanted out now. It didn't matter if these people around him saw him vanish into thin air.

He pressed the emergency call, and the LOC grew slightly warm upon his wrist. Relief coursed through him because until now he wasn't sure if his device was even functioning. A few seconds later he felt a tiny prick; numbness went through his veins.

The man helping him gave him a cup of water. Noel found it icy cold and clean, and drank thirstily. Deadened by the drug, the pain faded in his skull. He let out his breath in relief and focused for the first time upon his new friend's face. He had a few minutes before emergency assistance yanked him home. He did not want to think about the possibility that he might find himself trapped again between the time streams. The fear of once more facing that nightmare could not outweigh the fact that he was in serious trouble here, his mission out of control, and himself injured. Whatever the cost, he had to get out.

"Better now?" asked his benefactor.

Noel looked at the handsome, well-molded features beneath a rough-cut shock of thick chestnut hair. The man's eyes were as blue as the Peloponnesian sky. He was young, perhaps twenty to twenty-five—although with these people's short life spans that would be considered middle-aged. His face was tanned from hours in the sun, with tiny squint lines already cut into his skin at his eyes and mouth. A thick, puckered scar ran along his neck and disappeared beneath the embroidered collar of his tunic. His garb proclaimed him a rich man, for his heavy silk tunic was royal blue in color with purple lining the wide sleeves. His coat of arms was emblazoned at his collar and upon the hem of his tunic. His strong legs were encased in purple hose, and his shoes had been made from a heavy cloth that resembled tapestry. Thin, supple leather soles had been stitched to the bottoms for protection, and the points were fashionably long.

The man smiled and extended a well-shaped hand in friendship. Jewels made dull by the shade adorned his fingers.

"I am Theodore of Albania," he said. His smile grew wry. "I would introduce myself as Theodore, governor of Mistra, but that, alas, seems unlikely to come true."

Noel's eyes widened. "You're the prince who was ambushed last night."

"Yes," said Theodore. "Or at least I was. It seems you have caused them some confusion on the matter."

"I—I don't understand."

"Although you handle the Frankish tongue fluently, your accent is that of a foreigner. I heard you taunt the boy in Latin, and it is of a very old-fashioned derivation that would interest my old tutor greatly. He was an antiquary and fancied himself rather an expert in Roman Latin."

Noel wondered if he was hallucinating. Theodore's answer made absolutely no sense. Raising his hand to his eyes, Noel rubbed them a moment. How much longer until the recall happened? He was sweating lightly, from concussion or from nervousness he couldn't tell.

"I still don't—"

"No, of course not. I tend to ramble from my point. It is a fault of mine," said Theodore smoothly. "These bandits are a suspicious people. From something you said, I gather they are convinced that you are me."

Noel frowned, feeling his headache threaten to return. "I—what?" he asked stupidly.

"It seems that despite my finery and my good manners, they do not think I am Theodore. I suppose they wish to convince themselves that I am a servant masquerading in your place. While you, good sir, in your simple clothes and awkward tongue, are the governor. They seem to admire you for nearly escaping their clutches. I wish I had thought of the ruse." He made a comical face that had serious frustration behind it. "I might well be to the gates of Mistra by now."

Noel's hand fell to his lap. He frowned. "This is crazy."

"Have some more water," said Theodore. He put the cup to Noel's lips, his gaze watching the bandit guard who wandered close to survey them for a moment before walking on. "Now, listen, my friend," said Theodore in a low, urgent voice as soon as the guard was beyond earshot. "It is not such a crazy idea if we can make it work."

Noel nearly choked on his last swallow of water. He sat upright too fast, and had to shut his eyes against a wave of dizziness. "No—"

"Hear me, please," said Theodore, placing a hand upon his chest. "No harm can come to you this way, for I am too valuable as a ransom prisoner for killing. Convince them that you are Theodore the Bold, and I shall make you a rich man when this is over."

"Why?"

"Oh, come, man!" said Theodore impatiently. "Consider the situation. This province has gotten out of hand. Even the local Franks have sought audience with the emperor in Constantinople to request a stronger governor placed in charge over them. The tribes—these wretched bandits—are running wild, looting and preying upon weak villagers. The Greek families are feeling restive and think they can throw off the yoke of Byzantium, which is complete foolishness. The Turks are on the move again. A new wave of invaders is expected to strike the coast soon."

How long until recall? thought Noel wearily. He found it hard to concentrate although Theodore's blue eyes burned into him with penetrating force.

"I have been entrusted by Emperor Andronicus to put this province back into order. It will take a strong army and a strong sense of purpose to accomplish it. But I can't do anything as long as I am kept a prisoner. I *must* gain my freedom."

He gripped Noel's arm. "You can help me. You *will* help me. It's very little that I ask."

"You ask a lot," said Noel uneasily. "I have no political interest in Mistra. I am a traveler on my way to—"

"Hear me! They were about to kill you, were they not?"

Noel gingerly touched the back of his head. "I'd say they nearly did. What was it?"

"A pebble from a slingshot. A mere shepherd's weapon," said Theodore impatiently. "I tell you that you are expendable. Only the suspicion that you might be me in disguise has changed their minds about letting you live. All I ask you to do is bolster their suspicion into complete belief. Act like a prince for a few hours. Put on arrogance, a noble air, make demands . . . these actions will convince them. See how I act like your servant when they watch us?"

Noel looked past him across the camp, where the bandits were grouped idly. Some were cleaning their weapons. Others drank from a wineskin or argued. The boy Yani, who had felled him with a pebble almost as effective as a nine-millimeter round, paced back and forth as though waiting for something that had not yet happened.

Like my recall, thought Noel. It had been long enough. Was the signal jammed? Wasn't it reaching back to the time computer? Didn't they know by now that he was in trouble?

"Look," Noel said curtly. "There's one aspect of your plan that maybe you haven't considered. Like, if they start thinking I'm Theodore of Albania and you're my servant, what's to stop them from making you expendable and killing you?"

"I have considered that, of course," said Theodore. No trace of fear or self-concern showed in his eyes. "It is a risk, but I am not afraid to gamble. If you can focus their attention upon you, then less will be upon me. I shall find an opportunity to escape."

"I sympathize," said Noel, "but I can't help you."

"You must!"

"No. It's not my cause. It's not my involvement."

Theodore drew back. A frown darkened his face, and Noel wondered if Theodore was going to demonstrate princely temper. "Who are you?" he asked imperiously. "Where are you from?"

"I am Noel of Kedran."

Theodore's frown intensified. "I have not heard of this place. What country? Are you English?"

"No," said Noel hastily.

"The English have no interest in our affairs, and we pay our Venetian allies a great deal of money to make sure the English continue to stay away," said Theodore with visible displeasure. "To whom is your allegiance?"

"I owe no man my allegiance," said Noel. He didn't like where this interrogation was heading. He didn't like not having a thorough cover story at hand. Theodore could tell he was lying. "I am not a vassal."

"Odd," said Theodore, still subjecting him to that penetrating gaze. "Are you dishonored, then? Disinherited? Are you nothing but a vagrant, wandering the face of Europe? 'Tis dangerous indeed."

"I *was* on my way to Constantinople," said Noel, growing weary of having to repeat himself. "Apparently I am lost."

"Lost? Indeed, you are. One hundred fifty leagues if you go by sea as well as by land. You are too far north of your course."

Noel grunted. He made himself accept the fact that his recall wasn't going to work. That meant there was a ninety-five percent chance that his 1.67-day limit wouldn't work either. If so, he was trapped here for the rest of his life, with no way to get home at all.

He shivered. He wasn't ready to give up.

"If you help me," Theodore was saying, "I shall give you safe escort to Constantinople. I shall give you money and ample rewards. You may even gain an audience with the emperor."

It was tempting. Noel knew Theodore was being more than generous. But he could not interfere. Every dictate, every principle he lived by forbade violating the time paradox.

He met Theodore's anxious, persuasive gaze. He could almost feel the force of this man's will being thrown at him, urging him to agree.

"No," he said. "You make a good offer, but to my regret, I cannot accept it. My reasons are valid. I have an oath I must obey."

"What oath supersedes this?" cried Theodore. "Even God must look down from His heaven and know these times are fraught with upheaval and dangerous change."

"Change can be a good thing," said Noel.

Theodore drew breath with a hiss. "You believe in this cause of independence?"

"I didn't say that."

"What, then, say you? Have I spilled my confidences to a traitorous varlet? A knave without conscience or loyalty?"

"I won't betray you," said Noel, trying hard to hang on to his temper.

"Oh, yes, an easy assurance. No doubt you think you will now go and bargain with them at my expense. I shall strangle you here in the dirt before I let that happen."

Theodore's eyes blazed. His fingers curled into fists. Noel tensed, although he knew he was in no shape to defend himself from attack.

"Let's just keep things as they are, without complications, without intrigue, all right?" Noel said soothingly. "You're the prince. And I'm the simple traveler—"

"Indeed you are simple," muttered Theodore, shoving a hand through his hair. "And most damnably stubborn as well."

Noel glared at him and said nothing. Silence stretched out for several minutes, a silence in which Theodore sat on a rock with his blue eyes dark with anger and his jaw clenched hard. Noel studied the layout of the camp, although it was hard to concentrate when his own disappointment was choking him.

Wasn't there anyone listening in Chicago? Wasn't there anyone monitoring his mission? The LOC was recording the events happening here, and it was supposed to transmit back. If nothing else, they should be able to trace him to the wrong time. Weren't they *trying* to get him back?

All kinds of chilling explanations occurred to him: the anarchists had overrun the Time Institute and destroyed the equipment; a traitor had infiltrated the labs, sabotaging not only Noel's LOC but others as well; the time computer had malfunctioned. . . .

He could theorize all day, but what good did that do him? As long as he remained a prisoner with these other men, he couldn't access his LOC for much needed data. Aside from Theodore, four others had been taken prisoner. From the looks of their torn, drooping finery, they must be part of Theodore's personal entourage. Not one wore mail or showed signs of having borne arms. Scribes and toadies, thought Noel unfairly and tried to banish the grim memory of all those soldiers lying dead upon the mountainside. What had they died for? To protect this pathetic knot of courtiers now huddled in a dejected cluster?

Their prison was a goat pen, and the haphazard, rickety pole fence wouldn't hold an arthritic nanny goat, much less active, able-bodied men. But a boy in a ragged, homespun tunic and bare feet stood guard over them with a crossbow. He had the intense, eager look of someone anxious to practice his aim on a moving target.

Noel shifted his gaze back to Theodore and frowned. The worst part of it was that he wanted to help this man. There was something noble—for lack of a better word—about the prince, some aspect of character that shone from within him even when he was worried and abstracted, as now. That kind of charm was hard to resist.

The words of his mentor Tchielskov came back to Noel, haunting him: *"You must not involve yourself with the lives and concerns of the people you encounter. Change no course of events. That is our primary directive. Interfere, and you alter history forever. Meddle, and you might eliminate your own existence. Remember that when your heart urges you to practice compassion."*

"Something is wrong about this," said Noel aloud, still frowning.

Theodore's gaze swung to meet his. "Obviously."

"I'm not talking about morality," snapped Noel. "The ambush. Your men scattered upon the mountainside. How many? Fifty?"

"Seventy-two." Theodore's eyes held anguish. "All dead? Or any wounded?"

Noel thought of the scavenging dwarfs and their little daggers. He looked away first. "All dead."

Theodore remained silent.

Noel said, "But that's what I mean. Seventy men at arms, enough to man a garrison, and these hill bandits take them out? It doesn't add up."

"The Milengi did not carry the main brunt of the fighting," said Theodore, giving him an odd look. "It was that fiend, Magnin Phrangopoulos, and his army who came upon us like

the hounds of hell. To engage in combat without announce-
ment, to engage in combat from ambush, and at night . . . he
may call himself a knight, but God pity his black soul, if he
still has one."

"Look," said Noel, unable to resist his own curiosity, "your
pride is hurt right now. It was a nice post, being governor, but
your emperor will ransom you. At least your hide is still intact.
You'll get assigned another post. You don't have to take this
to heart—"

"Hell's teeth, how dare you tell me to fold my bones and be
grateful I can sit far away from the action while that damned
gasmoule bastard has Sophia in his clutches!"

His voice carried loudly enough to cause the guard and some
of the other bandits to glance their way. Noel reached out and
caught Theodore's wrist.

"Calm down," he said. "I just asked. Who's Sophia?"

Theodore shook off his hand. His eyes burned like fire. "The
Lady Sophia is my betrothed."

"Uh-oh. He grabbed her during the ambush and made off
with her? No wonder you're so upset."

"Upset? I—how can you be so ignorant of the world around
you? Lady Sophia lives at Mistra. Her father was its most
recent governor, and his death opened the post for my appointment. She is alone at the castle, defenseless save for the
garrison there that has probably surrendered by now to Sir
Magnin's forces. Who is to protect her?"

"Someone will," said Noel.

His quick assurance received the stony glare it deserved.

Uncomfortable, Noel shrugged but a warning twinge from
his skull told him not to move. "All right," he said with a sigh.
"You're saying she has no one to watch out for her? No trusty
servants?"

"I am saying that Lady Sophia is sixteen, fair, and innocent,
no match for a man who knows not God, who mocks all laws
save that which his sword arm makes for him, who pillages
and thieves and stirs people into revolt against their masters.
She . . . she is on yon hill, a half day's ride from me. I am this
close, and I can do *nothing*!"

Theodore's eyes were so raw with anxiety it felt like an
intrusion to watch him. "She is waiting for me to rescue her.
I am her only hope. How long can she hold out?"

"I do offer you my sympathy," said Noel, "but—"

"I am her protector!" cried Theodore. "If I fail her, *if* I fail her . . ." His voice quivered away and he put his hands to his face.

Noel frowned, disturbed by the man's weeping. A wave of compassion swept him and before he could stop himself, he set his hand upon Theodore's shoulder in silent comfort. Inside he raged at the imperative that kept him from getting directly involved in the lives of history. He hated inaction. He hated appearing cold and heartless before this man, who wept before him without shame.

Briefly he knew the temptation to strike back at fate. If he were indeed trapped here, then why not live as he chose? Why not interfere? After all, those who had sabotaged him would have to suffer the consequences, not him.

But once you adopted a principle you didn't throw it off just because the going got rough. Besides, he didn't want to think about having to spend the rest of his life here. It brought back that numb, crawling sense of hopelessness to the pit of his stomach.

Who was to say, however, that Sir Magnin's usurpation of power was the way history was supposed to go?

You are going to get in awful trouble for this, accused a voice in his head.

Noel hesitated a moment longer, but he hurt, and he was mad, and he was scared. Maybe the only way to get the Institute's attention was to kick the time paradox principle to hell. Maybe then they'd think about rescuing him.

"All right," he said. He tapped Theodore on the shoulder. "Come on. You've squeezed enough tears."

Theodore's chestnut head whipped up. "You think I am unmanly?"

"Where I come from we don't cry over trouble. We do something about it."

"Oh, brave words indeed," said Theodore, mocking him. "Having refused my request, you now choose to criticize—"

"I'll help," said Noel.

"What?"

Noel wriggled a little, feeling uneasy, but determined to go through with his decision. "I said I'll help. Briefly. If you think these Greeks are going to really believe I'm the prince, then I'll go along for a while. But only a short while, understand?"

Theodore gripped his hand, a smile shining from his blue eyes. "Only until I make good my escape. You have my thanks, Noel of Kedran." He glanced around swiftly to be certain they were unobserved, then shifted so that his back blocked the guard's view of Noel. Drawing something from a pocket in his sleeve, he passed it to Noel. "Here. My seal of office. Guard it with your life."

Uneasily Noel wondered what his impulsiveness had gotten him into. But he allowed Theodore to put the object in his hand. The seal was made of gold, and although small, it was quite heavy. He looked at the relief of a two-headed eagle and recognized it as the symbol of Imperial Byzantium. Tracing it with his finger, he shivered as a sense of history flowed from it into his flesh.

"I'll keep it safe," he said. "You have my word."

Theodore smiled, his whole face lighting up with a charisma that made Noel wonder how he had managed to resist the man this long. "I have a plan," said the prince in a low, eager voice. "It is a desperate one, full of risk, but with God's help we shall make it work. Listen closely."

Noel leaned toward him, but his attention was distracted by a horse and rider galloping into the camp and plunging to a halt in a dramatic swirl of dust.

Theodore turned to look also, and his face went pale.

"What is it?" asked Noel in alarm. "Who—"

"See the badge of the falcon on his left shoulder?" whispered Theodore in a hollow voice. "It is one of Sir Magnin's men."

A cheer rose from the gathering bandits, and Theodore's shoulders dropped. "God help us all," he said in despair. "He must have taken the castle."

The other courtiers came running from the far end of the pen. "My lord!"

Quick as lightning, Theodore whirled to his feet. "Nicholas, all of you, heed me," he said. "This is Noel of Kedran, a stranger who has agreed to join our cause—"

"But, my lord—"

"Silence! Listen well. We have little time," said Theodore rapidly. "All of you must pretend that he is Prince Theodore of Albania."

"But prithee, why?"

"He will explain it to you. The masquerade will free me from their attention and improve my chances of escape. As long as they consider me a servant, I hold little importance."

"But his clothes—"

"A disguise. The Greeks have invented this intrigue themselves. We need only capitalize upon it. No argument! Play your parts well."

Not giving them further chances to protest, Theodore swiftly tapped each man upon the shoulder as he made introductions. "Nicholas, my adviser of state. Stephen, my confessor. Thomas, my secretary. Guy, my gentleman in waiting."

The introductions were too fast and too brief for Noel to assimilate well. They bowed in their turn to him, their faces closed with suspicion and reluctance. Adoring suppliants they were not.

It wasn't going to work, thought Noel. Not in a million years.

"Theodore the Bold!" called an arrogant voice in French. "Stand forth from your men!"

Theodore milled with the others as they turned about. Of them all, only he sent one last beseeching look at Noel, who still sat upon the ground. The plumpish one called Thomas— already Noel had forgotten his job description—tugged unhappily upon Theodore's sleeve and shook his head. His eyes looked at his master with open despair.

"What is this cowardice?" demanded that arrogant voice. "Stand forth and face us."

Noel gulped in a deep breath and said, "Don't just stand there gawking. Stephen, Noel, help me to my feet."

The courtiers glanced down at him uncertainly, and their very bewilderment was perhaps the most convincing thing they could have done.

Theodore bent and helped Noel to his feet with a great display of solicitude. For an instant Noel was dizzy. He gripped Theodore's forearm hard to hang on. Then the tilted world straightened for him and he looked ahead to the knight who stood with legs braced and arms akimbo. The sunshine gleamed off his mail coif, glittered upon the signs of cadetship on his collar, and reflected from the burnished steel breastplate of armor that he wore over his surcoat and mail. His helmet, fastened to the breastplate by a length of chain, dangled at his side. He wore long gauntlets upon his hands and plated greaves to protect his shins.

Noel realized he was seeing armor in a transitional phase between mail and the heavy steel plate that would mark the epoch of the medieval era. Trojan could tell him what every single bit and piece of it was called. But Trojan was not here.

Slowly, Noel walked forward, trying to keep himself steady on his feet. When he stepped into the sunshine, its brightness made him wince.

Whoever he was, the knight was no fool. Dark, close-set eyes shifted from Theodore to Noel and back to Theodore again. The man frowned, and Noel halted just short of the pole fence. Weeds and some kind of flowering vine had grown over it. Bees swarmed busily.

Noel met the knight's suspicious gaze with all the arrogance he could muster. Without looking at Theodore, he waved him back. Theodore hesitated, then returned to the other courtiers.

"I am Theodore of Albania," Noel said in a voice of cold indifference.

The knight burst out laughing. "You?" he gasped finally, wiping his eyes. "Demetrius, I protest this joke has gone too far. Who thought to set this ragamuffin before me and call him a prince?"

Noel's face grew hot and he could hear a distant roaring in his ears, but he maintained his stony look. On a previous mission he had been privileged to actually stand in the same room as the Roman emperor Marcus Aurelius. At a party in his honor, the emperor had arrived already displeased over some matter of state. No entertainment pleased him. No conversation amused him. No flattery won a single smile from him. He had been chilly and distant, and by the time he left he had frightened his hosts half to death.

Now, Noel copied that behavior as closely as he could. He prayed he had enough acting ability to carry it off, or this was going to be his last role.

"No," said the knight. "I do not believe it."

Demetrius towered over the knight, his muscular arms bulging as he gestured. "Yani!" he shouted. "Over here. It is Yani's idea. Don't like it myself. Don't believe it. Yani is always too clever."

The redheaded youth who had brained Noel with his sling-shot strode over. He was smiling with confidence. "Look at him," he said. "No, really look."

The knight glanced at Noel briefly and shrugged. "I see a scribe badly dressed, missing a shoe, without hose, his cloak stained with blood. You tell me this is a prince? What about those bejeweled peacocks behind him? What about the big one wearing the insignia of—"

"Anyone can don clothing," said Yani. "Is it not said that Lord Theodore is a clever man? Why should he ride through hostile territory without resorting to disguise?"

"A cowardly trick."

"To a knight, perhaps." Yani shrugged. "But to me, it says here is a clever man. He was the only survivor on the battlefield this morning. With luck he would have escaped entirely."

Put that on my epitaph, thought Noel bleakly.

"And his speech," said Yani. "It is peculiar. We can barely understand him, even when he speaks Frankish."

"The others?"

"Polished, with fine airs. You know how professional courtiers are."

"Yes, I do know," said the knight with scorn. "What do you know of a court and its graces, bandit?"

Demetrius put his hand on his dagger with a growl.

Yani's smile disappeared. "I know enough," he said. "Explain to me a scribe found on a battlefield, without vellum or pens, a scribe who claims he has never heard of Theodore the Bold, a scribe who says he is journeying *to* Constantinople and is simply lost."

"A fool's tale!"

"That is what he told us."

"He's lying."

"Exactly," said Yani and shot Noel a glance of satisfaction. "He is too odd. Nothing about him makes any sense, except the explanation I have found. Talk to him yourself."

"I shall." The knight stepped closer to the fence, close enough for Noel to smell the unwashed sweat on him, close enough for Noel to see that he was hardly grown from boy-hood. But his eyes were as old as these mountains. They bored into Noel. "Theodore of Albania?" he said sharply.

"Yes," said Noel.

"You claim yourself as such?"

"Yes."

"What proof have you?"

Noel did his best to stare right through the man. "My men."

"Your men would lie like jackals. What else?"

"My word."

"I spit on your word."

Noel felt the heat rise in his face again. Behind him, the courtiers muttered angrily.

"Oh, come, sirrah!" said the knight with scorn. "Can you not think of another lie for me? I vow, you are a witty one, playing your master's fool this way. But we'll shave your tongue for the trouble, I promise you."

He gripped his sword, which hung low in its scabbard.

Cursing himself for getting into this, Noel reached for the only thing he had left. All the men tensed, but he drew only the seal from his pocket. Demetrius and Yani relaxed, but the knight leaned forward like a hound who has suddenly sprung a scent.

"Hold!" he said sharply. "What is that?"

Noel held it aloft to make the sun flash from its sides. "My seal of office as duly appointed and rightful governor of this province. You are advised to surrender your arms and your lives to me, and reswear your allegiance to Byzantium. Otherwise, you are criminals, guilty of treason against the empire, and your lives are forfeit."

The words rolled from him, making a heavy threat indeed in the ponderous phrases. The men stood frozen, and for a moment Noel thought he might actually pull it off.

Then the knight pushed back his coif, revealing a sweaty tangle of short-cropped hair, and laughed. "Well said, my lord! You almost made me fall on bended knee to you. But I serve a master who spits defiance at Byzantium, as do I."

He extended his hand. "The seal, please."

Noel did not have to turn his head to feel the tension emanating from the men at his back. He tucked the seal away swiftly and met the flare of anger in the knight's eyes with more courage than he actually felt.

"I am sworn to die before I surrender that seal to unlawful hands," he said. His gaze could not help but go to the knight's sword. He wished he hadn't mentioned death.

"Oh, you'll surrender it, my lord," said the knight. He awarded Noel a mocking bow. "I am convinced. But your trickery is over now. Yani, Demetrius, I have orders to bring Lord Theodore to Mistra. Sir Magnin wants to deal with him face-to-face."

Both bandits set up an immediate protest. "Sir Magnin promised us part of the ransom—"

"And you'll get it," said the knight impatiently. "But he must be secured within the castle dungeons. Here, despite your certain diligence, it is too easy for him to escape. We cannot have him causing mischief in the countryside and undoing the alliances we wish to forge. Bring him forth."

"No!" said Noel.

The knight's mocking gaze slid to him. "No, Lord Theodore? Did I hear you say no?"

"My, er, men—"

The knight laughed and turned away with a gesture. "Bring him. Make sure he is bound securely and get him mounted."

The bandits complied with a roughness that brought back Noel's headache. He managed to glance back once where Theodore and the courtiers stood helplessly. Theodore's face was filled with raw despair and frustration. Noel felt exactly the same way. So much for the plan, he thought with exasperation. If Theodore wanted to get inside the castle to rescue his lady love, he should have stayed away from trickery and scheming.

The dungeons . . . Noel knew about them. Trojan had recorded an entire torture session on the rack from the Spanish Inquisition. A cold shudder passed through Noel as he was lifted bodily and set upon a mule. All he had to do for this farce to end was to come face-to-face with Lady Sophia, who wouldn't know him from Adam.

She was bound to give him away.

Sick, Noel didn't want to think about what would happen next. It could get a lot worse.

CHAPTER 5

"Sir Geoffrey!"

The voice came from nowhere. It echoed off hill and rock swiftly, rebounding until it was impossible to tell from which direction it came.

The knight leading Noel's mule drew rein and glanced about with his hand upon his sword. They stood upon a narrow trail inches away from a sharp drop that plunged hundreds of feet into a ravine choked with fallen rocks and logs. On the other side, a limestone escarpment rose above them like a wall. In places it leaned over the trail, making the going almost impassable. The air smelled of heat, horse sweat, and orange blossoms, a wild fragrance unlike anything Noel had inhaled before.

"Sir Geoffreeeeeeeee!"

This time the call was plainly a taunt, teasing and shrill.

The knight swore to himself. "This is not a good place. Too close. Kick your mule, and let us ride on!"

Noel was in no mood to cooperate. The jouncing trot the knight had insisted on for the last half hour made his head throb like a bass drum. Looking down at the ground moving beneath his stirrup brought on dizzy nausea. The sun blazed at him without mercy. Noel just wanted to crawl into a dark hole somewhere and close his eyes.

"Come on, I said! Are you deaf?"

Sir Geoffrey tugged on the lead rope and the mule came forward with reluctance.

"Sir Geoffrey! Sir Geoffrey!" shouted two voices in unison.

There came the sound of men barking like dogs. The echoes created an unholy din that shuddered along the mountainside.

Noel winced. "The dwarfs," he said.

"What?"

"It's the dwarfs."

Sir Geoffrey stared at him as though he had lost his mind. "I know of no dwarfs."

"Elena's dwarfs," said Noel with the exaggerated patience one used with a half-wit.

"Who—"

"Sir Geoffrey!" said Elena, appearing above them on the lip of the escarpment. She crouched low on one knee, every movement quick and supple, and tossed back her wild auburn hair.

Her hose and tunic had been exchanged for an ankle-length gown of sky-blue. It was straight in cut, with long sleeves, and plain of any adornment except for simple embroidery at the collar and upon the narrow kirtle that drew in her waist. A necklace of dowry coins tinkled softly each time they swung against her breasts. She had washed her face, but her hair had bits of leaf and twig in it as though she had snagged her tresses more than once while running down the mountainside to waylay them.

She was still panting, and a touch of perspiration made her face glow.

Noel forgot his headache. She was the most gloriously alive creature he had ever seen. Her vibrancy and sheer animal magnetism struck an immediate physical response within him. He forgave her for capturing him earlier. He wanted to jump off the mule and grovel at her feet. He wanted to chase her up and down the mountainside, making her shriek with laughter. He wanted to kiss her full lips and taste their strength and eagerness.

"Sir Geoffrey," she said, her gaze for the knight alone. "Let me ride pillion with you to Mistra."

The knight looked her over with moderate interest. "Faith, but you are a bold piece."

Her eager smile faded. "I am Elena," she said proudly. "Sister to Demetrius and Yani. I carry a message to Sir Magnin."

Sir Geoffrey's mouth twisted into mockery. "Ah, now I remember you. I was just in your brothers' camp, and they mentioned no such message."

"That is why I have run all this way. Sir knight, please take me to the castle. It is an important thing I carry."

"The only message you have for Sir Magnin is an offering of your virginity," said Sir Geoffrey. "Go home, little maid, before your brothers find out what sins you plan and come avenging you."

She straightened with a jerk as though struck by a scourge. Her face flamed to the roots of her hair. Noel realized that Sir Geoffrey's remark—although cruel—was exactly on the mark. But it took a real jerk to say it to her face.

"You—you are a jokester, I see," she struggled to say. Tears made her eyes glisten, but she faced Sir Geoffrey's jeering grin. "You should trade jests with my dwarf Thaddeus. His fool tales have worn thin from too much use. We need fresh merriment around our fires at night."

It wasn't much of a comeback, but it served to wipe the grin from Sir Geoffrey's face. He said sharply, "You would do well to seek a confessor, little maid, and set your soul to rights. Not only are you playing with fire for your wanton ways and behavior, but a shrew's tongue will not get you a husband."

She spat at him. "Damn you!"

Sir Geoffrey spurred his horse and tugged the lead rope to move them on.

"Wait!" she cried, but Sir Geoffrey did not look back.

Noel did, however, and saw her scrambling down the escarpment like a monkey, fingers and bare toes finding holds he could not see. Her dress hiked up around bare, shapely thighs before she jumped the last bit and came running along the trail after them.

"Wait!" she cried again.

"Pull up," said Noel. "Or she'll run yelling after us the whole way."

Sir Geoffrey drew rein with visible exasperation. He shot Noel an angry look and shook his head.

When Elena came panting up to them, Sir Geoffrey leaned over from his saddle and spoke before she had a chance: "Go home, you fool!" he said harshly. "Sir Magnin will not see you. He is an important man. He has a thousand details to see to this day, and the next, and for weeks to come. I vow you are too scruffy to catch his eye even were he not thus occupied. Go home."

She glared at him. "I will go to the castle whether you give me a ride or not."

"Oh, aye, hike in and present yourself. Look at you," he said with a derisive gesture. "Ill-clothed, unshod, your hair hanging in your face. You might get inside the gates, but the seneschal won't give you entry to the hall."

His words hurt her. Noel could see her flinch although she glared fiercely to hide it.

"I can braid my hair," she said. "And I have shoes. I shall wear them when I arrive."

"Do not go to the trouble," said Sir Geoffrey. "You will be on your back within five minutes of entering the gates."

"Hey," said Noel, deciding this had gone on long enough. "She doesn't—"

"You may not care about a Greek maiden, Lord Theodore," said Sir Geoffrey with an ascetic frown, "but as a knight I am just as sworn to uphold God's law as I am to serve Sir Magnin. You know as well as I what will befall a maid like this in the castle. Our men are full of themselves. They had an easy time defeating your men, and the castle fell the hour they surrounded it. They have wenched and wined themselves all night. The townsmen have locked their women safely away, and the tarts left at hand are not enough to go around. A morsel like this, dirty as she is, is just too tempting."

Noel blinked. This was one aspect of medieval life that he hadn't considered. But he knew that Sir Geoffrey was absolutely right. The man's decency surprised him.

"Sir Geoffrey is right," said Noel, turning his gaze back to Elena. It felt odd to be lecturing her together as though they were colleagues instead of a guard and his prisoner. "It's for your own safety, Elena."

She tossed her head. "I can take care of myself. Last winter I killed a wolf while—"

"You cannot kill Sir Magnin's men," said Sir Geoffrey. "He would boil you in oil for it. That is the law."

"Not Milengi law—"

"But Frankish law and Greek law," said Sir Geoffrey. "Now go home."

"No," she said stubbornly. "I want to see Sir Magnin. I do have a message for him, and *not* the one you so crudely suggested. And as a member of the Milengi tribe, who caught this man when everyone else failed to recognize him, it is my right to see that our interest in him is guarded."

Sir Geoffrey opened his mouth.

"Sir Magnin could not have done this as easily as you boast without our support," she said. "If the Milengi think we are being cheated of our ransom, we will not keep our allegiance."

"It is your brother who should be making those threats, not you," said Sir Geoffrey.

She shrugged. "My brother has the wits of a log. Yani and I cannot always convince him to act quickly."

"And are you certain Yani knows what you are doing?"

She shrugged again. "I do not have to answer to you, Sir Geoffrey. Besides, if I ride in with you, no man in the castle will dare touch me. I will be safe. And Sir Magnin's order is enough to give me protection. But if I have to walk in, whatever happens to me will be on your conscience. Now what do you say?"

Noel started to laugh at the sour look on Sir Geoffrey's face, but swiftly changed it to a cough. Sir Geoffrey glared at him. He glared at her. Finally he gestured angrily.

"Very well. Get on behind Lord Theodore. I shall take you to Sir Magnin, but if he refuses to see you, little maid, you are on your own. I have other business more important than guarding your chastity, and you are no responsibility of mine."

She grinned, unimpressed by his threat, and climbed on behind Noel. The saddle kept them separated, but still he found his senses flooded by a lot of girl. Bodily warmth radiated from her. She smelled musky and sweet, all of herbs, woodsmoke, and the outdoors. The narrow cut of her gown made it necessary for her to hike it up to her knees. Noel gazed down at her slim, golden calf and foot dangling just inches from his own leg.

He swallowed hard, intent on controlling his heat. They went bouncing down the trail at that tail-pounding, head-numbing trot, and within minutes Elena's arms snaked around his middle to keep her balance. He could feel her breasts against his back. The wind blew strands of her hair against his cheek and they felt like twists of silk teasing and stroking his skin. His blood flamed to the boiling point.

"I'm glad you came," he said to her in a low voice so that Sir

Geoffrey could not hear. "You've improved what was turning out to be a bad afternoon. How about—"

"You," she said even lower in his ear, her breath a warm tickle that made his heart pound with pleasure, "are an impostor. George overheard everything that you and Lord Theodore plotted."

Noel went cold with alarm. When he could find his voice he said, "Hell is too nice a place for George."

She rested her chin upon the point of his shoulder. "I think he is a very clever dwarf. And Lord Theodore is a very clever governor. You are the fool."

Noel gritted his teeth. Every bit of attraction she'd held for him vanished. The mule picked its way around a tricky bend in the trail when for a moment they seemed to hang over nothing but air. Noel felt the urge to tip Elena off at that point, but, seething, he curbed it.

"We like this development, however," said Elena. "Yani and I are pleased because we still have Lord Theodore in our hands in case Sir Magnin decides to trick us. A man who steals another's castle will steal from his friends as well. You see?"

"I see," said Noel bleakly. Byzantine intrigue . . . now he knew why the term originated.

"So we want Sir Magnin to go on thinking you are Lord Theodore. I am along to make sure you do not lose your nerve and confess the truth to him. He is a very intimidating man."

"I'm not easily intimidated," said Noel.

He felt the prick of a knife point against his kidney, and stiffened.

"Good," said Elena, her voice like gold in his ear. "Because I will disembowel you if you betray us. Clear enough?"

"Very clear."

She laughed, obviously pleased with herself. Noel glowered at his bound hands resting upon the pommel. His knuckles had gone white. Anger blazed through him. He had never felt so damned helpless. Everything, from the moment he stepped through the time portal, had gone totally wrong. Someone unseen and unknown had sabotaged his mission. He was possibly trapped in this time and place for the rest of his life. And now he was being used as a pawn in a local game of politics and war. He wasn't used to being manipulated. He didn't like it. He wasn't going to put up with it any longer.

Ahead, Sir Geoffrey's attention was centered upon his own mount and the steep dip in the trail. There was no longer a precipice on Noel's right; the slope remained very steep, but it now looked navigable, if only by a mountain goat.

Not giving himself time to reconsider, Noel leaned forward over the mule's neck and grabbed the slack lead rope. One quick yank pulled it from Sir Geoffrey's grasp. The knight glanced back and shouted, but Noel had already turned the mule. He kicked it hard in the flanks, and the startled animal plunged off the trail into a thicket of brush that whipped Noel's face and arms mercilessly.

The angle was steeper than it had looked from the trail. The mule scrambled and lunged. Finding no bit in its mouth, it stretched out its nose and went where it pleased. Noel found himself pushing against the stirrups and leaning back against Elena to keep his seat. She clutched him and screamed a torrent of Greek in his ear too fast for his translator to handle.

Behind them, Sir Geoffrey yelled again, but Noel didn't look back. Breathlessly he concentrated on hanging on. The mule plunged through another thicket. Locust branches raked him with thorns. Elena screamed as they caught in her hair. Noel glanced back and saw a hank of auburn hair left hanging from a branch. She pounded on his back with her fist and reached around him, trying to snatch the rope he held in his hands.

"Stop the mule!" she commanded. "Stop it now! We cannot go this way."

The mule skidded to a halt at the edge of a gully, then jumped down into the bottom of it. Noel's bones rattled at the unexpected change of direction. He clutched the pommel while the mule scrambled up the other side of the gully. From behind them he glimpsed Sir Geoffrey forcing his horse down the hillside at a cautious pace. He could hear Sir Geoffrey cursing steadily.

"You will kill us," said Elena. "Stop the mule!"

"No!" said Noel. "I'm getting out of here."

"You forget I have a knife, to make you stop!"

Noel gave the mule another hard kick in the ribs. It responded with a half rear and picked up speed, jumping recklessly off an outcropping of rock and landing with a stumble that jolted Noel half from the saddle.

He caught himself and hung on grimly.

"Do you hear me?" yelled Elena. "I have a knife."

"Then use it," said Noel. He saw a branch coming and ducked flat to the mule's neck. It veered at the last moment and scraped his leg against the tree trunk. Noel yelled with pain and kicked the beast again. He realized now that it was doing its best to dislodge them. It wanted its freedom as much as he wanted his.

"Use it!" repeated Noel in a burst of complete recklessness. "But if I fall off you'll fall too."

"Don't count on it," she said and sank her teeth into his shoulder.

The pain was unexpected and intense. Noel stood up in the stirrups and twisted around, trying to grab her by the waist and sweep her off.

She clung to him, her nails digging in, her hair flying wildly.

The mule dodged to one side, and Elena slipped. She clawed at his arm, trying to pull herself back. Yelling and pleading in fear, her words were drowned out by the pounding of the mule's hooves and the throbbing desperation within Noel's ears. She was still sliding, her head dangling near his foot, near those dangerous hooves.

He thought about what it would be like to fall at a speed like this. He thought about what might happen if she happened to roll beneath the mule. He thought about slashing hooves cutting young flesh to ribbons, of smashing bones, of Elena being broken like a discarded doll upon the ground.

"Damn!" said Noel. He tightened his fingers around her own and heaved himself hard to the left in an effort to pull her up.

He nearly succeeded. She was sobbing "please" over and over again, struggling to help him, struggling not to pull both of them off. The nearly intolerable strain of compensating the balance eased off. She clutched his shoulder, then his neck. She settled herself astride, then screamed.

Startled by the raw terror in her voice, Noel looked ahead and saw the chasm yawning ahead. It plunged hundreds of feet down, a precipitous barrier effectively separating the base of Mt. Taygetus from its foothill Mistra.

Frozen, he stared at the looming disaster for an eternity. Elena's scream went on and on forever. He wanted to scream with her, but he hadn't the breath. The mule's head came up as though it too saw the gorge ahead. It slowed, but not quickly enough, not soon enough. The awful certainty that they could not stop in time slammed through Noel with the force of a sledgehammer. He hauled back on the rope with all his might, but the mule wasn't responding. The idiot animal actually tossed its head in protest.

"Stop!" shrieked Elena. "For the sake of God, *stop!*"

"I can't!" shouted Noel.

The edge rushed closer. Suddenly there was not enough time left for anything. It was coming, coming too fast, coming like a metro shuttle.

Elena shoved hard. For an instant he thought she was trying to knock him from the saddle. Then she went sailing off. He heard the thud and her cry of pain as she hit the ground. She rolled over and over and caught herself from going off the edge.

The mule's forefeet planted themselves, and the animal's rear sat down to create a drag coefficient. Impetus still carried them, in a choking cloud of dust, and Noel heard the animal scream in fear of its own.

"Jump!" called Elena. "Jump before it's too late!"

His feet were tangled in the stirrups. His grip on the rope had locked on so tightly he seemed unable to loosen his rigid fingers. He struggled, panic taking over. In the last possible second, he got free and hurled himself off to the left.

The mule's feet went over the edge, and he heard the animal scream again. The mule did an impossible twist and scramble, but it could not stop itself from going over. Noel missed the ground and fell into the chasm as well.

A yell forced itself into his throat and lodged there. He envisioned his body twisting and plunging for hundreds of feet. It was too far; it gave him too long to think, and to remember, and to regret. He didn't want to die, not here, not like this. Ending up mushed at the bottom of a ravine in the wrong century and the wrong country, his LOC crushed with him, all that he had learned gone to waste, all that he could still achieve unaccomplished . . . dear God, he didn't want to die.

A tree growing twisted and wind-carved on the side of the ravine caught his fall. Noel hit it hard and went crashing through the branches with a snapping, crackling velocity that slowed him down but didn't stop him. The tree, however, did deflect his body.

A few seconds later he hit the steep slope with a crunching thud that shattered the breath in his lungs and numbed him totally. He tumbled, picking up velocity again, but at this level there were too many fallen logs, spindly wind-blasted trees, and rocks choking the sides. He came to a stop at long last, halfway down, and lay there so dazed and disoriented he could not at first comprehend what had happened. His vision was a gray blur of shape, without color. His hearing was only a roar. He still experienced the sensation of falling, although another part of his brain knew that he had stopped.

He could not seem to draw breath, and he could not move. Paralyzed, he thought and felt despair.

"Theodore!" The sound came crashing and echoing down to him from far away. "Lord Theodore!"

Noel's eyes flickered open. He heard, but he could not make himself care. Wrong number, he thought.

The mule lay perhaps ten or fifteen feet away from him. The impossible angle of its head told him its neck was broken. Sunlight glistened on the blood that had flowed from one nostril. It had been a strong, good-looking animal, and he'd killed it.

Killed me too, he thought and wished it were over.

"Lord Theodore!" called the voice. Sir Geoffrey's voice.

"Lord Theodore!" called Elena.

Noel shut his eyes. They could not get to him down here. He did not care.

CHAPTER 6

He must have lost consciousness, for when he next awakened the sun no longer shone on his face. The air was cooler too. He could not remember why he was lying on this sloped, rocky ground. A distant memory told him there had been a purpose, but he'd lost it. There had been something to do, something urgent, something important. He *had* to remember.

A hand touched his face.

Noel blinked and sat upright, gasping and frantic. "Must get back," he said aloud. "Must hurry and get back. Something's wrong."

"The only thing wrong," said Elena, "is that you nearly killed yourself. How could you be so stupid?"

He did not know what she was talking about. He kept silent. After a moment his hand reached out to touch her cheek. "Pretty."

Her face flamed with color, and she slapped his fingers away. "Try that again, and you'll lose your hand," she said.

He smiled at her and sank bonelessly back to the ground.

"Theodore," she said, gripping his shoulder and leaning over him. Her face and voice were anxious. "I can find no broken bones, although you cried out when I felt your ribs. It is a miracle you are not dead after such a fall. Where are you hurt? Tell me. Theodore?"

"Not Theodore," he said in irritation. "Where's Trojan? Find him. Tell him something's wrong."

She bent even lower over him until her hair was a veil beside his face. It was tangled and snarled, but it smelled of the wind.

"You are Theodore," she said in a low voice. "Remember that, even if your wits have been rattled. Sir Geoffrey is within hearing, so guard what you say."

"I can't get home," said Noel worriedly. He wanted her to understand. "I need to get home. Call Trojan and tell him to help me."

She frowned. "You make no sense. You babble as though you have fever, but your skin is cool."

"Want home," he said, and then even talking was too hard. He shut his eyes until the sound of someone else approaching roused him.

"How is he?" said Sir Geoffrey.

"Not good," said Elena. "His wits are gone. He makes no sense when he talks."

"Small wonder of that," said Sir Geoffrey. "Your brother shouldn't have used a slingshot on so valuable a head. He must have been addled to even try such an escape. How many bones broken?"

"None."

"Impossible."

Elena shrugged angrily and gestured. "Examine him for yourself."

"I shall. Stand over there."

"Why should I?"

He pointed angrily. "Just stand over there!"

She flounced away. Noel gazed up into Sir Geoffrey's face. The knight's dark eyes were troubled. He had lost his habitual mocking expression. His mouth set itself in a thin line.

As his hands moved with surprising gentleness along Noel's limbs, he said, "Can you hear me, Lord Theodore?"

"I'm not—ow!"

"Sorry." Sir Geoffrey's hand came off his rib cage. "What were you saying?"

The pain of cracked ribs drove away the cloudy haze within Noel's mind. Behind it came clarity and renewed caution.

When he could catch enough breath to speak, he said, "I'm not dead?"

"No. God spared you. I cannot say why. A haze of unreason must have asserted itself upon your brain. Do you not know there is only one path to Mistra from this accursed mountain?"

"Seem to have forgotten that." Noel winced and reached his hand across his side, feeling gingerly. "Damn."

"If a few ribs are all that ail you, you are blessed indeed." Sir Geoffrey sat back on his spurred heels. "We are losing the day. It took the devil's own time to get down into the ravine with the horse. You must give me your word and bond that you will try no such stunts again."

"Why should I?"

Sir Geoffrey met his gaze with open exasperation. "Is dying a better alternative than being ransomed? Our terms will not bankrupt Byzantium. You had no cause to do such a foolhardy thing."

"Perhaps not," said Noel.

"Can you stand?"

Sir Geoffrey helped him sit up. Noel held his side and grimaced as he was pulled to his feet. The world spun around him. He nearly swayed over, but Sir Geoffrey steadied him.

"Let me go free," said Noel in a whisper. "Say I broke my neck in the fall and leave me here."

Sir Geoffrey met his pleading gaze for a long moment, then slowly he shook his head. "I must obey my orders," he said. "Elena!" he called, "help me get him on the horse."

There was something about the posture required to sit a horse that made Noel's side ache constantly. His head still throbbed, but that pain was almost an old friend compared to the newer discomfort in his ribs. He realized now he had used his emergency medication too soon. Now it was spent, and he would just have to grit his teeth through the rest of this ordeal.

Elena and Sir Geoffrey walked at the horse's head, leading it down into the bottom of the ravine. Gazing up at the vast mountain rising above him, Noel saw the buzzards still circling the sky. He shivered as though a hand had touched his soul.

Eventually, they emerged in the broad river valley where once, centuries ago, the proud, ancient city of Sparta had stood. Now there were only fertile fields and groves of orange and olive trees to mark the banks of the Eurotas River. Long rays of sun slanted shafts of gold and coral into the shimmering fields of tender barley. Twilight deepened within the folds at the base of the mountains. From the city of Mistra a church bell tolled.

As though summoned by the bells, peasants headed home from their fields. The men's tunics were grimed with dirt and sweat. Beneath the red, brimless caps that most wore, their swarthy faces shot Noel impassive glances. They kept their distance from Sir Geoffrey, with the cautious air of men who have lost their security. They looked tired; scrawny donkeys trudged behind them with heads low from fatigue.

Children carrying long staves made from the stalks of century plants ran for home, herding small flocks of goats or sheep before them. Noel listened to the rhythm of their chatter. They squealed with laughter or scolded an errant animal for trying to break away from the flock. The worries of war and revolt had not touched them.

Or perhaps it had. They did not pause to stare at Noel, perched on the horse with his hands bound in front of him. They did not trail after Sir Geoffrey in his mail and spurs, pestering him with questions. They dodged the trio and went on their way quickly, as though their parents had given them explicit instructions to avoid all strangers.

From up on the mountain came the lone cry of a wolf. The eerie, primeval howl sent prickles up Noel's spine. He could not help glancing over his shoulder. The mountain stood black in silhouette as the sun disappeared behind it; a corona of umber and crimson shone around its peak. Mt. Taygetus was where the Spartans had exposed children who were born with imperfections. Noel himself had arrived in the world with his left foot turned in. It had straightened itself out within a few months following birth, but the Spartans with their rigid codes of life would not have given him the chance to live. He heard the wolf howl again and shivered, imagining babies lying out there a thousand years ago, shaking in the cold, crying in fear and hunger, slowly being extinguished by the impartial elements.

Perhaps he should not have specialized in the ancient world. Right now he rode by the toppled drums of old temple columns. The horse's hooves scraped across pavement that had once been dressed marble. Now it was weathered and pitted from the years. Weeds choked the faint outlines of the temple steps. Noel saw a crumbling chunk of iron lying on the ground. The Spartans had used iron bars for currency, fearing that gold would corrupt them.

Iron money . . . iron bodies . . . iron minds. Where were the Spartans now? Not even their city still stood. At least in this century, primitive as it was, people understood the quality of mercy.

If he did not return by the end of his time loop, he must accept the fact that he was stuck here forever. Until he accepted it, he could not cope with it. If he could not cope, he could not survive.

Church bells stopped ringing. The chant of a religious order, voices smooth and controlled, lifted like smoke to God in the following quiet.

A peaceful scene spread before Noel. Sir Geoffrey led the horse across a stone bridge spanning the river. The road wound up through the walled gates of the town. A sentry called out to Sir Geoffrey from the gate tower.

Sir Geoffrey identified himself, then said, "Send word to the palace that I have come bringing Lord Theodore of Albania as my prisoner. He is injured and needs a physician ready to attend him."

The sentry saluted and turned to dispatch a boy.

"Let them pass!" came the cry.

The horseman's gate swung open ponderously to admit them. It was wider than the pedestrian gate where peasants and townfolk were streaming through. Noel ducked his head beneath the stone archway, although there was room for him to ride upright. The dark tunnel, though short, stank of damp stone, horse droppings, and something unpleasant that Noel could not identify.

Perhaps it was fear. He ran his fingers across the surface of his LOC, trying to draw comfort from its presence upon his wrist. As long as he had it, there was still a faint chance of getting home. He had to cling to that.

Tall, narrow cypress trees towered over rooftops of red tile. Sturdy houses of golden limestone looked prosperous and snug. Lights shone from their windows. Open doorways emitted sounds of chatter and laughter, smells of roasting goat meat and the spices of cloves and cinnamon. The town held a festive air as though Sir Magnin's usurpation of power had benefited it. Noel could see no signs of oppressed citizenry or despair or defeat.

Those who bothered to appear on balconies and stare at his passing did so in grave silence. He could tell nothing from their faces.

Partway through the steep streets, a small contingent of knights upon horses met them.

"This is he?" said one.

"It is," said Sir Geoffrey.

"We thought the Milengi had killed you. You're hours overdue," said another.

"I see no one came after me," said Sir Geoffrey in a voice dry and cynical.

The men laughed. "Oh, we would have in a day or so, once the grape ran out, and we had nothing better to do. And who is this damsel with you? Ah, Geoffrey, have you been sampling the best treasure of these hills?"

Elena stepped back until she stood pressed against the horse, her back next to Noel's leg. He could feel her tremble. Now, when it was too late, it seemed she believed Sir Geoffrey's warning.

"She is the sister of Demetrius Milengus," said Sir Geoffrey sharply. "She has brought Sir Magnin a message."

"A message. Oh, ho, and what might that be?"

"Never mind, Sir John," said Sir Geoffrey shortly. "Are you here to escort us up, or to block our path forever? Walking in mail has left me mortal galled, and I want my dinner. It is a damned big mountain to ride over."

"Aye, come then, and let us escort you in style. Give him your horse, Andre—"

"Nay," said Sir Geoffrey. "I'll walk it."

"Make way!" shouted a voice. "Make way for the Lady Sophia!"

The knights shifted aside for a retinue mounted on mules and dainty palfreys decked out in fine silver trappings and bright saddlecloths. Two guards in mail and red surcoats bearing the same falcon insignia as Sir Geoffrey and these other knights wore led the group. They were followed by a thin, elderly man in black cloak and tunic, a close-fitting cap of black tied over his skull and a cap worn upon that. His collar was made of fox fur, and he wore a heavy chain of office. His features were all bone and angle, the parchment-pale skin withered to nothing. His mouth was merely a slash set hard beneath a hooked nose. Jutting gray eyebrows concealed his eyes. He pretended to look only straight ahead, but Noel saw a glint of white as his eyes darted here and there.

Behind this official pranced a white Arabian mare that looked almost ghostly in the twilight. Her gliding stride made her seem to float above the ground. Pages dressed in particolored hose and red livery ran alongside the retinue with flaming torches borne aloft in their hands. The lady riding the white horse was too beautiful and too richly dressed to be anyone other than Sophia, destined bride of Lord Theodore.

She was very fair. Her skin glowed like milk and her eyes were as cobalt as the sky. A single curl of blond hair had escaped the headdress of pillbox hat and wimpled veil that concealed the rest of her hair, her ears, and her throat. She possessed a heart-shaped face with a hint of stubbornness at the chin. Sixteen, Lord Theodore had said, and she looked it. She wore a gown of dark green velvet. Her russet cloak flowed from her shoulders to spill across the horse's rump. She rode with the graciousness of royalty, her posture erect and poised. Her gloved hands upon the reins were dainty, yet it was she who controlled her mare and not the varlet trotting beside her.

She was accompanied by five other women, all in rich dress. A servant walked at the rear, bearing a locked Bible box made of olive wood. A strip of purple wool embroidered with the lady's coat of arms lay draped across it. Another servant carried a velvet pillow that presumably Lady Sophia had knelt upon during her devotionals. Two more guards brought up the end of this procession.

She was a prisoner too, thought Noel; despite all the pomp surrounding her, she remained a political pawn at the mercy of those who married her or controlled her dowry.

He stared at her because he could not help it. In turn, she gazed at him as the retinue slowed down to go past the knights. Her blue eyes took in his face and his bound hands; they widened. She seemed about to speak, then her rosy lips clamped firmly together, and she turned her face away.

They rode on in a jingling of bridle bells and the lingering aroma of incense pomanders.

Noel watched them until the shadows closed them from sight. Only then did he realize Sir Geoffrey was staring up at him closely, with the narrow gaze of a suspicious man.

"No greeting from your lady?" he said with his old mockery. "It would seem you have a cold night ahead of you, my lord."

Noel had not the faintest notion whether Theodore and Sophia had ever laid eyes on each other before. Not all medieval couples were engaged by proxy. He said, "Men who have taken vows of chastity should not snoop in the romances of those who haven't."

The knights howled with laughter. Red-faced, Sir Geoffrey started to retort, but before he could do so a balding man in a beautifully cut tunic of crimson, a measuring tape dangling from his neck, ran up to seize Noel's stirrup.

"My lord! Good news, my lord! I have finished your order and it is—"

Noticing Noel's disheveled appearance and bound hands, he broke off, blinking rapidly. "I—I seem to be mistaken. I was certain you were—"

"Stand away!" commanded Sir John. "You, tailor! Stand away from our prisoner."

The tailor bowed, his face pale with alarm. "Yes, indeed, gentle knights. Forgive me. I was mistaken. I—"

They rode on, leaving him standing in the street, wringing his hands and still bowing. Noel stared back at him, puzzled by the incident. The knights, however, immediately forgot him. They were still throwing jests at one another, distracting Sir Geoffrey's attention as they made their way up the steep hillside. Noel kept his forearm pressed against his side for support, and tried not to shiver. Now that the sun was down, the temperature had dropped sharply. He felt faint with thirst and hunger. His head throbbed mercilessly. These puzzles hardly mattered in his general misery.

Elena grabbed his foot and squeezed hard. "Take care," she whispered. "Theodore has visited Mistra and Lady Sophia at least twice before. It is rumored to be a love match with her."

Noel's spirits sank lower. That was all he needed. In a few minutes his dangerous game of pretense would be over. As soon as he entered the castle, Lady Sophia would give him away. Noel figured no one was going to be amused at the deception he'd practiced today. He didn't want to lay odds on being drawn and quartered at dawn.

Halfway up the hill, the chaotic clusters of houses and shops perched on every available bit of building space stopped at the base of another wall. Guards admitted them through a set of gates, and they rode through another tunnel into the spacious palace complex. No cramped round donjon here; instead, a rectangular palace of three or four stories formed a great L with numerous small outbuildings and miniature wings spreading out from it in a clutter of barracks, kennels, stables, kitchens, storehouses, armory, and the like.

The thing that struck Noel first and most unpleasantly was the noise. The greatest racket of off-key singing voices, raucous laughter, women shrieking jests and catcalls, babies crying, children calling out with shrill voices, geese honking in offense, cart wheels clattering upon the cobblestones, the rhythmic clanging of hammer upon anvil, a fistfight going on in the stableyard with cheers of encouragement from the watching crowd, fighting cocks screaming challenges at each other, dogs barking in an eager chorus for their supper, the creaking groan of the well pulley, doors and gates opening and slamming, a shoat destined for the butcher's knife squealing in its pen . . . in short, the normal bustle of castle life beat upon Noel's hearing and intensified his headache.

Torchlight blazed everywhere, and upon the battlements sentries paced slow and steadily. At the corners they called out, "All's well," and paced back. In spite of all the activity, a crowd of onlookers, chiefly knights from their surcoats and mail, gathered in the yard to watch a flogging.

When Noel was led up, the flogging had obviously been going on for some time. The man being punished was tied by the wrists and ankles to iron rings set in two massive square posts. He was bare to the waist, and his back was a bloody mess of raw welts. If he had not already lost consciousness, he was close to it. He sagged limply, held up only by his bonds. The whip whistled through the air and cracked across his back. He jerked and screamed aloud.

"Thirty-nine!" shouted the crowd in unison.

Many of them held huge tankards; their faces were shiny from sweat, excitement, and the effects of the ale. They slapped each other on the shoulder as though the gruesome spectacle they witnessed was a fine thing indeed, and called out encouragement to the man executing the punishment.

Elena squeezed Noel's foot, although this time it was plainly unintentional. She stared at the man, her face rapt, her eyes sparkling with the full gamut of her emotions. Just looking at her in that unguarded moment, with all her youth and vitality ablaze in the first headlong rush of infatuation, made Noel feel a hundred years old. He remembered his own first love, how unequal it was, how blissful at first, how humiliating at the end. He wanted to take Elena by the shoulders and shake some sense into her, but he knew she'd never listen. She couldn't.

The whip struck again.

"Forty!" shouted the knights.

It had to be Sir Magnin who was wielding the whip. Noel studied him while he had the chance.

Sir Magnin Phrangopoulos loomed at least a head taller than every other man present. Stripped to the waist, with only his hose on, a servant standing nearby with his shirt and tunic, Sir Magnin was magnificently proportioned with a tapering waist ridged and corrugated with hard muscle, a deep chest, broad shoulders, and a set of biceps that bulged and rippled effortlessly beneath skin like bronzed satin. The veins stood up all over him like taut horseflesh. With every crack of the whip, he put his full strength behind the blow, yet displayed a grace of form that made the other men around him appear to be clumsy, lumbering oafs.

His face was wide and sensual, with a large nose, full lips, and a deep cleft in his chin. His eyebrows were black and straight, slashing across his face above eyes like gleaming obsidian. He wore his ebony hair long. It swung chin-length in a straight bob. Heavy bangs fell across his brow in a style more Renaissance than medieval.

"Forty-three!"

He grinned, revealing large white teeth, and swung twice more in swift succession, giving the prisoner insufficient time between the two blows to catch enough breath to scream again. Then it was done. Coiling the bloody whip, Sir Magnin tossed it at a nearby varlet and swept the perspiration from his face with both hands.

"Take him down," he said. His voice was deep and rich. It flowed with confidence.

Why not? thought Noel. He'd just captured this castle and the province it represented for his own.

Sir Geoffrey stepped forward. "I have brought the prisoner, my liege."

Sir Magnin whirled like a dancer, panther quick, and regarded Sir Geoffrey with his intense black eyes. Beside Noel, Elena trembled visibly, still enrapt. She was panting as though she had run down the mountain. Noel put his pity aside. She was as vital and as physical as Sir Magnin. It was inevitable she be attracted to him.

Sir Magnin's gaze shifted to Noel, who promptly forgot all about Elena and her fantasies. He was taken down from the horse. The ground tilted beneath him enough to make him stagger. He dragged in a swift breath to keep himself quiet.

"What ails him?" demanded Sir Magnin, striding forward. He grasped Noel's chin with powerful fingers still slick with sweat and blood, and forced Noel to look at him. A varlet scurried forward with a torch. Sir Magnin's eyes flew wide. He stared at Noel as though looking upon an apparition.

"What trickery is this?" he whispered.

Noel's blood ran cold. So this was the end of his game. He imagined himself trussed to those posts and the whip whistling against his back.

"You look exactly like—" Sir Magnin cut himself short and frowned, his eyes boring into Noel as though to pry the deepest secrets from him. "Hmm," he said at last. "No, I think not. Not quite, yet this is most peculiar."

"What is it?" said Sir Geoffrey in bewilderment. "Do you say this is not Lord Theodore? The Byzantines did their best to conceal him by putting him in this coarse garb. Another even pretended to be him for a time. But we figured out the ruse. He carries the seal of office—"

"Does he?" Sir Magnin smiled, his good humor restored as though he had drawn on gloves to mask his claws. "Harlan, regard him and tell me if you are not astonished at the likeness."

The elderly man in clerical black, the one who had ridden ahead of Lady Sophia a short time ago, shuffled forward with his chain of office gleaming across his chest. He put his skull-like face in Noel's and peered at him. He reeked of camphor and pennywort.

"Indeed, it is most uncommon."

"Look," said Noel rather desperately as their faces began to spin around him. "This is the second time I have been mistaken for someone else. I don't—"

"Injured," said Sir Magnin. His gaze stabbed to Sir Geoffrey. "How? In last night's battle?"

"No," said Sir Geoffrey and explained in a low voice.

Sir Magnin's laugh rang out across the courtyard. "Jumped his mule into the ravine, by hell and divinity! Did you think God would let you fly, Lord Theodore? Ho, I have not heard such a jest in weeks! You must have more courage than good sense, my lord. Is it true, what he says?"

Noel managed to pull himself together. "Yes, it is true," he said quietly.

Sir Magnin's wide mouth spread in a grin that sent a chill coursing through Noel. There was a rapaciousness to his expression, a ruthlessness radiating from him, even in laughter, that betrayed what manner of man he was beneath the finery and the good looks. Noel did not want to be this man's enemy.

"I like the sound of this," said Sir Magnin. "So you are a brave and clever man, are you? I will hear this tale. But not here and now. Get him cleaned up, Sir Geoffrey. We are not uncivilized. We can afford to be gracious to those whom we have defeated. Bring him to my table tonight."

Sir Geoffrey bowed. "As you command."

"Harlan, make certain my little shadow hears of this," said Sir Magnin with a smirk Noel did not trust. "I want him at my side in a small audience with Lord Theodore before we dine. Oh, and Lady Sophia may be present also."

The official bowed reverently. "It shall be done, my lord."

"Good." Sir Magnin gazed into Noel's eyes, his own brimming with amusement. He burst out laughing again and walked away, shaking his head at the servant who tried to offer him his tunic.

Noel stared after him, and Elena came to his side.

"I *must* speak to him," she said in a low, frustrated voice. "You, Sir Geoffrey, you did not even give me introduction—"

"Why should I?" said Sir Geoffrey irritably. "Something is afoot. What trick have the two of you invented?" His eyes swept from Noel's face to Elena's. "I swear to God, if you have led me false—"

"If we have led you false," broke in Noel, tired and more worried than he wanted to admit, "it's him we'll have to fear, not you."

Sir Geoffrey ignored him and turned to the old man. "Lord Harlan, what amused him so? What is amiss?"

The official bared the few rotten teeth remaining in his mouth. "I am not at liberty to say, sir knight. Go and do as you have been commanded. When our guest is presentable, see that he is brought to the small antechamber behind the audience hall."

Cutting Noel a sly look, the official placed his clawlike hands importantly upon his chain and shuffled away.

CHAPTER 7

Noel went to sleep in his bath and nearly drowned.

Attendants jerked him out by his hair and pummeled him until, gasping and sputtering, he coughed up the water he'd inhaled. The tub was made of wood and large enough for several people to bathe in together. The water looked reasonably clean, and a blushing little maid in a headdress and saffron gown had scented the water with an aromatic mixture of herbs that she crushed with a marble mortar and pestle. She also added the juice of lemons and heated, fragrant oils. The steam soothed Noel's senses, and the warm water was heaven on his bruises.

When he'd been dried off, massaged, and had his ribs bound tightly, Noel put on hose of scarlet, shoes too short, and a scratchy tunic of blue that bore someone's coat of arms. A brazier fire kept the small stone room warm. Torchlight blackened the walls from iron sconces bolted into the stone, and cast a ruddy, flickering light over everything. His attendants did not talk, and their grim faces made him as uneasy as did the royal treatment he was receiving.

He kept thinking of Sir Magnin's laughter. It had been the wrong reaction. He knew he'd been found out, but he wasn't sure how. Nor did he understand why Sir Magnin was toying with him in this way.

The gold seal of office, naturally, had been scooped away by a servant as soon as his clothes were stripped off. His money and dagger were long since gone. All he had left was his LOC, and when the maid tried to take the copper bracelet from his wrist, she had received a slight electrical shock that obviously puzzled her but convinced her to leave it alone.

"Food, my lord?" she said softly. She clapped her hands, and a page entered with a laden tray. The maid directed him to place it on the wooden clothes chest, and while she busied herself pouring wine into a metal goblet, the other attendants filed silently out.

Noel took the cup with caution, half expecting the sour bite of retsina, but it was a full-flavored bordeaux, as fine as anything he had ever tasted.

"French wine!" he said in surprise. "Excellent!"

She bowed, a smile curling her tender lips. "Of course, my lord. We are civilized here in Mistra. The cellars hold the finest in French and Italian wines."

He drank deeply and let her refill his cup, then watched as she removed covers from dishes and set about seasoning them with herbs shaken out from small bottles sealed with cork stoppers. Oregano, basil, rosemary, cinnamon, a meager pinch of salt, and the juice of lemon were combined with dishes of steaming food. Noel's mouth watered. It was all he could do not to snatch a platter for himself and dig in.

There was something about time travel that burned excessive amounts of calories. Noel always found himself ravenous when he reached his destination. Today there had been no chance to eat. Now, rested and feeling better, his headache nearly gone, he could barely keep himself in his chair.

She drew out a tiny box carved from streaked olive wood and shook it so that the contents rattled. "Peppercorns. Do you care for ground pepper, my lord?"

"Yes," he said and bit off the urge to tell her to hurry.

She served him rice first, a pilaf flavored with tomato and cinnamon. Next came flaky, tender fish, grilled and delicious. He wolfed his way through roasted kid, served with chunks of onion, pepper, and eggplant. At the finish were flat cakes coated with honey and filled with raisins, a precursor of sorts, he supposed, to baklava. When she brought forth a bowl of figs, dates, tiny yellow plums, and oranges, Noel had to stop. He was too full to continue.

She poured him more wine, although his head was beginning to spin.

"It was a delicious feast," he said, growing sleepy again. "You are called . . . ?"

"My name is unimportant," she said, blushing. "And it is customary to serve a feast to a man who—" She broke off, and her dark eyes grew troubled.

Noel felt a coldness stab him deep beneath the well-being brought on by the bath, food, and wine. "—who is condemned?" he finished for her.

Her eyes lifted slowly to his. She nodded. "It is Sir Magnin's pleasure to treat noble prisoners well."

"I thought," said Noel grimly, standing up to pace about the small chamber, "that I was to be ransomed, not executed. Is there a way out of this place?"

"Oh, no. There is only this door, and a guard stands without." She came to him and placed her hand upon his chest. "There is not much time left before you go before Sir Magnin. All in this room is here for your enjoyment. Even I."

She stepped back from him, her face aflame, and her slender fingers fumbled determinedly with her headdress, until it came off and her brown hair spilled upon her shoulders.

Without the headdress she looked even younger—hardly more than a child—and deliciously tender, gentle, and appealing. But there was knowledge in her eyes that made them old, and with it lay fear.

Noel frowned at her a long moment, then put his hand upon her cheek. She closed her eyes and nuzzled his palm. For a moment he was tempted, then he jerked back forcefully enough to make her eyes fly open.

"I displease you?"

"No!" he said too vehemently. Anger pushed through him, and he paced about the room, raking his fingers through his hair and making certain he avoided looking directly at her.

"Another can come if you—"

He whirled to face her. "No! What is your name?"

She looked frightened. "I am not permitted to say it."

"Why not?"

"I do not know why. The seneschal gave strict orders. They will cut out my tongue if I say anything I am not permitted to."

"That's barbaric. They wouldn't—" He broke off, his eyes narrowing as he studied her. She was evading his gaze. She fidgeted nervously with the headdress in her hands.

In two steps he reached her and gripped her by the arm. She gave a frightened little cry.

"You're lying," he said. "No one has threatened to cut out your tongue. I'm not even certain you were sent here to—"

She fell at his feet and gripped the hem of his tunic. "Oh, please, my lord! Please do not betray me. The guard thinks I was sent in Katrina's place by the seneschal. Please, my lord, have pity on me."

Completely bewildered, Noel felt his anger fade. He placed his hand upon her bowed head and realized she was trembling.

"Stand up," he said softly. "Face me, and tell me the truth."

She rose to her feet, keeping her head down. He slipped his knuckle beneath her chin and forced her to look at him.

"What the devil are you up to?" he asked.

She glanced at the door as though she expected the guard to burst in at any moment. Then she drew a tiny, much-folded slip of paper from an inside fold of her headdress and pressed it into his hand.

"My name is Cleope, and I serve the Lady Sophia," she whispered. "She sent me here tonight in Katrina's place. Now all our lives are in your hands."

Noel unfolded the scrap of parchment that crackled stiffly against his fingers. A single line of laboriously printed Latin was all it contained. He frowned, struggling to decipher the message. His universal translator worked on audio mode, not visual.

. . . help you in any way I can . . .

At least he thought that was pretty much the gist of it. It was signed with the flourishing initial S.

"I guess she couldn't give me a signal when we met in town tonight."

"Met you?" said Cleope in bewilderment. "When, pray?"

Noel explained that he had watched her retinue pass by. Cleope shook her head. "My lady mentioned it not. Word was just brought to her that a man impersonating Lord Theodore had been brought to the palace. Then she sent me here to you."

He frowned.

"I am to ask you what has become of Lord Theodore. Does he live? Is he well? If he has been injured my lady will die of grief."

"He's fine," said Noel shortly. "It was his idea for me to take his place and distract Sir Magnin while a way is found to rescue Lady Sophia. But I've been caught by Sir Magnin already."

"It is not a wonder," said the girl, "since you are the very image of—"

A pounding on the door startled both of them. She clung to him, her face as white as linen. Noel's own courage sank. Options were running out.

"Time!" said the guard loudly through the door.

The girl snatched the piece of paper from Noel's hand and threw it on the fire, where it charred and disintegrated at once in a shower of sparks. She had time only to dash back to Noel's side and give him one last beseeching look before the door crashed open and a pair of burly guards peered inside.

"Out," said one to the girl. "Get yourself presentable and help with the serving belowstairs." He pointed at Noel. "You, come forth."

Noel's heart was thudding. There had to be a way out, had to be a way to escape. Sophia would help him, but he didn't know how he could reach her. The palace complex was an unfamiliar maze. He could remember the way he'd come in, but that was all. There were too many people, too many knights, servants, pages, squires, and God knew what else hanging around. He'd already tried one desperate getaway today and it failed spectacularly. He thought he needed a better plan in mind before he made another attempt.

The stairs themselves were narrow, winding, treacherous things, offering no chance for him to dodge free of his guards and run for it. He had a guard ahead of him and a guard in back. They were armed to the teeth and dressed in a formidable combination of mail and plate armor that protected vulnerable places like throats and kidneys. Even if he managed to take out the man ahead of him, the one behind him remained.

He sighed, his gaze darting everywhere in search of inspiration or a chance, however slim. There wasn't even a pike hanging on the wall. All the windows in the stairwell were little more than arrow slits, far too narrow to squeeze through. He had no options.

The sound of talk and laughter and a hideous kind of twanging music rose up the stairwell as he neared the bottom. He emerged into a dim, shadow-filled colonnade bordering the long, high-vaulted hall. Bright light and a scene of merriment filled the hall itself. Long trestle tables had been set up for all the knights to dine. Merchants, an abbot in travel clothes and his retinue, and others of unidentifiable trade or occupation sat at the foot of the tables, with the boisterous knights filling the center. They were laughing and jesting, hacking at platters of meat with their daggers, eating with their fingers, hurling morsels at dogs roaming behind the benches, slopping wine from their cups, belching, and in general ignoring the group of three acrobats in motley performing a series of tumbles and cartwheels for the evening's entertainment.

At the head table, facing the rest of the room, Sir Magnin sat with his own retinue of advisers and favorites. He was too far away for Noel to see him clearly. Just a glimpse of the huge, broad-shouldered man with the long black hair and cruel face was enough to send a shiver through him.

He noticed that Lady Sophia had not joined the company. Before he could decide whether that was a blessing or a hindrance, the guards shoved him on.

"Move! Don't gander all day."

They walked behind the columns supporting the vaulted ceiling high above. The torchlight flared bright in the hall but did not quite reach them along this colonnade. Noel was glad of the shadows, glad those eating took little notice of his passing behind them. A gaunt dog blocked his path, snarling and growling, but one of the guards swore at it and kicked it in the ribs.

Yelping, it slunk off with its tail between its legs. Sir Magnin noticed. He turned his head, and for a moment he and Noel stared at each other. The hairs on the back of Noel's neck stood up. Sir Magnin merely smiled and swung his attention back to Sir Geoffrey, who was speaking to him with many earnest gestures. Sir Magnin yawned widely, making no effort to mask his boredom.

On his other side, however, Lord Harlan lifted his head slightly from between his hunched shoulders and followed Noel with his gaze. He looked like a scrawny vulture, his white skeletal fingers tearing a joint of chicken apart, his cap clamped tightly to his narrow skull. For a moment he smiled at Noel, half toothless and malevolent, then dispatched a page boy on an errand.

Past the colonnade stood a door flanked by guards in livery. They let Noel and his escort pass through into what proved to be a narrow corridor. It ended at another guarded door, beyond which stood a short flight of about four steps leading through an open archway into a sizable chamber furnished with benches and massive chairs covered with carving. Byzantine frescoes and French tapestries decorated the walls. Tall, arched windows lined one side of the chamber. Noel stared at them, wondering what they overlooked, wondering how high off the ground this room was.

Queer, heavily swirled glass in tiny panes mirrored the chamber back at him. He could not see through them into the night. The guards released him and left him alone there. As soon as the door closed and was bolted, Noel hurried about the chamber in a quick circumference, peeking behind the tapestries for a hidden door.

He found it, but it was locked.

"Damn!" he said aloud.

A fire crackled upon the stone hearth, fragrant with burning apple wood and cedar. The benches lining the walls and the very sparseness of the other furnishings told Noel that this must be an antechamber, where suppliants waited for an audience with the governor.

The eyes in the faces of the frescoes seemed to watch him. He warmed his hands at the fire, then told himself to get on with it. Striding across the room, he picked up one of the two chairs, finding it heavy enough to wrench his side. He lifted it high with a grunt and swung it against the center window.

Glass shattered into a thousand shards, the brittle noise of its breakage crashing over him. Cold air rushed in, and the fire blazed up the chimney with a roar.

Shouts from without the door warned Noel he had only seconds. He bashed at the ragged edges of glass still jutting up from the sill and flung a leg over.

He was one story up, above what looked like a tiny, walled garden. A tree spread its branches close by, but it was too small to support his weight.

The door to the chamber burst open, and the guards ran inside with shouts. Noel swung the rest of himself out and dangled a moment by his hands in hopes of finding a ledge, however narrow, beneath him. His groping toes found nothing but the straight stone wall.

A hand seized his wrist. Fear and reflex enabled Noel to jerk free of those clutching fingers, but he lost his hold altogether and plunged straight down. He closed his eyes, certain that when he hit the ground he would shatter both legs.

Instead he crashed into a taut awning that sagged, groaning beneath him, then recoiled like a trampoline, hurling him sideways into a massive bush. Birds burst from their nests, chirping and fluttering in panic. Noel flung out his arms, seeking to grab anything that would stop his impetus. But the bush could not support his weight. He went crashing down through the center of it, limbs snapping beneath him like pistol shots, and landed on a hillock of pungent compost, straw, and crushed flowers that gave off a heavy fragrance. The jolt of hitting immovable ground knocked out the last bits of breath left in him.

He lay there, stunned and weary, his ribs protesting with every breath he attempted to draw. His head had had enough.

From above him, voices cursed and shouted, raising the alarm. Groaning, Noel forced himself to his hands and knees, then to his feet.

Stumbling over plants, flagstones, and something about the general size and shape of a sundial in the darkness, Noel searched for a gate in the garden wall and found none. A guard was climbing out the window. Noel's heart pounded harder.

There had to be a way out. He just had to find it.

The only door he discovered, however, was a narrow one that led back into the palace. It came open at his touch.

Reluctant, every instinct screaming at him that he was going the wrong way, Noel entered. He found himself struck in the face by a musty, ecclesiastical scent of beeswax, leather, damp wool vestments, and incense. A lone candle burned upon the small altar, casting a feeble nimbus of light at the feet of the madonna statue.

It was a tiny chapel, cramped and dark with wood and stone. A tarnished chalice and plate rested upon the altar cloth; cobwebs hung in the corners like veils. Noel crept between the pews and nearly stumbled at the sight of a boy stretched prostrate on the floor before the altar. He was dressed in a mail shirt, leggings, and coif, but he wore no surcoat, spurs, or weapons. A sword lay upon the floor inches from his head. He was muttering prayers to himself in a hoarse chant that sounded worn with fatigue.

Noel's heart seemed to stop; it was a hell of a time for someone to be having an all-night vigil.

The boy's eyes jerked open and stared up at Noel. He blinked and lifted his head, his eyes widening in obvious surprise. For a moment Noel thought he would speak. Noel opened his own mouth, but he'd lost his breath and his tongue felt stuck to the roof of his mouth. They looked at each other for what seemed an eternity, then the boy frowned and clenched his eyes tightly shut.

Pressing his face to the floor, he began a new prayer.

Apparently no distractions of any kind were permitted to interrupt a vigil. Noel dragged in a breath, giving thanks to tradition, and hurried to the rear of the chapel.

He eased his way out, leaping into an alcove dark with shadow as guards came trotting past. One of them entered the chapel with a bang of the door, only to emerge almost at once, shaking his head.

When they were gone, Noel touched his bracelet. "LOC," he said in a fierce whisper. "Activate. Show me the way out."

The LOC made no response.

"LOC!" he said with urgency. "Activate *now*."

It didn't. He could have wept with frustration. But more men were coming. Some of them had pikes and they were probing the alcoves along this passage with a savage clanging of steel upon stone.

Noel whipped from hiding and ran for it, hoping he could make the stairs ahead without being seen.

"Look yon! There he is!"

The shout brought a fresh rush of adrenaline through him. Noel picked up speed and drew ahead of them, for they were lumbering a bit in the weight of their armor. His only encumbrance was his exhaustion, but for the moment he forgot that and ran like the wind.

He started up the steps, then changed his mind and went down, plucking a torch from its wall sconce as he did so. The narrow steps spiraled tightly. He prayed he would not

slip and tried to hold the torch at an angle to keep the breeze
from extinguishing it.

Going down didn't look like such a good idea. Wiping
sweat from his eyes, he thought about cellars and dungeons.
He thought about being trapped like a rat down a hole. He
thought about never seeing daylight again.

But going up into the main part of the palace offered no better advantage. He figured he had a ninety-five percent chance
of being caught, no matter which way he went.

Voices came from behind him, drawing closer. They must
have split up, taking both directions on the stairs just in case.
Noel reached the bottom, finding himself in a low-ceilinged area
supported by posts of rough-hewn wood. He started toward the
open passageway at the far end, then caught himself with one
hand on a post and swung himself around in a slingshot effect
toward a row of huge fermenting vats along the wall.

Fashioned of aged oak staves bound with iron rings, the
casks stood upright on end. Each was taller than Noel and
large enough to hold half a dozen men at once. Noel ran from
one to another, searching for enough clearance between their
sides and the wall to wedge himself into. He even tapped their
sides, seeking a hollow thud that would tell him the cask was
empty, in hopes of being able to hide inside.

The smell of wine emanating from them was almost strong
enough to overwhelm his senses. Slinging perspiration from his
eyes, he stumbled into a stack of mead barrels, nearly knocking
them over, and found himself at a dead-end corner.

All hope in him sank. He heard his pursuers coming down
the stairs, and at once he threw his torch upon the ground and
stamped it out. The darkness blinded him, then he saw the glow
thrown forward by his pursuers' torches and the long shadows
cast upon the floor.

"He must be down here," said one.

"Aye, he's here right enough. Search it well. Sir Magnin
won't take kindly to this goin' on all night."

Noel squeezed himself into the corner and tried his best to
shift the huge cask over enough to let him behind it. Of course
it would not budge. He crouched down in despair, breathing
hard, his heart hammering wild, and tried to think.

Only then did he notice that this cask was set up on support
pillars above a stone-lined pit cut into the floor. He ran his arm

under it and felt about. There was about three feet of clearance beneath the cask. Without hesitation, he thrust his head and shoulders between the bottom of the cask and the edge of the pit. He scraped his cheek and felt it sting, but he didn't care. There was just enough room for him to slither in.

It was awkward, going in and down head first. He had to twist himself about in order to bring his knees around in the right direction. That made his ribs catch on him, and he nearly gasped aloud.

At the last instant, he held back the sound and bit down hard on his lip. Safely down in the shallow pit, he breathed hard through his mouth, and sweat bathed him in a river. He coiled himself against the wall, keeping his head low, and watched the swing of light and shadow as they walked closer.

They did not find him. They searched every nook and cranny. They went through the dungeons or whatever lay beyond the passageway he had first started down. They stuck their torches behind the casks. They even found a hiding spot up in a niche behind the stairs and spooked a family of rats that chittered and hissed furiously at the disturbance. His concealment was perfect, and as they finally started up the stairs to leave, he felt his thudding heart slow down. His breathing grew calmer. His tense muscles slackened.

He rolled onto his back and lay inert for several minutes, basking in the sheer relief of it.

But of course he could not remain in that hole forever. He debated with himself over waiting through the rest of the night, or of trying to slip from the castle now while there was still plenty of confusion.

He decided finally that he could not wait. By morning, the castle would be more secure. Men would be organized. The searches would become more thorough. In the darkness, he had a slim chance to slip away unseen. In daylight, he would have none.

Getting out was easier than getting in. He squirmed his way out and finally kicked free. His clothing was coated with dirt and cobwebs. He slapped and brushed as best he could in the darkness. He had to look presentable enough to blend in with the crowd if necessary. If he could find a servant about his size, he would ambush the fellow and make a quick change.

Fumbling his way to the stairs, he groped about until he found the bottom step. It was not until he placed his foot upon it that he heard a faint sound.

Noel froze, his blood turning to ice water in his veins. It seemed to come from the direction of the passageway behind him. Every instinct he had urged him to dash up the stairs for his life. But with all his willpower he forced himself to look back. His eyes strained to see through the darkness.

There must have been a torch burning far away down the passageway, for the faintest hint of a glow came from that direction. After a moment he could see the vague outlines of a figure standing there. He swallowed, forcing himself to wait.

The watcher did nothing, said nothing. Noel's sense of alarm tamed down. Maybe this was a friend.

He hesitated, but he had to risk it. "Help me," he whispered. "Whoever you are, I need your help."

"Theodore?" said a woman's voice, all atremble.

His head came up. He said, "Sophia?"

She ran to him, heedless of the dark, and gripped his arm. Fragrant and soft in folds of velvet and fur, her beads clicking upon her bosom, she leaned close.

"God have mercy!" she said. "Who *are* you?"

"A friend."

"Is he here? In the castle?"

"No."

She gasped and began to weep. "He is dead. He is dead. I know it. I have dared to hope, but now I know it must be so."

"No, he isn't dead," said Noel with irritation. He checked himself. "At least he wasn't when I saw him last."

"When?" she said eagerly. "When did you last see him?"

"This morning, late. About noonday."

She thought it over a moment, then twisted with rich rustles of cloth to push away his arm and stand free of him. He could smell the clean scent of verbena upon her. She had skin as cool and smooth as silk.

"You sent your handmaiden to me, didn't you?" he whispered. "You offered to help me."

"Yes, I thought you must be here to help Theodore. I couldn't imagine another reason why they should mistake you for him. He is—" She broke off.

"His only thought is to rescue you," said Noel, feeling like Cupid on a bad day. "He is trying to—"

"But he mustn't," she said in fresh alarm. "Sir Magnin will only entrap him. Theodore must send word to Byzantium for a *sebastocrator* and reinforcements. He must retake the castle and subdue the rebels before they incite the entire Peloponnese to revolt."

"Fine," said Noel. "Whatever. I must get out of the castle. Can you help me?"

"But who are you?" she asked again.

"My name is Noel of Kedran. I am a traveler who has been caught up in these events. Will you help me get away? Is there some secret passage out that I can use?"

She drew in a sharp breath. "There is."

"Great! Show me—"

"No!" Her hand closed hard upon his, her nails digging in. "I cannot. I swore to my father upon his deathbed that I would not reveal the secret of its location to anyone."

"Oh, for God's sake," said Noel, losing his temper. "What good is a secret passageway if it isn't used in times of need? I have a great need to escape Sir Magnin, Sophia. He wants to kill me, and I would rather stay alive."

"And what have you to do with Theodore?" she asked.

He frowned. The girl might be pretty, but her wits were not quick. "As I have said," he answered with all the scant patience he had left, "I am a friend. I switched places with him to give him a chance to escape the Milengi—"

"No! The Milengi!" she cried in distress. "They will torture him. They are animals—"

"Hush. By now he's probably escaped them and is on his way here to rescue you. In the meantime, I have to get away. It would probably be wise for you to come with me. Then Theodore won't have to risk his neck by entering the castle, and the two of you can go back to Constantinople together."

"This is his plan?" she said doubtfully. "It seems poor-spirited."

"It is a very practical plan, designed to save all our necks," said Noel in exasperation.

"Theodore the Bold should come storming Mistra with all his men and retake it," she said.

Noel very nearly said something unwise. Curbing his temper, he said, "Theodore may be bold, but right now he has no men. Sir Magnin wiped out his entire force."

"Oh," she said. "Oh, I see. That is why they have been feasting. The garrison here did not fight very well. It surrendered here almost at once. My captain-at-arms should be horsewhipped for his cowardice. Had I been a man, I could have led them in resistance and Sir Magnin would have had to besiege us. Our walls here are very strong. We do not even fear the Turks who are marauding the coasts, according to the latest word from Monemvasia."

"My lady," said Noel, rolling his eyes. "Forgive me, but armies, Turks, and cowardly captains-at-arms do not matter very much right now. Will you get us out of here?"

"Yes," she replied. "But it means that I must reveal to you the location of our secret treasury. You must swear your most sacred oath that you will never betray this secret to another soul. Kneel and swear."

Time was ticking away. Noel, however, knew that to argue with her would only delay them more. He knelt upon the hard stone floor.

"I do most solemnly swear," he said, "by my honor, my rank, and my position in the realm of Kedran that I will hold this secret fast within my heart and reveal it to no one."

"Very well said, Sir Noel."

He jumped to his feet and grabbed her hand impatiently. "Come on! Which way?"

"Through here," she whispered and led him toward the passageway.

The light grew stronger as they progressed. So did the smell. Noel wrinkled his nostrils at the fetid stench from something dead or unspeakable that came wafting along the tunnel.

"What is it?" he finally asked. "That stink?"

"Oh, just the dungeons," she said casually, still leading the way. "It is always worse in the spring. The thaw, you know. The garderobe is worse."

The dregs of macho pride still in him would not let him place his hand over his nose and mouth or even make gagging noises while she was so unconcerned. He wondered what else could be found in the dungeons besides rats and rotting corpses. The sewer?

She stopped and pointed at a flight of straight steps leading up toward a torch burning on the wall. "Up them. Quickly. And mind, good sir, that you make no noise, for we can easily be heard along this way. If we are stopped, you are my ser—"

As she spoke she glanced over her shoulder at him. Her eyes flew wide, and her scream rent the air.

Startled, Noel seized her by the shoulders and shook her hard in an effort to shut her up. "Are you mad? What the hell are you doing?"

"You!" she shouted in a fury and began pounding on his chest with her fists. "You evil, treacherous dog! You lying, filthy, wicked *brute!*"

She screamed again, so enraged he could do nothing with her. Hearing the sound of running footsteps and a voice raised in query, Noel shoved her away from him and looked about for a way to escape.

But guards seemed to appear from nowhere, surrounding him. Noel found himself pinned against the wall with the barbed tip of a pike held to his gut. He glared at Sophia, who stood there glaring back with her fists clenched and her beautiful face red and contorted with rage.

"You sought to trick me!" she said. "You called on my pity, and you twisted every word into such persuasion I nearly undid the secret that I have sworn to protect unto my dying breath. Oh, how clever you think yourself, Lord Leon, but you are evil through and through. God shall surely strike you down one day for what you do!"

"What?" said Noel stupidly. "But I'm not—"

"At last!" said Sir Magnin's voice, booming off the stone walls as he descended the steps. He looked resplendent in his pierpoint tunic cut of heavy silk that shimmered richly in the torchlight. His sleeves were very wide, revealing the snowy cuff of his linen shirt as he raised one hand to quell the noise. "Our fox is run to earth at last, and such a chase you have given us. For an impostor you amuse us greatly."

"Who says I'm an impostor?" said Noel, but it was false bravado, and he and Sir Magnin both knew it.

Sir Magnin merely smiled and turned to regard Sophia, who had run out of breath and epithets and now stood like stone, her blue eyes wide and accusing behind the sheen of tears, her skin so pale she looked ghostly. Her blond hair flowed down her back nearly to her knees, and she held it bound back from her face with only a narrow circlet of finely worked gold filiagree. She looked like a queen, but she had the intelligence of an ant. Noel watched the bewilderment and doubt flow into her face, and nearly lost his temper again. What in the world had possessed her to bring everyone down on them like this?

She was staring up the stairs at the small crowd of onlookers who had clustered there. If possible, she grew even paler. "I do not understand," she whispered. "Is it sorcery you practice, Sir Magnin? How can you command two such creatures?"

Sir Magnin's robust laugh echoed loudly. "Oh, my dear lady, you have tricked yourself, it seems. What a perfect joke. Such exquisite irony. I really don't know when I have enjoyed myself more."

He glanced at Noel, who was frowning at him without comprehension, and snapped his fingers at the staircase in a summons. "Come down, my shadow, and meet your counterpart."

A figure detached itself from the others and came down the steps into the clear light. Noel stared into his own face, into his own eyes, and could not believe what he saw. It was not possible. It couldn't be.

"Lord Leon," said Sir Magnin in a voice like cream, "come and allow me to introduce you to—I don't believe you have given us your true name, sir."

Noel felt as though he were standing over his head in water. Everything had a bent, unfocused quality to it. His hearing seemed to be fading in and out. He could not feel anything in his body except the pulse beating hard in his left temple.

Somehow he managed to speak. "I am Noel," he whispered.

"Ah," said Sir Magnin. "Lord Leon, I give you Noel. Truly, the likeness is most amazing."

The twin, the duplicate called Leon, stared back at Noel with equal astonishment. It was like staring into a mirror. He frowned at Noel, then seemed to realize that Sir Magnin's brows were raised, signifying that he awaited a response.

Leon nodded to his master. "Indeed, I am sore amazed by this."

His voice jolted Noel, for it was like hearing himself on a recording. A dozen questions flashed through Noel's mind, but he had no time to speculate, for Sir Magnin's smile had changed to a scowl.

"And why did you not tell me about this brother?" he demanded.

"Nay," said Leon nervously, backing away from Sir Magnin. "I did not know I had a—a double. We were not born this way. I swear to you that I didn't—"

"You lie!" said Sir Magnin in a voice like thunder. He gestured at his guards. "Throw both of them into the dungeon."

CHAPTER 8

Narrow, tanned faces with straight noses and angular jaws. Crisp black hair, gray eyes widening in turn each time they looked at one another.

The shock of recognition traveled between them again and again as they were escorted down into the putrid depths of the dungeon. Noel barely noticed the stench that was now thick enough to make him cough. He saw the rack standing in one corner, with old bloodstains soaked into the wood. The iron maiden dangled from the ceiling beam overhead; its occupant moaned softly as they entered. The thumbscrews lay neatly arranged upon a table. The boot waited for its next victim. A fire burned in a raised, circular hearth, and branding irons and pokers for the putting out of eyes lay with their ends red-hot in the hissing coals.

Beyond the torture area stood the cells, black, airless holes cut into the bedrock of the mountain itself, ripe with the stinking filth of all the occupants who had been there before.

"It's full," said the jailer, gnawing on a cud of something stuck in his jaw. "Where do I put 'em, eh? Answer me that."

"Sir Magnin says put 'em down here, so we put 'em down here," replied the guard. He stuck out his jaw and faced down the jailer. "You want me to tell him you can't do the job?"

"No, no call for that," said the jailer hastily. He chewed a moment, his gaze vacant in thought. "We'll put 'em in together, see? And double up another cell."

It took time for this to be arranged. Prisoners suffering terrible, untended wounds were dragged out. One man screamed horribly each time he was touched. His right foot was swollen, bloody, lacerated to the ankle. Noel averted his gaze, certain the injury must have been caused by the boot.

He caught Leon staring at him and the shock came again. Where had Leon come from? Was he created by whatever anomaly had upset the time stream? But how? Or was it the anomaly that had brought Noel and his twin together? There was an ancient theory that said each person had a twin somewhere in the world. Was there also a twin for each time?

Now that his initial amazement was fading, Noel noticed that his duplicate was not quite as tall as he. Leon's features were less chiseled. His jaw had a blurred line to it; the skin of his cheeks bore a few pitted scars from acne or smallpox. His eyes were not as deep-set, and their color was paler, almost silver. He held his mouth in a perpetual hostile sneer. It was like looking at oneself in an imperfect glass, where a small ripple in the surface put the reflection off kilter.

"We'll have that dagger from you, my lord," said the guard.

Leon's brows drew together. *Is that the way I look when I frown?* wondered Noel, only to drive the thought away. Leon said nothing, but he pulled his dagger from his belt and surrendered it.

He used his right hand.

Noel himself was left-handed. He blinked, putting it all together. Even their names were reversals of each other. Noel and . . . Leon. This duplicate *must* have been created when he was going through the time stream.

But they hadn't come through to reality in the same place, unless Leon had regained consciousness first this morning and come straight off the mountain to Mistra before the dwarfs started scavenging among the bodies. Was Leon merely a clone? Did he have the same personality, the same way of thinking, the same thoughts? Or was he his own person, a duplicate only on the surface?

The whole idea was chilling.

"Inside, both of you!"

Hard shoves sent Noel and Leon staggering into the cell together. Their shoulders bumped, and as one they whirled away from each other, taking opposite sides of the cell. It was furnished with a pile of dirty straw in one corner, a pair of ring bolts to fasten shackles to, and an open grille in the door to let light stream in.

Noel sucked in a breath. His voice seemed to have deserted him. "You are Leon of . . . Nardek?"

Leon's glare intensified. "I am," he snapped.

Noel forgot the listening jailer and turnkey outside. He took a step closer to Leon. "This isn't supposed to happen," he said in half a whisper. "You shouldn't—"

"—exist?" finished Leon with a sneer. "Shouldn't I? Next will you say I should plunge back into the ether that created me? Am I going to be too much of an inconvenience to you, Brother Noel?"

Noel blinked, surprised in spite of himself. "You know about the—"

"Of course I know! I went through it, didn't I? I know everything you know, Brother Noel. I am everything you are. You can't put me back. You can't make me disappear. I'm real now, and I'm going to stay real."

"We've got to go back," said Noel. He rubbed his bracelet. "Somehow—"

"Go back to what?" said Leon angrily. "I exist *here*."

"You shouldn't."

Leon swung at him, but Noel ducked beneath his arm and slammed him against the wall.

The jailer kicked the door. "You there! Stop that fighting."

"Stay out of this," said Noel and Leon simultaneously.

The jailer backed away. "Mind you keep quiet," he said.

Noel paid him no attention. His gaze fastened on Leon. This was just a copy, an imperfect one, some twisted, angry version of himself. They shouldn't think alike. They shouldn't speak at the same time.

Yet they did.

Noel set his jaw. "We've got to talk."

"There is nothing to say," said Leon, still pressed against the wall although Noel had retreated. "You have everything . . . a real, working LOC, memories of your own past, even—"

He broke off, breathing raggedly.

Noel watched him. "Even what?"

"I have only now," said Leon. "I was born today. That is all I have. Today. No yesterday. No past. But I can make a future for myself, in this time, in this place."

"No," said Noel in horror. "You can't interfere with history. The paradox—"

Leon laughed, a scornful, cutting blare of sound. "Do you think I care? I can do anything I want, and how will you stop me?"

"You must not interfere," said Noel urgently. "You could destroy the future, change it irrevocably—"

"Then let it change! Let my name be written in their history books. Let my descendants fill the world. How else can I *be*?"

"No—"

"Yes! Damn you, *yes*! I have already made it so. And if you are wise, Brother Noel, you will not seek to stop me."

He whirled away before Noel could reply and banged on the door. "Jailer! Jailer, I want another cell. I demand it! Jailer—"

"Be quiet," said Noel. "He isn't going to accede to your demands. You're a prisoner, just like me."

"It's your fault I'm here," said Leon. "I was already Sir Magnin's favorite. He likes my company. I amused him. I gave him good ideas. But you have spoiled everything, turned him against me, made him distrust me."

"Good," said Noel. "We both have to find a way out of Mistra. Recall will come any minute now. We mustn't interfere more than we've done already. You know that."

"I've already said I do not care. I will regain my position with Sir Magnin. I can offer him skills that no one else can."

Foreboding filled Noel. "What do you have in mind?"

"Oh, no, I am telling you nothing about it."

"You had better."

"Go to hell, Brother Noel."

Putting his back to the door, Leon rolled his eyes up in his head and stayed that way for several seconds. Noel watched him with concern, wondering if he was crazy in addition to his other problems, but before Noel could think up another approach with Leon, the jailer came to the door and unlocked it.

"We've got another cell for you, my lord," he said. His eyes looked slightly glazed. His voice sounded wooden. "Better if the two of you stay apart. You might cook somethin' up."

Noel stared, too astonished to act. Grinning broadly, Leon strolled from the cell. Noel stepped forward, but the door was slammed in his face.

"Wait," he said desperately. "You must listen to me—"

Leon only laughed as he walked down the cell block and was locked away. Noel hammered on his door.

"Jailer!" he called. "Jailer!"

But a brick came hurling at his door, striking it with such a savage thud Noel was startled into leaping back.

"Shut that noise!" yelled the jailer. "Pipe up again and I'll have your tongue out."

Noel frowned, his mind awash with worry and the implications of what he'd witnessed. What had Leon done to convince the jailer to move him? What kind of mental powers did he possess? Noel knew that he himself lacked any kind of telepathic skills. He'd been rigorously tested before he was allowed to enter the training program at the Time Institute. How could Leon be a duplicate copy and possess different abilities? Was there something latent in Noel that the duplication had picked up and amplified?

He could ask himself questions like that for an eternity and come no closer to getting any answers.

Clearing off a space on the floor, Noel settled himself gingerly there and leaned against the wall. It was cold and hard against his shoulders. His problems were getting worse, and he was further from solving any of them than he'd ever been.

His hand closed over the bracelet on his left wrist. He had to make the LOC work. He needed answers, and he needed them soon.

Worried and tired, Noel dozed until the dungeon grew quiet and the fires burned down to low embers. Then he went to work.

"Come on, LOC. Come *on*, LOC!"

Shivering with cold upon the dank stone floor, Noel hunched himself up in a knot to conserve body warmth and tried to crush the fear gnawing the pit of his stomach.

"LOC, activate," he said.

The device did not respond. Apparently it was jammed in disguise mode. He knew part of it was still functional, for its warmth on his wrist told him it was monitoring him and operating its recorder. Unless he could access its data retrieval banks, he would be forced to continue without any information on this time and place. It was like being blind.

"Last chance," he muttered and twisted the bracelet in an effort to find the concealed manual override switch that would respond only to his imprint. The LOC was isomorphic, and only he could operate it, but it was acting as though it had its defenses up against him as well. That minuscule depression on the side had to be it, but when he pressed it nothing happened, just as nothing had happened to his emergency recall signal, just as the end of the time loop had come and he was still here.

Sweat dripped into his eyes despite the cold. He felt suddenly clammy and without hope.

For all his complaining about life in the twenty-sixth century, for all his disparagement of modern people's life-styles, for all his criticism, it was still his time. He cared about it; he wanted to make it better; he needed it for his own identity. Never to go back. . . .

He shoved the growing fear away, not wanting it to paralyze him. He had to keep his mind clear and his hopes up.

"Damn you!" he said and chopped down on the bracelet with the heel of his hand. "*Activate!*"

With a low, almost inaudible hum the LOC came on. The bracelet's copper image dissolved into the reality of its Plexiglas sides. They revealed the pulsing optics and complex circuitry that made this small device capable of such wondrous things.

Noel closed his eyes a moment and sagged in relief. He felt as though he'd just been thrown a lifeline. But there wasn't time to waste. At any moment he might be overheard or discovered.

Collecting himself, he said softly, "Scan. We are at Mistra in Greece, era medieval. Determine date. Identify and correlate all important historical events for this time and place. Begin."

"Scanning," said the LOC's toneless voice in acknowledgment.

Noel wiped the sweat from his face and waited. As long as his LOC functioned, he was not helpless. He could get himself out of this mess. He just had to take it one step at a time.

"Ready," said the LOC. "Specific date 1332 A.D. Location Mistra. Important historical events . . ."

It stopped talking. Noel frowned in alarm.

"LOC," he said, trying to keep anxiety from his voice. "Are you malfunctioning?"

"Negative."

"Are there no important historical events?"

"Affirmative."

"None?"

"Affirmative."

Noel's frown deepened. "That's not possible. The fourteenth century marked a lot of political power struggles in this part of the world as well as in Asia Minor and Europe. There's a power struggle going on right now, and someone mentioned Turkish pirates making raids on the coast. Scan again."

"Scanning," said the LOC. It paused. "Anomaly warning."

"Well, isn't that amazing," said Noel, then caught himself. The LOC did not respond to sarcasm. "Specify."

"Time split. Parallel alternatives."

He swore. "Of course. LOC, this is the situation. A duplicate of me has been created during our journey through the time stream. That duplicate is called Leon."

"Reversal of Noel," said the LOC.

"Yes. I'm left-handed; he's right-handed. He's telepathic or something. I'm not. I don't know how many other comparisons we can make. That's not important. What we've got here is someone who looks like me who wants to change history."

"Acknowledged."

"LOC, give me data on the history parallels."

The LOC hummed but made no reply.

"Are you malfunctioning?"

"Negative."

"You can't specify the alternative lines of history?"

"Not at this time."

"Since when?"

"Negative."

Noel's frown deepened. The LOC wasn't making sense. "Run diagnostic codes," he said. "Scan for registering malfunctions. Identify."

"Scanning . . . destination codes," said the LOC.

He felt that cold shiver of fear again. "Obviously those are shot to hell. Look where we ended up."

"Date codes."

"Yes. What else?"

The LOC did not reply.

"Are you malfunctioning—"

"Retrieval codes. Systems . . . nine, four, zero, two date. Two date. Error. Scanning . . ."

It was getting warmer on his arm. Noel touched it. "LOC," he said urgently, afraid it would crash on him. "LOC, stop internal check. Run hypothesis."

"Ready."

"What if Leon didn't affect history? What if Leon didn't exist? What would be the important events happening here at this time? List them without dates."

"Theodore of Albania named governor of Mistra. Rules province five years. Marriage of Theodore and Lady Sophia. Three children produced. Invasion of Turks under Umur, the Emir of Aydin, stopped at walls of Mistra. Bulgarian uprising is—"

"Stop," said Noel. "What about Sir Magnin? What part does he play?"

The LOC did not reply.

"Are you malfunctioning?"

"Negative."

"Run another hypothesis."

"Ready."

"If Leon changes history here, what part does Sir Magnin play?"

"Sir Magnin the Black usurps rule of Mistra, leads Peloponnese in revolt from Byzantine rule. Lady Sophia dies of suicide before wedding. Umur leads Turkish janissaries up river and conquers Mistra. All holdings of Peloponnese and Athens fall into Turkish hands within—"

"Stop," said Noel. "Question. What action does Leon commit that changes history?"

The LOC hesitated. "Action already committed."

Noel sat up straight. "What!"

Something stirred outside his cell. The man in the iron maiden moaned, and Noel hunched over his LOC in frustration, reminding himself to keep his voice low.

"Repeat."

"Action already committed."

"Damn," said Noel. "Damn, damn, damn, *damn*."

He couldn't go back and undo it. With date and destination codes malfunctioning, he certainly couldn't expect to do the kind of tight maneuvering required to create that short of a time loop. Besides, the LOC wasn't being specific enough. Apparently it wasn't programmed to handle the kind of contingency Leon represented. No one had ever been duplicated while going through a time stream before. For that matter, no one had ever been sent to the wrong time and place either.

"All right," said Noel, thinking rapidly. "I can't stop Sir Magnin from taking Mistra. That's already happened. But can I help topple him from power and keep him from trying to marry Lady Sophia? Will that pull events back into proper line?"

"Unknown."

"You must know something!"

"Unknown."

"Damn!"

The LOC remained silent, its circuit lights pulsing steadily.

"All right," said Noel, drawing a couple of breaths in an effort to regain control. "All right. Maybe I should forget the whole thing. Maybe all this is supposed to happen. Why don't we get on with our original mission? Can you reprogram to original destination? Location Constantinople. Date 634 A.D."

The LOC did not reply.

"LOC!" he said sharply. "Respond. Are you malfunctioning?"

"Negative."

"Then reprogram, dammit!"

"Wait," said LOC. It almost sounded sullen, although that was impossible.

"Come on. Come on," said Noel impatiently.

"Reprogramming not possible," said the LOC.

"Why?"

"Malfunction in destination and date codes. Date two, zero, four, four, four . . . scanning time retrieval scramble not found, not found, not found—"

"Stop," said Noel. "Let's try again. Reprogram. Location Constantinople. Date 633 A.D. Run."

"Wait," said the LOC. It hummed briefly. "Reprogramming not possible."

Noel swore. His hands were shaking. He rubbed the moisture from his palms. Forcing himself to remain calm, he said, "Reprogram. Location Byzantium. Date now. Run."

"Wait."

He waited, listening to faint snores and the suffering whimpers of the man in the iron maiden. The LOC kept humming, but it did not respond.

"LOC," he whispered. "Are you still reprogramming?"

"Affirmative," said the LOC.

Noel's spirits rose. His confidence came back in a rush. "Good. Let's travel there *now*."

The LOC did not reply.

"Are you malfunctioning?"

"Affirmative."

Noel's heart hit his shoes. "Reprogramming is impossible?"

"Destination of Byzantium is impossible. Destination codes malfunctioning. Retrieval scan—"

"Stop," said Noel. "Question."

"Ready."

"Is reprogramming for destinations other than Constantinople possible?"

"Unknown."

"Oh, hell!" Noel started to cancel in frustration, but forced himself to wait. He thought a long while, then sighed. "Run hypothesis."

"Ready."

"Input this data. My time loop should be near its end within an hour or two."

"Mission time scheduled to end in exactly three hours."

Noel grinned. "That's more like it. Input this. Emergency assistance recall failed. Question: will my time loop end with recall?"

"Negative. Anomaly warning."

Noel's frown returned. "You're saying that because of the duplication and the changes in events that have already taken place, I have nothing to return to?"

"No return. Anomaly warning."

"So much for getting yanked away from this mess," muttered Noel. He rubbed his forehead. "What's the length of my safety chain?"

"Safety chain programming intact," said the LOC. "Derive the square root of the forty-nine-minute time ratio to—"

"Seven—yeah, then what?" Noel did swift figuring in his head. "I make that about, what, twelve extra hours?"

"Twelve hours, nine minutes," said the LOC.

The safety chain was a highly complex contingency program intended as a fail-safe device in times of emergency, when a time loop did not end with a proper recall. It was not inconceivable that something might go wrong on a mission, involving, say, the temporary removal of a LOC from a traveler's possession. The safety chain consisted of several miniature time loops built in to expand the main loop and thus allow the traveler some leeway in straightening out problems. But its length was limited because access to a time stream could only be maintained for a certain duration.

As far as Noel knew, only one traveler had ever had to use the safety-chain program. Now, it was about to be two travelers. He swallowed hard, and thought there must be an easier way to make history.

"I'm not certain I can fix the problems in just twelve hours," he said. "How many links in my chain?"

"Standard."

That meant three links, and a link consisted of seven times the number of hours within the loop. He had about ten and a half days before . . .

"What happens if I don't fix the anomaly by the end of the safety chain?"

The LOC did not respond. It didn't really have to. Noel knew the answer. The time stream would snap shut, and the alterations to history would be permanent. No other historians could journey back to this time and place to attempt further repairs. The future, for better or worse, would be changed.

It also meant he would be trapped here for the rest of his life.

He rested his forehead on his knees, trying not to let his emotions give way. Whoever had sabotaged him had done a hell of a job.

The rules and his operating principles had just changed. He could no longer remain an uninvolved observer. Leon had to be stopped, and nothing—not pity, a sense of unexplainable obligation toward his twin, or anything else—could be permitted to deflect Noel from that purpose.

"Deactivate," he said.

The LOC disguised itself as the bracelet of hammered copper and shut down. Noel stared at the wide band spanning his wrist. It tapered to two narrow ends at the heel of his palm. The hammered surface looked dull in the shadows. He grimaced and pulled his sleeve down over it. Time to go.

Rubbing his eyes that were gritty from insufficient sleep, he said softly, "LOC, activate but retain disguise mode."

The LOC did nothing at first. Just as he felt his tenuous hold on his temper slip, the bracelet grew warm upon his wrist and hummed quietly. It did not assume its true appearance.

He sighed in relief. "Project external electrical field. Unlock this door."

The device grew warmer on his wrist, almost unpleasantly hot. A hinge bolt flew through the air and struck the wall with a loud ping. Noel jumped, his nerves on edge.

"Stop!" he whispered and listened to hear if anyone had been awakened.

No alarm sounded. He let out his breath. His heart, however, kept on pumping too fast.

"Continue," he said and braced himself.

The next hinge bolt went flying. He ducked and heard it whistle over his head. It landed at the back end of the cell, the sound of its impact muffled in the pile of straw.

Noel tugged at the door, working its heavy weight off the hinges slowly, silently, making sure he did not strain the lock itself into creaking. When he had maneuvered himself enough space to squeeze through, he whispered to the LOC: "Engage external electromagnetic fields, human body level. Dampen."

The LOC grew hot again on his wrist, busy controlling the alertness levels of the men sleeping within the cells and within the jailer's quarters. It would not keep them from awakening if Noel made a lot of noise, but it would prevent them from being disturbed by any subconscious registering of his stealthy exit.

He crept through the near darkness, the torture area lit only by a few dim coals still glowing on the ash-filled hearth. It seemed as though he held his breath the whole way; his nerves stretched into taut wires, ready to snap at the least provocation.

No one heard him. No one came awake. No one raised the alarm. He crept, ghostlike, up the steps into the palace itself and emerged into the cold, clean air of the night.

CHAPTER 9

Pressed against the door of his cell, his shoes soaking up squalid mud, the snores of his cellmates rattling the air, Leon watched through the grille as Noel slipped away to freedom. Leon battled the urge to sound the alarm. It was almost more than he could bear to see Noel escape, but he pushed down the hatred surging through him. If Noel was caught now, they would likely maim or kill him.

Unconsciously Leon rubbed his right side where his ribs felt bruised and sore. Noel might have the injuries, but Leon felt them. Not strongly, not enough to incapacitate him, but he feared what might happen to him if Noel died. Just how closely were they linked?

He hated the thought of being dependent upon Noel. The fact of Noel's existence was enough to pour rivers of anger and hatred through him. When they first came upon each other tonight, it had been all he could do not to seize his twin by the throat and choke the life from him.

He could not bear the fact that Noel was the original and he the copy. *Copy* . . . something less than whole . . . something imperfect . . . something that could never stand alone as long as the original existed for comparison.

He tipped back his head and shut his eyes a moment, try- ing to slow his breathing. Even now, emotions boiled raw and furious within him. His legs were unsteady at the knees, quivery, as though he had been running for miles. His heart jerked too fast. He rubbed the right side of his chest to slow it down. Although he had known he must soon meet Noel, he had been filled with a mixture of dread and excitement. Nothing, however, had prepared him for that actual moment of standing face-to-face with him. Because while gazing into Noel's gray eyes, so steady and keen, like tempered steel, he had been filled with the dreadful certainty that he should not exist at all.

Then Noel had actually said the same thing.

"I live!" said Leon through gritted teeth. His fingers dug at the coarse, mildewed grain of the door as though to claw his way to freedom. "I *belong*."

But in his heart he knew better, and that made him all the more determined to get rid of Noel. For if there could only be one of them in existence, then Leon intended to be the one who survived. He had to figure out how to do it, how to put an end to Noel that would not kill him as well. There had to be a way to cut the link between them.

Was it the LOC that made Noel special? Leon had listened to him consulting it. He knew the LOC had made it possible for Noel to escape.

Leon frowned at the copper bracelet on his own wrist and rubbed it angrily. Why couldn't he have an operable LOC? Why did he have only this fake copy?

Because you are an anomaly, a freak, an accident.

He shoved the thought away with fresh resentment. Very well. He might not have a LOC of his own. He might have come into this world with a purse of fused, unusable coins. He might have other flaws—other *differences*—but he could make a place for himself here. He liked Mistra, liked Sir Magnin and the events that were happening around him. He liked shaping history, feeling it flow and re-form under his influence like modeling clay.

The key to success lay in possessing Noel's LOC. The knowledge it contained would give him almost limitless power. And because he was Noel's duplicate, the isomorphic properties should work for him. The LOC would protect *him,* and Noel could be eliminated.

It was indeed poor jail design to have the hinges set on the inside of the door, but Leon was unable to remove them anyway. They had long since rusted into a solid mass with the hinge, and even prying and scraping with the thin edge of his bracelet could not budge them.

Gasping and fatigued, he finally gave up. Thirsty, he went to the water pail and scooped some of the water into his mouth. It was probably stale, but it had no taste to him. Earlier in the day he had drunk wine for the first time, and it had had no taste either. Cold and wet, going down his throat; that was all. He had eaten with Sir Magnin's men. They proclaimed the steamed grape leaves stuffed with seasoned rice to be delicious. Leon could feel the textures upon his tongue, but there was no taste for him, no enjoyment.

It seemed there were other flaws besides the lump of fused, unusable coins in his purse and the inoperable LOC on his wrist. Flaws in *him*.

He felt panic unraveling the edges of his mind and shoved it away hastily. Not flaws, he told himself with all the force he could muster. *Differences.*

A trickle of sound caught his attention. Cat-quick, Leon went to the door and listened. It was the turnkey, yawning and shuffling, his torch flaming high in the cross drafts of air. No more than half awake, he made his rounds slowly. At random he inserted a long staff through the door grilles and poked an occupant. Curses, moans, or dead silence responded to this ploy. He twisted the iron maiden about on its chain, then let it spin free, chuckling softly to himself as the occupant sobbed in agony. Then he came over to the last cell block.

By now, Leon had his plan worked out. He reached his hand through the grille. "Turnkey!" he called softly. "You there, listen. He's gone."

The turnkey stared at him and scratched his head. "Eh?"

"He's gone. My double is gone."

"Be it so?" The turnkey peered at Noel's door, half ajar, and scratched his head again.

Sweat broke out upon Leon as he pressed with all his might. But this man's mind was too simple to be affected. "He's a sorcerer," said Leon urgently. "I heard him calling on his demon, and it answered him plain as plain. It opened the door for him. He's free. Don't you understand?"

"Got loose, eh?" The turnkey finally seemed to comprehend. He touched the door with wonder, then backed away. "Jailer!" he shouted. "Jailer!"

He ran for the jailer's quarters, crying out loudly.

In moments both of them returned. The jailer took one look at the empty cell, and his craggy face turned grim. "Roust the guards," he said to the turnkey. "Hurry, man! Don't stand there gawking."

The turnkey shuffled off, and the jailer stared at the empty cell with his torch held aloft. He crossed himself.

"Aye," said Leon eagerly, pressing hard. He could affect this man's wits. He'd already done it once, and that made new persuasion easier. "Sorcery. I heard him at it. I heard the demon talking to him. It tore the hinges off the door for him, and none of you heard."

The jailer was sweating. He bent and picked up one of the bolts from the floor, turned it over in his thick fingers, then dropped it. "Witchcraft!" he whispered.

Leon had been experimenting all day. Already he had found that when he willed it he could walk past people without them able to remember seeing him. He could also persuade them to do what he wanted, regardless of where their own best interests lay.

"Witchcraft," he echoed now, feeding on the jailer's fear as though it were ambrosia, taking small sips, drawing out the moment to its fullest. "He's called his demons down upon Mistra. Sir Magnin must be warned. Only I can protect him from the sorcerer."

"You!" The jailer blinked and came over to stare very hard at Leon through the grille. He put the flaming torch close to the grille, and the heat drove Leon back. "You are his double. If he is a sorcerer, then so are you."

"I command no demons," said Leon sharply, displeased by this argument. "Unlike him, I possess no special powers. But because I am his—"

"What is all this?" demanded Sir Magnin's voice, booming loudly enough to awaken all the inmates. He strode in, a long, billowing cloak draped over his bare shoulders. Guards with drawn weapons trotted behind him. "Jailer, an explanation. Your minion has broken my sleep with the babblings of a madman. Who has escaped and how?"

The jailer bowed low. "My liege, forgive me for failing my duty. I do not know how this man—"

"Who, blast your eyes? Who?"

"Noel of Kedran," said Leon.

Sir Magnin's black eyes narrowed. He pursed his lips thoughtfully, and the expression on his face boded no good for Noel. In his heart Leon laughed.

"Did you drop your keys in his hand? Are these cells not secure? How was this accomplished? Did he bribe you to help him, jailer?"

"No, my lord," said the jailer with a frightened gasp. "I swear to God, my lord. I had no part in it. Look for yourself. The hinges have been taken apart by no means that I understand. The bolt is still fastened."

Scowling, Sir Magnin took the torch from his hand and entered Noel's cell. When he finally emerged, he held all the bolts in his hand and hefted them absently. "Where is Leon?"

"Here, my lord," said Leon eagerly. He pressed his face to the grille where Sir Magnin could see him. "It was sorcery. Noel is evil in heart; his soul belongs to Satan."

"God help us!" cried the jailer.

"Rubbish," said Sir Magnin. "I want solid answers from you, my lad, not superstitious twaddle."

"I heard him call upon a demon," said Leon, pressing although he dared do little tampering with Sir Magnin's mind. The knight's thoughts were like steel traps. He was quick, with an agile intelligence, and suspicious. "I heard the voices. You must take care, my lord. He means to do you great harm."

"And what do *you* intend?" asked Sir Magnin. "You are his twin—"

"Do they not say twins are two sides of the same coin?" cried Leon hastily. "One good, the other evil? Has he not shown he is against you? Have I not sworn my loyalty and allegiance to you? I can protect you from him. I know his ways. I know what he intends. He stands on Lord Theodore's side. That has already been proven."

"You talk in circles," said Sir Magnin, but he was listening. "Why did you not cry out while he was escaping? Why did you wait?"

Leon frowned, but he had a lie ready. "I could not. There seemed to be a pressure upon my throat, paralyzing my speech, until he was well gone. I spoke the warning as soon as I was able. The turnkey himself can testify that I told him what happened before he discovered it himself."

"This the turnkey has said, my lord," said the jailer quietly.

Sir Magnin nodded. "And what assurance do I have that you can be trusted?"

"My word, my oath—"

"If the devil commands your heart, you can lie," said Sir Magnin harshly.

"Then bring a priest and let me swear before the cross," said Leon. "I do not fear the sacred relics of God."

Sir Magnin snapped his fingers, and a minion ran to fetch the priest. He came at last, sneezing, yawning, and looking frightened. His cassock sat crooked on his shoulders, and his tonsure needed clipping.

"Yes, my lord?" he said in a quavery voice, puffing hard.

Sir Magnin gestured at the jailer. "Bring Leon forth."

The jailer looked at the turnkey, who fumbled his keys with such shaking fingers that the jailer finally snatched the ring from him and unlocked the door himself.

Leon emerged, taking care not to look smug. He knelt before the priest and kissed the cross extended to him. The priest led him through a recital of his vows to God, and nothing struck him dead. His lips were examined to see if they had been burned by contact with the cross. They were not. He was given communion, and the wafer and wine did not poison him.

"I see no fault in this man or in his soul," said the priest at last.

"It seems we have misjudged you, Leon," said Sir Magnin. He smiled and threw his arm across Leon's shoulders, leading him from the dungeons. "Tell me of your twin's plan and what he intends against me."

"He must not escape the castle," said Leon swiftly. "A thorough search must begin now."

"It is under way. Sir Geoffrey has charge of that."

"When he is caught, he must be stripped," said Leon. "There is a bracelet that he wears, similar to mine." He held up his right arm.

Sir Magnin frowned. "Of what significance is this cheap jewelry?"

"None, save that it is a mark of our family. I would have it, to be sent home. That is all."

"Yes, yes, no matter. About the precautions to protect my men . . . if he can call on demons to serve him, how do we fight him?"

"The dark powers do not always obey him. You know they are treacherous and love to betray those whom they serve. He must be stripped, then thrown into anointed water to see if the possessing spirits can be driven from him. If not, then he must—he must be burned."

Leon's head rang with the word. He felt as though his throat was scorched, as though he had swallowed the very fire he called for.

Sir Magnin's hand tightened upon his arm. "You still care for this brother, do you not?"

Leon lifted his head with an effort. "I am afraid," he said honestly. If the LOC was not the link that bound them, then he would perish with Noel. It was an awful risk. But he felt driven to take it.

"There is nothing to fear," said Sir Magnin softly, kindly, "as long as you serve me true. Never lie to me again."

The threat in those black eyes struck to Leon's heart. He bowed. "I swear I shall not, my lord."

"Good. I had a brother once whom I loved with all my heart. He died when we were boys. I wept upon his grave. Thanks to God I was never faced with your choice, but you have done well to put a stop to Noel's evil." He smiled. "You will have your reward when this is done."

"Thank you," whispered Leon. He still felt cold. Now that he had set this in motion, he wondered if he had gone too far. But when he thought of a lifetime linked to Noel, of watching him from afar, never a true part of life, he knew he could never escape the conviction that there should be only one of them.

I shall be the one, Leon thought with fresh determination.

He looked up. "Lady Sophia must be well guarded. She betrayed him tonight. He may seek revenge there."

Sir Magnin's face darkened. "My own hand will guard her. Go, Leon, and join the search."

"Wait," said Leon, remembering something he had overlooked. "I do not want to be mistaken for him by your guards." He glanced back at the priest. "Is there some badge I can wear, to mark me as different?"

"Give him your cross," said Sir Magnin.

The priest's palsied hands lowered the cross by its chain over Leon's head. It hung upon his chest, its silver shape cold and heavy.

He put his hand around it and smiled. "That will do perfectly," he said.

Outside, running across the courtyard through the crisp night air, Leon threw back his head in triumph, wanting to howl aloud. It was so easy to manipulate these people, so easy to find their weaknesses, their superstitions, and twist them into whatever he wanted. Within a short time it would be he, Leon Nardek, who ruled Mistra, and not Sir Magnin the Black.

He ran because the others were running. Guards had sleepy, frightened servants rousted from their beds and lined up shivering in the night air. Sir Geoffrey, dressed in full mail and surcoat, his spurs jingling with every step, strode about directing a systematic search.

Leon watched, but he knew too much time had passed since Noel had escaped. It was doubtful he had managed to get past the guards at the main gates, but he was clever, resourceful, and he had the LOC. Leon worried, and moved into the shadows to search ferretlike in the small crannies and dark corners. With his mind he swept out, hoping to find Noel in that way, although so far Noel's mind had been completely blank to him.

Concentrating, he found instead a scurry of thought somewhere ahead of him. Someone, not Noel, was concealed behind the ovens where the bread for the castle and town was baked. Leon could feel the warmth still radiating from the round stone sides of the huge ovens, although their fires had long since been banked down for the night.

A rickety shed projected from one side as a wooden appendage where loaves were cooled and business was conducted. Leon's quarry hid inside it, hardly breathing, frightened, all thoughts banked down like a fire covered with ashes for the night.

He made his way to the shed on silent feet, drawing the dagger one of the guards had returned to him. He eased open the half door, and it groaned upon its leather hinges.

There came a swift furtive rustle from the back, a whispered, "No."

His nostrils widened. He sniffed the air and detected the delicate scent of . . . woman. Yes, he was certain. This one smelled of the forest, of pine, of innocence. He licked his lips and went forward.

When he got close, she came at him in a rush, striking him with her shoulder, and nearly overbalancing him. He caught her by the hair, yanking her around so roughly she cried out.

Swiftly he clamped her against him, and she struggled and kicked like a wild creature until he pressed the point of his dagger between her breasts. She went absolutely still; only the sharp jerks of her breathing betrayed her.

"Nom de Dieu," she said, using a French oath although he knew at once she was Greek. "Do not hurt me with that. Please do not—"

"Silence."

There was cunning in her voice beneath the pleading. He hurt her just a little to get her attention. "You are the girl from the mountains?"

"Yes. I—I am Elena Milengus."

"Very good. And what are you doing hiding out here in the darkness, Elena? Are you waiting for your lover?"

She choked and began to weep.

He squeezed her. "None of that! I do not want you. Pay attention to me. Everyone is looking for the man called Noel."

"I know," she whispered. "That was why I have been hiding. We tricked Sir Magnin because we thought he would cheat us of our share of the ransom money, and now he is angry."

"What do you expect, you stupid fool?" said Leon. "No, listen to what I have to say. There is a way for you to redeem yourself."

"I won't—"

"Listen! Noel has probably escaped the castle by now. He will seek your help tomorrow or the next day. He will want you to help Theodore recover Mistra."

"The Milengi do not serve Byzantine puppets!"

"But your alliance with Sir Magnin has been broken. Isn't it better to change horses before the one you have falls beneath you?"

She remained silent, but he knew she was listening. This girl was shrewd. He liked her.

"Well, Elena?"

"My brothers will never support Lord Theodore. They want Greeks to rule the Peloponnese. Sir Magnin is half Greek, and that is better than nothing."

"Better perhaps to have Byzantine rule than Turkish," said Leon with a low laugh.

"The Turks will not dare come this far—"

"I think they will. Perhaps there is a way to make Sir Magnin happy with you again."

"How?"

"Help us catch Noel."

He loosened his arm, and at once she sprang away from him. He caught her wrist, however, and swung her around. Moonlight glimmered upon the blade of his dagger. He sheathed it, but he did not release her wrist.

"If you should find him," said Leon, feeling his desire burn like fire within his veins. He put his hand upon the girl's face, driving in with his mind and his will until he felt her facial muscles go slack against his palm. "If you should find him, steal the bracelet from his wrist and bring it to me. That is all you have to do."

He took his hand away and Elena's face remained slack. Her dark eyes were glazed, shimmering reflections of the distant moonlight. Her mouth trembled. Leon touched those voluptuous lips with a tender finger.

"Do it for me," he whispered.

In silence Elena nodded. She looked drugged. Slowly she lifted her gaze to Leon's, and her eyes were docile, submissive eyes. Satisfied, Leon kissed her, but there was nothing in rubbing his mouth against hers that affected him. Nothing at all. If he wanted to feel the heat of passion, he had only to think of his hatred for his twin.

Angrily he shoved the girl away. "Go," he said and watched her run from the shed with her long hair streaming out behind her.

He paced there, shivering in the cold, rubbing his hands together, and felt hollow as though he were only a shell pretending to be a man. Was he doomed forever to be only half alive? Would eliminating Noel really make him whole?

No answers came to him, no assurance, no peace. He shivered in the night, and felt afraid.

CHAPTER 10

Noel's hand closed over Sophia's face. "Don't be afraid," he whispered.

She awakened with a muffled gasp and thrashed against him until he pressed her hard into her pillows.

"Hush," he said. "It's Noel. Don't be afraid."

She went stiff and silent for a moment, then struggled harder, trying to throw herself off the bed, trying to kick him, trying to wrench her mouth free to scream.

Exasperated, Noel wrestled with her despite the fact that he was hampered by his desire not to hurt her. She drove her fist hard into his stomach, and while he doubled, choking, she reached beneath her pillow and drew forth a tiny dagger that she slashed across his arm.

The pain was swift, like a razor cut, and the blood came welling up hot and vital upon his skin.

"Damn you," he said in a choked voice.

She struggled free of his grasp and opened her mouth.

"If you scream," he said desperately, ripping the knife from her hand, "I swear I'll kill you."

Kneeling upon the bed, she faced him with her hair streaming like silver in the moonlight. "Get away from me, villain," she said in a low voice choked with loathing and fear.

"We made a bargain, my lady. I gave you my word I would not betray you. And you promised to show me how to escape the castle."

She made a sound of denial, and he yanked her close against him. "I am not Leon," he said. "You know that."

120

"You look alike," she retorted, her breath warm upon his face. "I think it likely you act alike. How dare you come into my chamber—"

"Shut up, and consider," he said sharply. "I can help you and Theodore. But only if you help me. I have to get away. Will you keep your end of our bargain?"

The pain in his arm intensified as he flexed the limb and more air rushed into the wound, but it was a minor cut. Already it had stopped bleeding.

He tossed the dagger on the bed between them. Sophia watched him, saying nothing, doing nothing. He couldn't tell if she was thinking it over or awaiting her chance to yell.

"My lady?" came a soft, sleepy voice from the outer chamber. "Is all well?"

Noel's heart leapt into his throat. For a moment he thought he would choke. He froze, his gaze on the flimsy door between him and discovery.

"Yes, Cleope," said Sophia. "A bad dream, that's all."

"Do you want some heated malmsey?"

"No, thank you. Go back to sleep."

"Yes, my lady."

Noel shut his eyes a moment. The relief was almost too much. He was so tired he could barely think. He knew he was bound to make a fatal mistake soon, if he didn't find refuge.

"Please," he whispered. "*Please*."

"If Theodore is still a prisoner in the mountains," she whispered, "will you help free him?"

"Yes."

"Do you swear?"

He wanted to shake her. "Yes, yes. Hurry. Get dressed in something simple. They're going to know soon that I've escaped."

"How did you—"

"Just hurry."

She nodded and swung aside a tapestry to reveal a narrow servant's door. "Go through," she whispered. "Wait. I shan't be long."

He hesitated, wondering if he dared trust her. But he had little choice at this point. He went through the door, which she closed after him, and found himself in a musty space too tiny for comfort with shreds of old cobwebs that floated against his face like gossamer. The seconds ground by, each one an eternity. He leaned against the wall, feeling the coldness of it through his tunic.

The door snicked open and Sophia joined him in a faint rustling of cloth. Her hand groped across his sleeve to his wrist.

"There can be no light. We must stick close to the wall and not turn loose of each other. Come," she said. "Make no sound, for some of the walls are thin."

The darkness was total most of the way. Now and then their passageway had small open chinks in the wall mortar that let torchlight from some other area of the palace shine through. Sometimes Noel's feet crunched over what sounded like small, brittle bones. They snapped like twigs.

He did not like the darkness, the dank, tomblike smell, the dusty cobwebs that touched his face and hands like insects, the tiny rat skeletons on the floor. Yet at the same time he kept telling himself that it could not be this easy. The secret way to the concealed treasury, the secret way of escape from the palace could not simply lead from this girl's bedchamber.

The floor angled down after a while. He remembered the dungeons, and had to fight his reluctance to go near them.

Finally, after his legs were dragging with weariness and he felt they had gone at least a mile, Sophia stopped. "The end," she said softly.

She pushed his hand out through the air, and his knuckles rapped against the wooden rungs of a ladder.

"We must climb," she said. "Take care how you lift the trapdoor."

He struggled up the ladder until his head bumped the trapdoor. It was lightweight, requiring little effort to shift. Easing it open cautiously, he heard a rhythmic crunching sound, heard rustles, stamps, and snorts, inhaled the aroma of horse droppings and straw.

They were in the stables. Specifically they were in one stall, and its occupant, looming large in the dapple of moonlight shining in through the windows, stood near the manger as though quite used to strange people appearing in his stall in the dead of night.

Sophia climbed out with more agility than Noel expected and helped him lower the trapdoor into place. She pushed straw across it and went to pet the animal while Noel peered out at the courtyard. A man carrying a torch went running across it, calling out to the sentries patrolling the wall.

"Damn," said Noel. "We're in for it now."

"Find a torch," she said, and drew the hood of her cloak over her shining hair. "We must get to the mews. This way."

He snatched up an unlit brand soaked in pitch and followed her as she walked purposefully through the stables and out through a side door. A man ran past them in the darkness and gave Noel a shove.

"No time for dallying in the hay, man! There's a villain escaped from the dungeons. A sorcerer, they say. Report to Sir Geoffrey at once and join the search."

"Aye," said Noel, and the man ran on, leaving him to follow Sophia with his tunic soaked in cold sweat and his nerves raw with strain.

They made their way to the wall's southeast corner and entered a squat turret. The stairs spiraling up were made of wood and they swayed beneath Noel's weight. The place smelled of vermin and bird droppings.

At the top of the stairs, Noel discovered why. Large windows all around filled the space with moonlight. Row after row of small perches held an array of falcons, hawks, eagles, and owls. Leather jesses adorned with bells hung from their legs, keeping them bound to their perches. The floor was littered with bits of fur, feather, and broken bones from hundreds of meals served here.

Some of the predators were hooded; others were not. The latter watched Noel with large yellow eyes, aware and silent in the darkness.

Sophia went to one of the birds and pulled off its hood. She stroked its proud head, preening it with her fingertip. "There, my beauty," she crooned. "There, my love. Have you missed me?"

"For God's sake," said Noel, losing patience. "Are we getting away or visiting all your pets?"

"We need Sian," she said, replacing the bird's hood and untying her jesses. "She belongs to me. If necessary, she will hunt for us in the wild. There are some old weapons stored in that chest, if you want any."

He wanted to protest about the bird, but she was right in saying they needed weapons. In silence he made a swift search and found a broadsword for himself that weighed nearly a ton. He fitted a dagger and a war axe into his belt also, and found a moth-eaten cloak that smelled as though cats had been born on it years ago.

"Ready," he said, returning to Sophia. "Now what?"

She led him back downstairs. Outside, Noel could hear increased commotion. It sounded like the whole castle had been alerted. The searchers were coming closer all the time.

"Hurry," he said.

Holding the hawk upon her left hand, now swathed in a heavy leather gauntlet, Lady Sophia pointed at the floor.

"Open the trapdoor. See the ring?"

He knelt and pulled it open.

"Light the torch," she said.

"With what, my teeth?"

"Don't you carry a spark box?" she said.

"A what—no, I don't."

"We can't follow this passage if we can't see. Do something."

He peered outside and saw a torch burning at the base of the wall about halfway to the next corner. Noel's spirits sank. He felt that if he went running out across the open, it would mean his end. Yet there were men running everywhere, most in stages of half dress, torches flaming in their hands. It looked pretty chaotic.

Not giving himself time to dally longer, he left the turret and ran along the length of the wall, stumbling over holes pitted in the ground. Two knights and a page boy converged on the same torch just before he did. One was there to replace it with a fresh one; the others lit their brands from it.

"Any luck?" asked one.

They all, Noel included, shook their heads.

One of the knights spat. "I'll tell ye this, sirs. I didn't change my allegiance to Sir Magnin's banner just to spend my nights running about in search of some crazy varlet. It's my bed I want."

"It's your head you'd better care about," retorted one of the others. "His word is law, and he don't care how much he puts you out."

They scattered, Noel heading back toward the mews.

A hand grasped his shoulder. "Here, you. Act with some

wits. You just came from that way. What's the point of searching it again?"

Noel's mouth was drier than powder. "I just—I heard something up in the turret. I couldn't see, so I came to light the torch."

"Oh?" The knight leaned close, and Noel could smell the wine fumes on his breath. "Then we'd better both check on this noise, eh, lad?"

"Uh, yes."

Noel led the way, hoping Sophia was hiding. He opened the door and stepped into the darkness, the knight following right on his heels. Noel whirled and thunked the man between the eyes with the butt end of his torch. The knight staggered and fell.

Noel handed the torch to Sophia, who was standing there in plain sight, staring, and dragged the man inside so that he could close the door. Panting, he rested his cheek a moment upon the splintery wood. If he had felt a hundred years old earlier tonight, he was up to three hundred now and counting.

The temptation to sit down and go to sleep was so strong he could barely fight it off. Rubbing his eyes, he took the torch from Sophia and pointed at the stairwell.

She hesitated. "What about this man?"

"Leave him."

"But he may—"

"Just leave him," said Noel angrily. "We don't have time."

She climbed down the ladder awkwardly, balancing the bird that fluttered and fussed on her arm. Noel followed and shut the trapdoor, closing them in.

The torchlight filled the small well at the bottom, showing him smooth walls on all sides, but no tunnel.

"What is this?" he demanded. "A dead end?"

"Hush," she said sharply. "I must think."

She closed her eyes and held out her right arm. Counting slowly, she swung herself to the right, nearly striking Noel, who dodged.

"Here," she said, and opened her eyes. "Push on the wall where I am pointing. Push as high as you can reach. Yes, isn't there a depression in the stone?"

He groped, cursing softly to himself because the stretch awakened the soreness in his ribs. After a few moments he found the depression. He pushed, and it gave slightly as though fitted to a spring.

"Now straight down near the floor," she commanded.

He found that one and pushed.

There came a sharp click and a narrow section of the wall sprang open. Noel caught the edge of the door with his hand to keep it from closing again.

"Marvelous stone masonry," he said. "I couldn't see the lines at all—"

"Never mind," she said now, stepping into the passage ahead of him. "Hold the torch high and let us go through quickly. I hate this part."

He soon found out why. The tunnel was apparently hewn directly into the mountain. The ceiling dipped low in places, making him stoop to get through. The floor was rough, and Lady Sophia stumbled more than once. In places water seeped through the walls. The tunnel had the damp, mossy smell of wet rock. He knelt and sampled the water once, letting it trickle into his palm.

It tasted like cold crystal and numbed his teeth. Sophia drank also and gave some to her bird. It cheeped mournfully beneath its hood.

"How far?" asked Noel, keeping an eye on how much torch they had left.

"Far. We must hurry."

She led the way. There were branching tunnels, but Sophia never hesitated and Noel trusted her to take them safely through. This time they really did go a mile.

"Here," she said at last and ducked beneath a low over-hang.

Following, Noel straightened on the other side and found himself in a small, natural-looking cavern filled with a store-house of riches.

Iron-bound chests displayed mounds of gold coins. Small caskets of jewels stood stacked everywhere. Bronze or marble statues from antiquity lined the walls. Cups and plates of gold, jewelry set with precious stones, gold death masks, lifesize hounds carved from silver . . . Noel stood and stared, unable to believe his eyes. It was a jumble of precious relics spanning several centuries. It was a priceless treasure trove. It was an archaeologist's dream.

He picked his way over to a marble Kourus statue of a young man, long hair rippling down his back, with an owl carved upon one shoulder and a serpent coiled upon the other. The statue's vacant eyes stared into eternity. His faint, mysterious smile seemed to say that he knew all the answers man could ever seek. The colors painted upon him looked as fresh as though the sculptor had just finished.

In wonder Noel ran his fingers over the cold, smooth surface, feeling the depth of the carving, experiencing the skill. He had never seen a statue representing this symbolism. He hoped the recorder on his LOC was getting everything.

"Sir Magnin would take this wealth and spend it," said Sophia. She dipped her hand into a chest of coins, each stamped with the head of Caesar, and let them spill from her fingers. "Just spend it. He would never count the beauty. He would never consider the wonder of how such things were made. The little lady would be melted down."

Sophia glanced at Noel and smiled for the first time. The expression transfigured her face, made her seem younger and even more beautiful. "Come and see," she said.

They made their way to the rear of the cavern. There, resting upon a squared stone about waist-high, stood a small statue of a nymph fashioned of solid gold. Poised on her toes, she stood with her back arched, one hand lifted to the heavens, her head tilted up as though in ecstasy.

"She is a pagan thing," said Sophia quietly. "Very improper, but I love her so much. She is dancing, you see? She looks happy as though all the sunshine in the world has poured itself into her heart."

Surprised to hear Sophia say such a thing, Noel looked up. "She is exquisite," he said quietly. "I have never seen her equal."

"So many statues of the old times are broken up now," said Sophia. "The priests say we must destroy all things pagan. I understand why, but still it is sad to ride through the ruins of their temples and their houses, sad to see floor mosaics where perhaps a baby or a little girl played happily long ago. They were just people, as we are people. Surely they were not as evil as we are told."

"They weren't evil at all," said Noel. "They weren't any different from you or me. They lived, and loved, and went to war. They got married and had children and lost their teeth in old age. They tried to worship as best they understood. And some of them made art like this."

He traced his fingertip along the side of the little nymph, wishing he could take her home with him. But she'd only be incarcerated in a museum, a glass case erected around her, security beams scanning constantly. He liked to think of her here, at home in the mountains where she belonged.

"Thank you for showing me this, my lady," he said with a smile.

Sophia's gaze softened. For the first time she looked at him with warmth and possibly liking. "Thank you for understanding what kind of treasury this really is."

"I do."

"Come. We have farther to go."

The tunnel meandered on beyond the little cavern. Once they had to crawl several feet on their hands and knees to pass through. The torch burned lower and lower; its light grew steadily more feeble despite Noel's efforts to nurse it. He should have brought two, but he hadn't known it at the time.

"It's going out," he said grimly, worried about becoming lost in these caves forever.

"I see the stars," she said and hurried ahead of him.

He stumbled after her, anxious not to be left behind. The torch failed with a final pop, and for a moment he couldn't see anything. He blundered forward, then he too could see stars and the moon going down into a bank of clouds on the horizon.

They emerged through a narrow cave entrance and stood on the side of Mt. Taygetus, overlooking the ravine that divided it from Mistra.

The ravine, thought Noel, where he had nearly ended his life yesterday.

He braced himself against a rock and gazed out into the night. Wolves howled in the distance, whether in triumph or hunger he could not tell. Below them, torches flared upon the ramparts of Mistra. He smiled, feeling good despite his tiredness. Across the broad valley the stars shone down, their constellations so clear he felt as though he could reach up and scoop them into his hand.

Sophia unfastened the jesses and drew off the hood of her

falcon. She threw the bird up, and with a cry it unfolded its wings and caught the wind currents, sailing out into the night.

"My lovely Sian," said Sophia with a sigh. "She will follow us. Do you remember the way to the Milengi camp? We must find Theodore without delay."

Noel stared up at the black, forbidding shape of the mountain. "Let's rest first."

"Rest?" she exclaimed, starting up the slope with her long skirts gathered in her hands. "Why? There is no time to lose. We have a battle to plan, and we cannot do that without Theodore. Come."

CHAPTER 11

The next day they found the Milengi camp by virtue of the vultures circling overhead. Weary and footsore, they stood in the small protected canyon and stared at the scene of carnage. Men and women alike lay sprawled where they had fallen. Most had been hacked up by swords. A few were brought down by crossbow shafts.

Stunned, Noel could not avert his gaze from the mutilated corpses, the sightless eyes staring into eternity. The tent shelters had been torn down, their belongings strewn. The horses, goats, and chickens were all gone.

In the soft, early morning light when the rising sun cast a rosy hue upon the ground, and the clouds concealing the peak of the mountain gleamed pearl-white, something seemed unreal about so much death. Other than the circling buzzards, there was not a sound of life. No insects, no birdsong. Even the breeze lay still. Only the stream splashing over its bed of stones kept touch with reality. He heard himself swallow. Beside him Sophia whimpered.

He glanced at her, and saw that she was staring with her hands pressed against her mouth.

"Theodore," she whispered.

With a meager amount of sleep and a long night of hiking through rough country, maintaining a constant alert to avoid the search parties riding over the trails, her beauty had worn badly. She might be eager to find her fiancé, but she hadn't stamina. It had taken all her strength to keep going; by will-power alone she had managed the last leg of their climb. Now she stood aghast, all hope drained from her dirt-stained face.

Noel's heart filled with pity. "Stay by the stream," he said. "I'll search."

Wordlessly she nodded and seated herself upon a rock. She worked to arrange her torn skirts in proper folds over her feet. Noel knew the activity was a mindless one, a subconscious reaching for what was conventional and safe in a world that had turned upside down.

He did not want to walk through the camp, but he forced himself to do it. The sun overhead was growing hot. The still air within the canyon was too heavy, too oppressive. Then the smell hit his nostrils: a thick, wet, salty-copper odor that made him think irrationally of the ocean.

It was the smell of blood. He found himself standing next to a headless man in hose and jerkin. The pool of blood beneath him was too great to soak entirely into the ground. The edges had started to coagulate, but the rest was still wet.

The green figs Noel had eaten for breakfast came up in a choking rush. He stumbled away, coughing and shuddering, and wiped his face with unsteady hands. It was tempting to run from this canyon of death and never look back. He saw Sophia's figure still sitting upon the rock, posture perfect, hands folded in her lap. Her eyes were closed and her lips were moving as though she prayed.

Noel ran his sleeve across his clammy forehead and forced himself to continue the search.

Thaddeus, the dwarf he disliked so much, was the first person he recognized. The tiny man had been shot in the back with an arrow. His dagger lay in the dust beside him. Noel squinted ahead and walked on. It was worse to see faces he knew. He was afraid Elena would be here, and that fear grew with every step.

He found Yani next, the young, slim, red-haired brother who had been so clever in mind, so practiced with the slingshot. He had died with a sword in his hands. Blood smeared his face and chest. A dead horse lay half on top of him, its entrails spilling from the great wound Yani had cut in its belly. The rider was gone. Not a single casualty from the attackers remained behind.

Noel hurried on, not wanting to linger, determined to get this over with quickly. There were no survivors here. He went on peering at faces, sick outrage building beneath his horror.

Demetrius lay facedown like a fallen tree, his muscles bulging in the rigor of death. An axe had cleaved the side of his skull. His arms and torso held numerous wounds that bore mute witness of how long it had taken them to kill him.

One of the Byzantine courtiers lay draped over the broken poles of the goat pen, an arrow in his throat. Of the others there was no sign. Noel sighed and trudged back to Sophia. He started shaking his head before he reached her.

She rose to her feet. Her face was as white as marble. "He—he is not dead?" she said with trembling lips.

"He is not here," said Noel. "I'd say Sir Magnin's boys did this, came in and took the Byzantine prisoners by force." He frowned and glanced at the cliff face. "I thought it was against the rules of chivalrous battle to attack a sleeping camp by night."

"No honest knight fights at night unless provoked," she said. "What do you mean?"

"I mean it's early, just an hour or two since dawn. They're long gone. We didn't even hear this happen. That tells me they struck at night, like guerrilla fighters."

Her expression turned cold and hard with hatred. "It is a new trick invented by Sir Magnin, this night attack. The men boasted of it after they took the castle. That is why Theodore was ambushed on the road in the darkness. Sir Magnin is no honorable knight. He is a treacherous, conniving brute, a coward afraid to face true men of valor in the light of day."

Noel's frown deepened. "Has he always fought like this?"

"No," she said. "I have never heard so. But when my father died, his ambition to rule this province must have clouded his judgment. He has become utterly ruthless, and that horrible creature who follows him . . ." Her voice trailed off, and she avoided Noel's eyes.

Ambition was only part of it, thought Noel. The suggestion must have come from Leon. His duplicate was turning out to be a sociopath, without morals, scruples, or conscience. *Am I like him? Did he grow from some dark part of me?*

"Leon," he said heavily.

Her gaze came up. "Is he your brother?"

The answer stuck in Noel's throat. He turned away from her, scratching the itchy beard stubble upon his face. "There's no way to know if Theodore got away before this raid, or if they took him."

"At least he is not dead," she added, accepting his change of subject. "What do we do now? What can we do for these poor, unshriven souls? The wolves . . ."

"The ground is too hard for grave digging, even if I had a shovel." Noel sighed, dreading the task ahead. "I guess I can pile rocks over them. Some of them."

"I shall help you."

"Nay. 'Tis no task for a lady."

The voice came from the left. Noel spun around, reaching for his sword, and faced the figure walking toward them. The sun was at his back, putting his face in shadow, but Sophia gave a glad cry.

"Theodore!"

She ran toward him a few steps, her arms outstretched, then she stumbled and fell to the ground in a swoon. Noel and Theodore reached her at the same time.

"Let me," said Theodore, shouldering Noel aside. He carried her to the shade of the olive tree guarding the spring. Laying her gently upon the bank, he cradled her against him and poured a palmful of water between her parted lips.

She coughed and sputtered, coming around. Her eyes fluttered open and gazed up into Theodore's. Such a look of tenderness passed between them that Noel felt compelled to turn away and give them their privacy.

He grabbed the foot of the nearest corpse and dragged it next to another, on and on, trying not to look at their faces or their wounds if he could help it. After a few minutes Theodore joined him in the task. The bodies were stiff and unwieldy.

"We dare not take too long at this," said Theodore. "They may double back in search of me again."

"I know," said Noel. "There are too many bodies. It will take a full day of hard work to cover them all, but she's worried about the wolves."

Theodore met his eyes, his own blue ones a little suspicious, probing, doubtful. "Tell me all that has happened. Why is she out here wandering in the wilderness without protection?"

"What am I, chopped liver?" muttered Noel.

"What did you say?"

Noel straightened and glared at him. "I'm protection."

"You are not her father, brother, or husband," said Theodore shortly. "I do not think you qualify as protection."

"Oh, hell, are you worried about her virtue? I haven't touched her, you jealous idiot."

"So she assures me, or you'd be dead by now."

The rock in Noel's hand nearly went flying at Theodore's ungrateful head. Instead he slammed it on the ground. "Look, my friend, I got her away from the castle. Yes, she knew the way out, but if not for me she'd still be sitting there waiting for you to come along."

"I was coming," said Theodore stiffly.

"Really? Well, in the meantime I rescued her from Sir Magnin's less than savory attentions. Did you want me to leave her there so she could throw herself from a tower rather than be forced to marry him?"

"It had come to that?" said Theodore in outrage.

"Close enough. Why don't you quit thinking with your glands for five minutes and consider the situation rationally? Magnin's got your castle. He damn near had your woman. The Turks are coming, and he'll surrender to them or at best strike an alliance that will give them the foothold they've been seeking in Greece."

"Your wits are woodly," said Theodore with a frown. "The Turks have raided the coasts for years, but they never come this deep into the Peloponnese."

Noel thought of what the LOC had told him. "Care to wager on that?"

"I do not understand you. By what authority do you know how Magnin will act? You said yourself that you are a stranger to these parts, caught up in this by accident. Now you—"

"Let's just say my perspective has changed since I took your place and got incarcerated in the dungeons for a while."

"*Jesu mea!* I am sorry for that, my friend. But how did you escape?"

"It's a long story."

Noel bent over to place more stones upon the mound, but Theodore gripped his shoulder. When Noel glanced up he saw Theodore smiling down at him. The sun glinted off his chestnut hair and made his blue eyes sparkle with life.

"Thank you, friend Noel," he said. "If nothing else, you have given me Sophia's safety. We shall wait until nightfall and make our way southeast. There are fortresses whose lords are still faithful to the emperor. We shall find refuge and assistance in abundance."

"And what about Magnin?" said Noel.

Theodore set his jaw. "This is a rich, powerful province. Mistra and Athens are the two most important cities in all of Greece. I do not intend to let a minor half-caste baron unseat me from my rightful place."

"Good enough," said Noel. He glanced at the tree, where Sophia sat. "She cannot travel fast."

"No," said Theodore worriedly. "And there is another, who will slow us more."

Elena, thought Noel. He straightened with his hand on the small of his aching back. "Who?"

"I will show you," said Theodore. "Come."

He led them up beyond the canyon to a narrow incline and pointed at a series of cave mouths. "They are shallow, most of them. Animals have used them for dens. I have him hidden there."

"Who?"

Theodore shook his head. "He has not said his name."

It was George, lying in a bloodstained blanket like a child, his craggy face gray and cold with death.

"Oh, the poor child," said Sophia, but Theodore held her back while Noel knelt at the dwarf's side.

"He's not a child," said Noel. He unwrapped the blanket slowly. "His name is—was—George. He belonged to Elena."

"That girl," said Theodore in a tone that made Sophia glance at him sharply. "A vixen, a mountain nymph as wild as the wind itself."

Noel had to stop a moment and draw a deep breath. His hands were shaking with relief. "I thought she might be here," he said finally. "I didn't see her in the camp."

"No," said Theodore. "She never returned. She is blessed to have escaped this."

Noel shook his head and carried George outside to be placed with the others.

Theodore followed. "He was alive when you came. I meant to cauterize his wound. It might have saved him."

Noel squinted into the distance, feeling grim. "No surviving witnesses of this massacre. No one to testify."

"Except me," said Theodore harshly. "I hid in the rocks like a base-born coward."

"But you're alive," said Noel.

Theodore crossed himself. "Yes."

In silence, they finished their burial work, then rested by the stream and ate what food they could scavenge. When the heat of the afternoon lessened, they set out, keeping off the trails and as much to cover as possible.

By nightfall, Sophia was weeping quietly with fatigue. The courage she had shown earlier seemed to have faded now that she had Theodore to take care of her. They found shelter of sorts in the ruins of old Sparta, a city Theodore said had been abandoned after the Franks first came and built Mistra a hundred years or so before. Gradually the Greeks had left Sparta to live in the hill town where the air was better.

The evening temperature was slightly warmer here in the valley, but not much. They dared not build a fire, and although Theodore and Sophia could wrap up together beneath their cloaks, keeping each other warm, Noel found the ground hard and increasingly cold. The remnants of a marble wall at his back offered no comfort.

By the time dawn shone golden over the horizon, Noel was stiff and cramped. His admiration for the ancient Spartans had dropped considerably. If these were the kind of camping conditions they thrived on, he'd take modern life any day.

Everyone's face looked old and grainy in the dim gray light. In silence they set out again.

That day was spent mostly hiding, for dispatch riders galloped the road almost every hour. Two search parties nearly caught them. A peasant and his half-grown sons watched them go by as though they were ghosts, then turned again to their weeding.

Beyond the valley, the hills rose again, not as steep as the Taygetus range, but difficult enough. They scavenged olives and figs, although none of the figs were ripe and usually gave them the bellyache. Sian the hawk brought in a rabbit, but by the time they got the mangled carcass away from her and saw her fed, what remained was scarcely enough to go around. They fished streams and had good luck, but that took time. Noel found honey dripping from a hive in a cave and got desperate enough to rob some of it. They encountered a band of Jewish merchants in peaked, broad-brimmed hats traveling together for protection and were given provisions of cheese and bread.

By the time they crested a green hill overlooking a beautiful narrow valley with well-tended fields and a small round fortress with tall stone walls, Noel's hose were nearly falling off his hips, and his shoes were worn through. Four days of steady walking had brought them to the castle of Sir Olin d'Angelier.

"But," said Theodore, lying flat on his belly to survey the castle below, "has he maintained his fealty to Emperor Andronicus or has he joined Sir Magnin's revolt?"

"Sir Olin is very set in his ways," said Sophia shrewdly. With her finery in tatters, her hair hanging in matted clumps, and her face streaked and gaunt, she resembled a mummer in rags trying to portray a great lady. "He dislikes change. I doubt Sir Magnin will find him very supportive."

"But his garrison is small," said Theodore, "and he is not a rich man. He may find it easier to give in than to resist being crushed by Sir Magnin's forces."

"Someone," said Noel, "has to go down there and ask."

"You can hardly expect Lord Theodore to take the risk," said Sophia. "He would be immediately recognized, and if Sir Olin is hostile, he would find himself a prisoner again."

Theodore started to climb to his feet. "It is my cause and my appointment. I shall go."

Noel gripped his forearm to hold him in place. "She's right. You would be recognized."

Theodore fingered his ruddy beard and laughed. "Like this? Hardly."

"You're not expendable," said Noel. "You must regain the governorship. You have to rule this province; otherwise—"

"Otherwise the Turks will take over," said Theodore indulgently. He shook his head. "So you keep saying, but I do not see where you get your conviction."

Noel stared intently into his eyes, willing this man to believe him. "You must trust me," he said. "Please. I swear to you that I know this."

"Credo semper," said Theodore flippantly. He cocked his head to one side. "Go then. But take care." He rested his hand briefly upon Noel's shoulder. "You have shown yourself a

good friend. As soon as you are certain of a welcome reception from Sir Olin, signal to us."

Noel grinned. "Count on it."

Sir Olin's castle bordered a narrow mountain stream that looked swift and deep. A short arched bridge of stone wide enough for two horsemen to ride abreast spanned the water. The wooden drawbridge connecting the stone bridge to the castle's single entrance was down, but alert guards in brown surcoats and old-fashioned conical helmets with steel noseguards instead of visors stood with tall pikes crossed.

"Halt!" said one the moment Noel set foot on the bridge. "Name yourself and your business."

The hostility in that command made Noel wary. He rested his hand on his sword hilt and said in calm, even tones: "I am Sir Noel of Kedran. I have an important message for Sir Olin, if he will receive me."

"And to what reference is this message?"

Without moving his head, Noel glanced up at the battlements and saw more sentries standing between the crenellations with crossbows. He swallowed, preparing himself to dive off the bridge if necessary.

"I carry a message from Lord Theodore, rightful governor of Mistra, to Sir Olin d'Angelier, who was once counted his friend."

The guards conferred. Noel's senses strained to pick up the least hint of trickery. Someone was dispatched to the keep.

"Will you wait, Sir Noel?" asked one of the guards politely. "These are anxious times. We have orders to be careful."

"I'll wait," said Noel.

Five minutes later a boy in a long brown tunic overlaid with a tabard bearing two crimson griffins hurried out to meet him. He had short curly brown hair, cropped up nearly to the crown in the old Norman style, and warm brown eyes.

"Welcome, Sir Noel," he said in a voice that had just begun to change. "I am Frederick, Sir Olin's eldest son. Come inside. If you bring good news of our friend Theodore the Bold, you are more than welcome."

The boy's voice rang with sincerity. Noel's instincts said trust him. He swung his hand away from his sword hilt and walked forward.

Frederick clasped both his hands in greeting. Close up, he had an open, guileless face with a snub of a nose and a chin to match. He smiled, his eyes studying Noel frankly.

"You look as though you have had a hard journey. Come inside. Let us ply you with meat and drink. My father is engaged with another visitor at this moment, but he will be with you as soon as he can."

Noel started forward, but the boy hesitated with a frown. "Have you no mount, Sir Noel?"

"No horse, no baggage, no companions," said Noel, deciding to remain cautious awhile longer. He forced a smile, but it was not a very good one. "As you say, a hard journey."

"And fraught with much misfortune from the little we have heard. News comes seldom to our corner of Greece."

Their footsteps echoed hollowly over the drawbridge. Then they were within the walls surrounding a small, almost claustrophobic yard paved with cobbles. The keep itself looked squat and massive, with thick impenetrable walls and nothing better than arrow slits for windows. The doors stood wide open, probably to let in light.

Noel let himself glance around as they walked toward the keep. The barracks were in good repair. The stables were tucked beyond them. A cluster of women stood gossiping at the well. Geese puttered in piles of straw that had fallen off a cart. Barrels of provisions were stacked in plain view, but otherwise the place had an oddly empty feel. It was too quiet, too watchful. The faces he saw were grim and wary.

They expect a siege, he realized. Or some kind of attack.

Frederick led him into the gloomy hall of the keep. It was perhaps a third the size of the one at Mistra, a cramped rectangular room with a low, heavy-beamed ceiling from which the family banners hung. A coat of arms decorated one wall. Weapons filled another. The spreading antlers of a stag hung at one end over the tallest chair. Rushes cushioned the floor, rustling softly beneath Noel's feet. Near the unlit hearth, a gaunt deerhound with a white muzzle and blurry eyes lifted his head.

"Easy, Torquil," said Frederick. "It is but us."

The dog went back to sleep, and Frederick smiled. "Poor old fellow. He is blind and can barely walk, but Father won't have him put down, and all of us would raise an outcry if he did. Have a seat. Peter! Maria!"

Leaving Noel, he went off through an arched doorway into an even gloomier section of the keep. Noel stood by the scarred trestle table and stared around. Although outside the day was warm, this hall held a perpetual chill. He would hate to spend a winter in this place. It was crude, primitive, and out-of-date. Compared to Mistra, it was something from an entirely different, darker era, but it would be easy to defend.

He longed to finish his business and get out of the place.

"Here you are!" said Frederick merrily, returning with a serving boy in tow. The servant was small but quick. He put a tray before Noel laden with generous slabs of roasted pork, apples, and something that looked like boiled fennel. Frederick himself poured mead into plain goblets, and drank while Noel devoured the food.

"Aye, I thought you looked hungry. Did you walk all the way from Mistra?"

Noel nodded, his mouth too full for an answer.

"And Lord Theodore is well? God's wounds, but is this not an astonishing business? We thought him dead at first, I can tell you. Father went about as grim as a hornet, shouting for his shield and weapons. But by then it was pointless to ride out with the men. Magnin Phrangopoulos has always been a troublemaker. Too ambitious, Father says. I wouldn't dare what he's tried, though, thumbing his nose at Byzantium. A fine time to offend the emperor, Father says, what with Turks coming in. We got word that a force of pirates has started up the Eurotas. They nearly flattened Monemvasia. At a time like this the whole province should be banding together, and here is Sir Magnin wanting to hold a jousting tournament. Witless."

"He's mad and power-hungry," said Noel between mouthfuls. "He had the Milengi on his side—"

"They're a fierce lot."

"Not anymore. He turned on them. Wiped out their camp."

"They have many camps," said Frederick, although he was frowning. "They live scattered all through the Taygetus range. Their leaders, Demetrius and Yani—"

"Dead."

"God's wounds! Is it so?"

Noel emptied his cup and nodded.

"There will be an uprising. They will cause trouble all across this side of the Peloponnese. They may even stir up some of the other tribes. But Lord Theodore, is he—"

The sound of approaching voices made him break off. Frederick rose to his feet, and Noel reached for the last piece of meat when two men entered the hall. One of them was short and stout with a barrel chest and an ample stomach. His white hair was cut much like Frederick's, and his beard was trimmed to a sharp point at his chin. He could be no other than Sir Olin.

His companion, however, was lithe, young, and austere, wearing mail with his coif shoved back on his neck.

Noel choked on his food in dismay. He and Sir Geoffrey stared at each other like two hounds defending their territory.

"Is this how you maintain neutrality, Sir Olin?" said Sir Geoffrey, his dark eyes never leaving Noel's face. He reached for his sword, and Noel stood up so fast he toppled the bench over behind him.

He drew his own sword with a ring of steel through the scabbard.

"Hold!" shouted Sir Olin in a voice that shook the rafters. "What manners have either of you, drawing swords in my house? Sir Geoffrey, mind your place! As for you, monsieur, what business do you bring here?"

"Father!" said Frederick in dancing impatience. "Have care. He is—"

"He is our enemy!" said Sir Geoffrey. His gaze narrowed on Noel. "We have searched long and hard for you. Now to find you turning up here, in the protection of a man who professes himself to be our friend—"

"Father!" said Frederick in outrage. "We will not ally ourselves with that dog Magnin—"

"Hold tongue, boy!" said Sir Geoffrey like a whipcrack. "You insult my liege—"

"You are on my ground, Sir Geoffrey," said Sir Olin sharply. "Before you challenge my son, remember that."

Sir Geoffrey's anger flickered and faded back under control. His face was as white as flame, however, and his gaze held no quarter for Noel. "Well, sorcerer," he said with mockery a lash in his voice. "Have you put them under your spell already?"

"Sorcerer?" echoed Sir Olin. His gaze sought Noel, who shook his head.

"I am not. I am a friend to Theodore the Bold, who lives despite Magnin's treachery. I seek to help him recover Mistra. And I have come to ask your support in that cause," said Noel.

"Watch him!" said Sir Geoffrey, holding his sword so that the grip and the curved quillons formed a cross of protection at his face. "He can entrance men. His very tongue is black with guile."

"Frederick," said Sir Olin in alarm. "What have you brought through our gates?"

Frederick himself looked uneasy, but he said, "A man who professes himself loyal to Theodore of Albania. Do we trust him, Father, or this man who serves a proven villain?"

Sir Geoffrey growled something and swung his sword at Frederick, who scrambled back just in time. Sir Olin caught at Sir Geoffrey's arm, distracting him long enough for Noel to move forward. Noel's sword caught Sir Geoffrey's with a clang that rang through the room. Sir Geoffrey swung again, and again Noel parried, though clumsily. The broadsword was heavier than he was used to, and although he knew swordplay, it was primarily with the short Roman gladius.

He fell back, and Sir Geoffrey came at him hard, driving him to the wall with blow after blow. Cornered, Noel had no choice but to go on parrying desperately. He knew he could not escape unless he somehow seized the offensive from Sir Geoffrey, but it was all he could do to keep from getting himself hacked into pieces.

Sir Geoffrey got too eager. His sword tip crashed into the wall, striking off sharp splinters of stone. Noel ducked and scurried around, seeking to reach Sir Geoffrey's back, but the knight recovered and whirled with him. He lifted his sword again just as Noel stumbled over the fallen bench and lost his balance.

In that moment time slowed to a crawl. Noel went sprawling, caught himself desperately on one knee, and struggled to bring up his sword.

"No!" cried Frederick over the frenzied barking of the dog.

Sir Olin was shouting too, but for Noel there was only the break in his wrists as his weapon was knocked aside, and Sir Geoffrey's sword came slashing down like an executioner's blade.

CHAPTER 12

"Eeeraaagh!"

From nowhere, a pike crashed between Noel and Sir Geoffrey with enough impetus to knock their crossed swords to the floor. Sparks flew from the scrape of steel against stone and set the rushes to smoldering.

Sir Olin twisted the heavy pike and sent both swords skidding to the far corner, then stamped out the fire. "No one sheds blood in my hall!" he shouted, his face crimson beneath his white hair. "Hell's teeth! Do I have to run you through to prove it?"

"You disarmed me," said Sir Geoffrey as though he could not believe what had happened. "I had engaged weapons and you disarmed me—"

He reached for his dagger, but both Noel and Frederick held him back from Sir Olin.

He struggled against them. "Let me go, you heathenish—"

"Are you witless?" bellowed Sir Olin. "Have you taken complete leave of the few senses God gave you, monsieur? What do you mean by this conduct?"

Still struggling, Sir Geoffrey ignored the old man. His eyes—dark with irrational fury—blazed into Noel's. "Stay away from me, sorcerer. Play no games with my mind."

"I'm not a sorcerer, damn you. Stand still," said Noel breathlessly.

Sir Geoffrey strained for Noel's throat, and only Frederick's desperate grasp on his wrist held him. Little flecks of saliva flew from his lips. "Must kill you. Must make you pay for Elena—"

143

"What?" said Noel. He gave Sir Geoffrey a shake. "What do you mean? Explain."

Sir Geoffrey growled something inarticulate and lunged at Noel, sending him staggering back despite Frederick's efforts to hold him. Sir Olin waded in and seized Sir Geoffrey by the shoulder.

"I'll kill you," said Sir Geoffrey, his eyes only for Noel. "I have sworn it. I'll kill you."

The others pulled him off, and Noel frowned with growing concern. "Why?" he said. "Tell me! What's happened to Elena?"

Sir Geoffrey abruptly stopped struggling and became still. His face twisted into grief too raw to witness. "Do not mock me!"

"I'm not mocking you," said Noel. "If something has happened to Elena, I'd like to know what it is. She's—"

"You are surely damned for what you have done," said Sir Geoffrey in an awful voice. "If God will not let me be the instrument that smites you from this world, I pray someone else will—"

"Oh, be quiet," said Noel, losing his temper. "For God's sake, what am I supposed to have done to her? I give you my word, it's a lie. I haven't seen her since—"

"The word of a consorter with demons is nothing but putrescence!"

Noel punched him in the mouth, sending him reeling into the long table. Sir Geoffrey straightened slowly, his hand exploring his lip, which was already puffing up.

"That's enough from you, you damned coward," said Noel furiously. "You stinking, dirty coward. Did you have to kill women and children? Did you have to slaughter all of them like dumb cattle? With their slingshots and bows, what match were they for trained knights in armor? Were you so afraid they might fight you with courage that you had to attack them under cover of darkness—"

"What is this infamy?" said Sir Olin in astonishment. "Is this true?"

"Were you afraid to let them see you?" said Noel, while Sir Geoffrey turned crimson. "Or were you ashamed—"

"Enough!" cried Sir Geoffrey. "You goad me too far with these accusations—"

"But they are true accusations," said Noel. He longed to choke this self-righteous hypocrite by the throat, to dig his fingers into the resistance of flesh and cartilage, to will more strength into his fingers until they crushed air and life from the knight. Memories of the dead tribespeople flooded him, bringing back his sick disgust at such waste and brutality. "I helped bury those people. A whole camp attacked in their blankets and left to rot where they died." He swung his glare to Sir Olin, who looked shocked. "These are the caliber of men Sir Magnin has collected about him. Do you want to be allied to baby killers?"

"We killed no babes—" said Sir Geoffrey indignantly, then choked off the half admission. He dropped his gaze.

"Monsters," whispered Sir Olin, and Frederick's eyes were wide.

"It is not so," said Sir Geoffrey, but without conviction. "This creature twists the truth for his own—"

"I counted the corpses," said Noel hotly. "*They* are the truth. And with every rock I stacked over every mutilated body, I gave thanks that Elena was not among them. What happened to her? Didn't you protect her while she was at Mistra? She asked you for the courtesy. Couldn't you do even that? Or were you so busy murdering her brothers—"

"No!" Sir Geoffrey slammed his fist upon the table. "I had no part in the attack on the Milengi. I spoke against it, but the orders were given. I could do no more."

"You spoke against it," said Noel in a soft, mocking voice. "Do you think that absolves you from blame?" His question drove in like a sword thrust, and Sir Geoffrey flinched. "They told me to do it, so it's not my fault? Oh, come! That excuse has never worked. Are you really that weak-willed?"

Sir Geoffrey went white to the lips. He lifted his fists. "You think you can bend words and make them serve you just as you bend people to your will. You accuse me of this villainy, but it is *you* who put the spell on Elena."

"I—"

"Yes, you! Did you not escape the dungeons by supernatural means? Your cell door lifted off its hinges, your jailers mesmerized and unaware of your escape until it was too late? You spirited away Lady Sophia with the help of your demons and turned Elena into a mindless, speechless creature of pity, lacking any will of her own."

Noel frowned, bewildered. It sounded like shock trauma, and if Elena had seen the massacre of her family that might have put her into such a condition.

Before he could speak, however, Sir Olin lowered his pike to a ready position. "We serve God in this house," he said sharply. "All my household hears mass daily. There will be no witchcraft under my roof."

"Then drive him out swiftly," said Sir Geoffrey, pointing his finger. "Let him not put his curse on you."

"Nonsense!" said Noel. "I don't practice witchcraft, you idiot. The bolts and hinges were falling apart with rust. As for Lady Sophia, she showed me a secret passageway from Mistra—a passageway, I might add, that Sir Magnin would pay dearly to find since it also leads to a fabulous treasury."

Both Sir Olin's and Frederick's eyes grew large. "Lord Gerrard's treasury?" said Sir Olin.

If he'd been a dog his tongue would have lolled out. Even Frederick's eyes were gleaming. Noel remembered Theodore's comment that Sir Olin was not a wealthy man.

Sir Geoffrey stood silent. He swallowed several times as though struggling to control his emotions.

"And," continued Noel, "the Lady Sophia is safe and with Lord Theodore even as we speak. Should she not escape unlawful confinement to be with her rightful protector?"

Sir Geoffrey frowned. "He is nearby?"

"Yes."

Sir Geoffrey swung away with a gesture of frustration. *"Jesu mea,"* he said to himself. "What trouble will he cause for us now?"

"All he can," said Noel. "Depend on it."

"Hmm," said Sir Olin, his gaze darting between their faces. "Hmm. It would seem there is much to discuss. I would see Lord Theodore."

Noel kept his own attention on Sir Geoffrey, and saw the quick changes of expression registering there. The young knight had himself under control at last, icy and aloof, and he was once again acting in Sir Magnin's interests rather than his own. Noel was not happy to see the change. He still didn't know what was wrong with Elena, and he wasn't sure Sir Geoffrey would tell him now.

"Well?" said Sir Olin. "I assume you have a signal that you can send to Lord Theodore?"

"Wait," said Sir Geoffrey hastily. "I beg you to consider the terms—"

"I am considering your behavior as well as Magnin's terms," said Sir Olin with asperity. "Remember, monsieur, that I was seigneur here when Magnin was only a babe clinging to his mother's skirts. I am considering all I have seen and heard."

"No signal," said Noel.

They all stared at him.

"This is not neutral ground as far as I'm concerned," he said. "Not neutral enough to guarantee Lord Theodore's safety."

The wooden end of Sir Olin's pike thudded into the floor. *Nom de Dieu—*

"Sir," broke in Noel to stop the explosion. "No offense to you, but with this hothead around . . . well, you understand."

The wrath faded from Sir Olin's face. "Yes, I do," he said thoughtfully.

Sir Geoffrey lifted his head proudly. His face had gone stiff with anger. "I must repeat my earlier caution to you, Sir Olin. Constantinople is far away. Sir Magnin is near. He has offered you friendship in return for your fealty. He has offered you generous terms of alliance. The more we unite the stronger we shall be. We *can* have independence from the Byzantine stranglehold. No more foreign governors appointed at the emperor's whim. No more calls to arms for causes that do not affect the Peloponnese—"

"No more protection from the Turks," said Sir Olin gruffly. "Don't repeat your speech. I said I would consider Sir Magnin's offer—"

"Father, no!" said Frederick.

"Silence," snapped Sir Olin. "I will also consider what Lord Theodore has to say. That is only fair."

Sir Geoffrey scowled. "If you grant Lord Theodore asylum, then you are Sir Magnin's enemy."

Sir Olin scowled back. "Heavy words, monsieur. Are you certain you want to force my hand?"

Sir Geoffrey glanced at Noel, who shook his head. Sir Geoffrey flushed, but before he could speak further, Sir Olin gripped his shoulder and steered him from the hall.

"Patience, monsieur," said the older man. "You are young and fiery. So is your master. But I have lived a long time and survived many campaigns. I did that by keeping my head and deciding wisely. Give me until the tournament. Then Sir Magnin will have my decision."

Sir Geoffrey replied, but his voice was too low for Noel to hear. When the two men were gone from sight, Noel walked over and picked up his sword. Sir Geoffrey's weapon still lay upon the floor. Noel picked it up as well and raised his brows to Frederick, who took it gingerly from his hand.

"I'd better return this before Father sends him across the drawbridge."

"Wait," said Noel, reconsidering. "Let me."

Frederick frowned. "I doubt that is wise."

"I'll return it." Noel took the sword from Frederick's unresisting hand and strode outside into the welcome sunshine.

Sir Geoffrey was already mounted. Noel called out to him, and Sir Geoffrey turned his head. His eyes narrowed.

"You forgot this," said Noel and handed the sword up to him, hilt first.

Sir Geoffrey hesitated only a moment before his gauntleted hand gripped the hilt. He swung it up, and Noel saw in Geoffrey the desire to decapitate him. Noel tensed, but kept his gaze locked on the knight's. Sir Geoffrey sheathed the sword violently. His mouth twitched with visible resentment, but he said nothing.

When he reached for the helmet that hung on a chain attached to his breastplate, Noel gripped his stirrup.

"Please," he said, keeping his voice low so Sir Olin and the others watching would not overhear. "What happened to her?"

Sir Geoffrey snorted. "What game do you play with me, sorcerer? You bring back my sword, which probably now has a spell cast on it, and you persist in this pretense of ignorance."

"Damn you," said Noel angrily. "No one's casting spells. If you don't trust your sword, throw it in the moat. How can you people go around believing such stupid superstitions? Can't you just answer my question?"

"If a girl is as full of life as a mountain stream," said Sir Geoffrey passionately. "If she has a heart like the wind and glows like sunshine upon the sea, then overnight turns to wood, what is anyone to think?"

"Maybe it's grief," said Noel with more sharpness than he intended. "Grief over her brothers—"

"She does not care about her brothers, you fool! She doesn't know."

"Are you sure? Maybe she witnessed the massacre—"

"No," said Sir Geoffrey. "She stands in a daze, staring at the mountains. She speaks to no one. She listens to no one. She is dead inside, witless or possessed. And you did it to her, you—"

"Why the hell should I?"

Sir Geoffrey glared at him. "There is no logic to the works of Satan. Stay away from me, sorcerer. I vow the next time we meet I shall kill you, and no man will stay my hand."

Fitting on his helmet, he lowered the visor with a clang and galloped across the yard to the drawbridge. Well after the hollow thud of hoofbeats upon the bridge faded, Noel stood there frowning. Elena possessed . . . poppycock. A wandering hypnotist might put her in a light trance, but Noel wasn't sure hypnotism was known to the charlatans of this century. Besides, it made no sense.

Had Leon done something to the girl? Why should he bother? Had Sir Magnin tortured her? Had he taken advantage of her infatuation and hurt her; had he broken her spirit?

Rage boiled in Noel at the thought. He—

A hand settled upon his shoulder. "Sir Geoffrey's warnings notwithstanding," said Sir Olin, "I doubt you've come to bewitch us, eh?"

Noel pulled his attention to the here and now. "Of course I haven't," he said shortly. "I'm just a traveler caught up in this mess by chance."

"By God's will, monsieur," said Sir Olin in reproof. "There's no such thing as blind chance."

"Whatever."

"Go out and bid Lord Theodore to come inside for talk. There are four days until the tournament. We have little time to lay our plans." Sir Olin frowned, looking troubled. "And I would not put it past young Geoffrey to shorten the time he gave me. Now that he knows Theodore and Lady Sophia are here, he is bound to—"

"Sir Magnin doesn't exactly play by the rules, does he?" said Noel.

"No, that he does not. The whoreson ought to be taught a lesson. *Parbleu*, we may just have a way to do it. Frederick!" he bellowed. "To horse, lad!"

Frederick came running. "Yes, Father?"

"To horse! Waste no time. Ride to Geraki and tell Peter Phrantzes what's afoot."

"But he wants independence," said Frederick, wide-eyed. "He is married to Sir Magnin's sister."

"He also fears the emperor," said Sir Olin. He rubbed his hands together. "After all, he's applied to Andronicus for the adjoining estate to his east holdings. He can hardly afford to offend the empire."

Noel smiled. "A poor time for a brother-in-law to go rampaging."

Sir Olin smiled back. "Aye. If Lord Theodore were dead or captive, it would be different for all of us. I cannot stand alone, you see. But I would talk with him, monsieur. Go and tell him my castle is open to welcome him and his lady." Sir Olin rubbed his hands together again and chuckled. "Especially his lady."

An hour later Noel sank breathlessly onto the knobby roots of an age-twisted olive clinging precariously to the bank of a gully and met Theodore's intense blue gaze.

"And that's what happened," he finished. "I'm sorry Sir Geoffrey knows you're here, but there was no help for it."

"No damage was done. He does not have sufficient time to spread a warning to his master," said Theodore.

Lady Sophia smiled at Noel. "You did your best. I wish, however, you had brought us food."

Noel looked at her smudged, travel-weary face, and at Theodore whose red beard hid the ravages his eyes betrayed. Noel thought of his own hearty meal at the castle and felt guilty.

However, he returned her smile and brought from his sleeve pocket two apples and a chunk of cheese.

"It's bad manners to steal from your host's table," he said, grinning as she exclaimed and snatched the items from his hands, "but I managed to overcome etiquette—"

"You are wonderful!" said Sophia, laughing. "I am ready to die for a morsel of cheese. How good it looks." She divided the food between herself and Theodore and tried to coax her hawk into eating some of the cheese.

While he munched his apple, Theodore paced back and forth. His head remained bowed in thought.

"It's plain that Sir Olin has his eye on your treasury," Noel said to Sophia. "Mistra is rich, and he's not."

She frowned. "That is my dowry. It is not to be handed over to any—"

"Quite so, my dear," said Theodore. "I think Noel fears another ransoming?"

"Yes, maybe," said Noel. "You probably know how far you can trust him or we wouldn't be here in the first place. But if he's smart he knows he won't get a reward with you locked in his dungeons. He might get Sir Magnin to pay him for Sophia—"

Theodore's fists came up. "That cur!"

"Easy. I'm only speculating. Remember that Sir Magnin doesn't know where the treasury is," said Noel. "That gives us an ace in the hole."

Theodore frowned. "A what?"

"Uh, an advantage."

Theodore went back to pacing. "You may be sure he is searching for it. With time and perserverance, it can be found."

"But Magnin's got a lot on his plate right now," said Noel. "He's trying to pull in more allies. I don't know how long it will take for news of this to reach your emperor—"

"A month at best," said Theodore gloomily. "If a messenger has been dispatched at all. I, naturally, can send no one. By the time word reaches the court, Sir Magnin will be well entrenched. To lay siege to Mistra and its walls . . ." He shook his head.

"All right, no help from the emperor," said Noel. "A couple of cannonballs would do wonders to Mistra's walls, but they aren't invented yet, are they?"

Everyone was silent. They stared at him blankly.

Irritated at himself for that frivolous slip, Noel scowled. "Uh, taking the castle by force is too hard. Let's think of a better solution."

"No," said Theodore. "We shall fight. If I must, I can fill Sir Olin's coffers from my own fortune. I must have an army, and he can help me raise one."

"That will take too long," said Noel.

Theodore stared at him. "What constraint does time have upon our actions? I do not understand your urgency in this matter. It is spring yet; we have until late autumn to mount a campaign. Sophia's safety is no longer at risk and while I should prefer to settle this dispute without appealing to the emperor, if necessary I can call on—"

"No, no, *no*," said Noel, punching his fist into his palm for emphasis. "We have four or five days at the outside. You must have command of Mistra before the Turks come this far upriver."

Theodore sighed. "Noel, truly you are a wonder. The more I think on the matter, the less I fear their arrival. We have until autumn, and that is plenty of—"

"You *don't* have until autumn," said Noel. He wanted to knock Theodore's thick head against the tree. "What am I, Cassandra crying the doom that no one will hear?"

"Do you have the sight?" asked Sophia, dusting cheese crumbs from her dainty fingers and clutching his hand. "Have you seen a vision? Did a golden light shine upon you? Did you hear a voice beyond all understanding? Did you see God?"

Aware of Theodore's jealous eye, Noel detached his fingers from her clasp and cleared his throat. "Uh, what I've experienced, uh, I cannot explain. There are no words to describe it."

That, at least, was the truth. His translator had a built-in protection device that caught words like fiber optics, microchips, interdimensional physics, and the like, and threw them into gibberish to avoid contaminating history with advanced technical terms. If he said computer, his listeners might hear spoon or something equally nonsensical.

They stared at him, however, with disappointment and skepticism. He realized he had to tell them something.

"There was gray mist," he said, "and a sense of being lost. I could hear nothing, feel nothing. After a while I could see nothing. But I was not . . . entirely alone. I remember . . ." He blinked, unconsciously rubbing his left arm above the bracelet. "I remember terrible pain. I remember being afraid."

Sophia touched his arm, stopping him from rubbing it. "What happened then? Did the vision come?"

Noel sighed, pulling himself back from the memory, and met Theodore's gaze. "You promised to trust me," he said with all the persuasion he could muster. "You have to act this week, or it will be too late."

Sophia went to stand at Theodore's side with her arm around him. They made a striking couple, with their handsome faces and blue eyes. They belonged at Mistra—that beautiful Frankish fortress overlooking its fertile valley, a place peaceful beneath the two-headed eagle banner of Byzantium.

"Too late for whom?" she asked. "For us? For you? Be less cryptic, if you please."

Before Noel could answer, Theodore chuckled. "Cryptic is the way of prophets and oracles, my dear. Very well, friend Noel, if I am to use guile rather than force to retake my fortress, what do you suggest?"

"Get Sir Olin on your side," said Noel without hesitation, "along with as many of the other local nobles as you can muster. Get equipped with a horse and armor. Go to the tournament and—"

"He will be captured!" cried Sophia.

"Not if I ride nameless under Sir Olin's pennon," said Theodore thoughtfully. "Once the jousting has begun, the rules of chivalry demand that all comers may compete without fear of seizure."

"The rules," said Sophia in dismay. "Sir Magnin does not follow the rules."

"Alas, that is true."

Thank you, Leon, thought Noel in exasperation. He said, "Yes, that's a good point and something to keep in mind. But with everyone in the province there watching, do you think he'd dare try anything?"

"Yes," said Sophia.

"No," said Theodore.

The two lovers glared at each other.

"You must not fight him—" began Sophia.

"It would be an ideal solution," said Theodore. "The leaders of the province will be assembled. I shall ride in and make public challenge to Sir Magnin. He cannot refuse—"

"He will kill you!"

Theodore's expression grew chilly. "My lady's confidence in my prowess overwhelms me."

"I do not doubt you, my darling!" she cried, clinging to his arm. "But Magnin the Black is champion of the province."

Theodore merely shrugged. "It is settled. I shall challenge him, one to one. The outcome will decide who governs Mistra and"—a muscle flexed in his jaw—"who weds Lady Sophia."

Noel raised his brows. "Strong terms."

"Do you see a better way to tempt him into fighting?"

"No, but make sure you win."

Theodore grinned, but Sophia struck him in the chest without warning, making him flinch. He frowned at her. "What was that for?"

She was tight-lipped and fuming. "So I am to be the prize, awarded to the victor like a piece of chattel—"

"That's what you are, mademoiselle!" said Theodore sharply. "When your father died, the stipulations of his will made me your legal guardian. Our betrothal gives me further rights to dispense your future and your dowry as I see fit."

"And I am to have no say—"

"No say whatever."

She glared at him, spots of color burning in her cheeks. "Then our vows, our love are as nothing. You are not my champion, but my keeper. I wonder you bothered to woo me at all."

"And I wonder why you do not bother to look beyond your own selfish concerns to the larger picture," Theodore retorted. "Mistra is the capital of the largest, and richest, province in Greece. There's more at stake here than just—"

"You talk of politics and I talk of love," she broke in heatedly. "I see I mistook the former for the latter. I see I have been a foolish child."

"No, but you are certainly acting like one now." Theodore gripped her by the arms. "You are willfully misunderstanding me. Try, Sophia, to see your future if I am defeated. As a prize, your future is protected. Otherwise, he can rob you of your lands, imprison you in a tower, and leave you to rot out your years alone—"

"Unhand me! I will not discuss it further."

He released her, and she stumbled back. When she turned from him and headed down the gully, Theodore went after her. He caught her from behind and spun her around. "It is only for your own protection, Sophia," he began. "You are—"

"No!" She swung at him, sobbing, but Theodore restrained her easily. With his arm around her, he glanced back at Noel and gestured for him to follow. Sophia wrenched away and walked on alone.

Aghast at the harsh one-sidedness of conjugal laws and rights, Noel joined the prince and shook his head glumly. "I thought you had more tact than that," he muttered.

"The lady is mortal spoiled," said Theodore coolly. "Sixteen and not married, that is what ails her. Worse, her father gave her too much independence. She expects to speak up and be listened to the same as a man."

"Why shouldn't she?"

Theodore scowled. "When I was a stripling and had not yet earned my spurs, I remember my sister being wed and bedded on her thirteenth birthday."

"That's too young where I come from."

"Verily? Let them go longer, my father used to say, and they are hard to train into an agreeable wife." Theodore sighed and plucked a leaf off a tree. "God's wounds, but I have been patient beyond what any man should have to endure. Her father bade me wait a year when I first sought her hand, and the emperor bade me wait another while I attended his court. And now see what we have come to. Were she my wife, the law would protect her as my widow. But as an heiress, she is so vulnerable—"

"I think she loves you a lot," said Noel carefully.

Theodore looked ahead at Sophia's stiff back, and his gaze softened.

"I think she's angry because she's scared."

Theodore did not reply. As they walked down the road to Sir Olin's castle, Noel watched Sophia wipe her tears dry. Her face grew set and cold and about ten years older.

"Aren't you going to talk to her?" asked Noel in concern. "You know, end this quarrel?"

"To what purpose?" asked Theodore haughtily, his eyebrows raised. "She is a spoiled child, who wants only the moonlight and none of the reality. I shall not change my stance on this matter."

Noel whistled silently. "Hell hath no fury like a woman dumped," he muttered.

"What say you?" asked Theodore.

"Nothing."

"Why do you talk to yourself so much? I fear for your reason at times."

"I said it's nothing. Forget it."

Theodore stared at him. "I know this look upon your face. You are troubled. Do you believe she will overset our plans? Fear not. She will recover her temper soon. Besides, what harm can she do?"

Noel frowned. He wasn't sure, but Sophia was not the sort of girl to sit by tamely with her hands folded.

"You'd better win," was all Noel said, however. "You'd better win."

Theodore smiled, his blue eyes serene with confidence. "Doubt me not. I shall not lose her to Magnin, for all my practical talk. He may be champion of the province, but I won three jousts at the emperor's court last year. Now tell me, Noel. Will you wager on a provincial baron or on a prince?"

Reluctantly Noel returned his smile, not wanting to jinx the outcome by getting cocky too early. "My wager is already laid," he said.

Theodore laughed. "So it is."

CHAPTER 13

Mistra made merry with fairgoers and revelry the night before the tournament. Red and white pennons fluttered over the steep, narrow streets. Faces peered down from garden walls, pointing and calling out at the processionals winding past with Sir Magnin's effigy atop a cart festooned with flowers and richly embroidered cloths. A varlet in livery beat upon a huge drum, and people streamed into the church where the competing knights had left their helmets on display. Ladies laughingly pointed out the helmets of those who had offended them in the past year, and those knights were struck from competition until they had righted the wrong. Comfits and sweetmeats were offered for sale at every corner. Peddlers sold strings of amber beads to blushing maidens hanging upon the arms of their stalwart swains.

Sir Magnin had opened his purse in lavish offerings of food and entertainment to win the townspeople to his side. Great feasting tables groaning with generosity filled the town square, and upon a crudely built stage a company of mummers performed busily to the delight of the crowd.

From the looks of the wine-flushed, happy faces that Noel saw as he rode through the crowded streets, Sir Magnin's plan was succeeding. Besides, thought Noel cynically, the man could always make back his expenditures later by raising taxes.

"Will you never lose your sour looks?" asked Frederick.

The boy rode beside him on a massive brown destrier that pranced and snorted with excitement. Beneath his cap with its jaunty feather, Frederick's face was alight. His eyes darted, and his head swiveled back and forth constantly.

"Mistra is a wondrous place," he said. "I have heard about it all my life, and now to see it . . . Noel! Look yon at that! Did you ever see so many people? Is that the palace over there? They say it took a thousand men to build it. Do you think that is true? How far is it to the ramparts at the top of the hill? Look! A pie seller. Let us buy our dinner. I am fair famished. Are you?"

"We should make our camp first and settle the horses," said Noel, keeping a sharp watch around him. He had long since given up trying to answer Frederick's constant barrage of questions. "Then we can explore the town."

Frederick turned around in the saddle to look behind him. "I vow I saw a fortune-teller back there."

"I wouldn't be surprised."

"Should I have my fortune told?" asked Frederick. "Father Thomas says it is wicked to seek to know God's plan ahead of time, but I think we should be prepared for what may happen on the morrow. Since it is so important, I mean."

Despite the fact that his nerves were stretched taut, Noel had to smile at the boy's eager naiveté. "Save your pennies, Frederick. Tomorrow will be here soon enough. It's Sir Magnin who should be consulting his horoscope tonight, not us."

"Even so—"

"No, Frederick," said Noel sharply. "We've enough trouble on our plate without getting in the clutches of gypsies and charlatans."

Frederick glared at him, looking sulky and mutinous. "You need not speak to me as though I am your dog, monsieur."

Noel closed his eyes a moment and counted to three. Blowing out a breath, he forced himself to adopt a conciliatory tone. "Sorry. I don't mean to yell at you, but if I'm recognized here it's—"

"You need not worry," said Frederick. "I am keeping sharp watch for Sir Geoffrey although there is no sign of his self-righteous face yet. Perhaps he's too pious to leave his prie-dieu at night and come down to the fair among the common folk."

In the face of the boy's ready optimism it seemed pointless to remind Frederick that Sir Geoffrey was not the only enemy.

Leon walked these streets as well. Noel couldn't tell if he actually *sensed* his duplicate's nearness or if it was just his imagination working overtime. But he dreaded meeting his twin again with an intensity that increased with every forward step of his horse.

Torches set on tall poles or in sconces bolted to the walls of houses kept the labyrinth of streets lit with a ruddy, surrealistic glow. Figures streamed from shadow into the irregular pools of light, only to vanish again. Faces, concealed by hoods and mail coifs, were only shadowed blurs. The pageant of heraldry, men and women in festive garments, jewels glittering from collar chains and fingers, silver trappings on horse bridles, the constant jingle of spurs, the mingled stench of horses, gutter dung, and pomanders filled Noel's senses. In other circumstances he would have drunk it all in like wine.

At the moment, however, he felt detached and far away as though he floated through their midst without substance. The old worry surged back, filling his throat, and he clamped his free hand over his bracelet to calm himself. He badly needed to consult his LOC for reassurance. With only twenty-four hours remaining until his time ran out, he still didn't know whether he could set everything right. Even if he succeeded, he wasn't certain the safety-chain feature would work. Only one traveler had ever experienced it.

Tolence O'Brien had been observing the Battle of Waterloo and making splendid recordings of the event when he was struck by a stray cannonball. Delirious in a field hospital, the screams of wounded men around him, filthy overworked doctors who had no awareness of germs or how infections were spread bleeding him regularly, Tolence had crawled from his filthy cot and searched the jumble of personal effects in the surgeon's desk until he found his LOC. The safety chain had snapped him home as soon as he held his LOC in his hand.

He later described the experience as madness, as being jerked backward through a tunnel where everything else hurtled in the opposite direction. When he returned in one piece, intact, and finished his debriefing, Tolence O'Brien resigned.

"Wise man," muttered Noel aloud. "But it couldn't be worse than how I got here."

"You said something?" asked Frederick.

Noel shook his head. He had to stop talking to himself, or the d'Angeliers were going to think he was nuts.

Although the tournament field had been set up across the river in the valley, the competitors pitched their tents within the secure walls of Mistra. To Noel, it felt more like a trap than a place of safety. He and Frederick followed another knight's entourage along a short lane to a rocky space where tents stood precariously upon every available foothold.

Frederick nudged Noel in the ribs. "We shall sleep vertically tonight."

Noel could not bring himself to smile at the joke. "Looks that way."

He glanced ahead, where a guard in Sir Magnin's livery was questioning the knight in line before them. The handful of d'Angelier knights behind Noel fidgeted and talked among themselves. They were along to spread word among the competitors that Lord Theodore was free. Tired mounts pawed restlessly, eager to be stabled for the night and fed.

The dread in Noel resurfaced. He glanced around, wondering if he dared slip off between the walls of the last house and the tent enclosure.

A squire walked by, water pails sloshing from each hand. He was puffing audibly. The guard did not even glance at him.

That's it, thought Noel. *Carry a bucket and you can go anywhere.*

He shifted in his saddle, loosening his right foot in the stirrup so he could swing down. His muscles—unused after seven months' layoff to spending long hours in the saddle—protested with enough soreness to make him wince.

"Ride on!" said the guard.

The entourage of destriers and baggage mules ahead moved on, and Noel's chance to slip away went with them.

"Damn," he breathed. His fingers tightened on the reins, and his horse tossed its head restively.

"Do not fear," said Frederick as they approached the guard. "Father coached me in what to say."

Noel felt no reassurance. He pulled his cloak hood forward to cast his face in shadow and halted his mount where the guard's torchlight came no farther than his hands and forearms.

"I am Frederick d'Angelier. With me are knights under fealty oath to my father's service, their horses, and servants. We come ahead of my father, Sir Olin, who will arrive tomorrow for the competition."

The guard said something to a scrawny boy in a herald's tabard. The herald consulted a list on parchment and made several rapid notations. Noel watched without blinking until his eyes felt on fire. He dared not breathe.

The guard laughed. "Your father is getting too old for jousting. Why don't you take his place in the lists and give the crowd a better spectacle?"

"I—"

"Ride on!" said the guard and slapped the flank of Noel's mount to jolt it forward. "Go to the left and set your camp there." He pointed vaguely at the darkness.

The d'Angelier train trotted into the tent enclosure, where all was purposeful bustle as knights and their squires made ready for tomorrow's contest.

"Impudent lackey," said Frederick, fuming. "As soon as I receive my spurs, I shall represent my family, but Father is not too old. He could outride that—"

"Easy," said Noel, aware of the silence falling ahead of them like a carpet unrolling. Squires looked up from polishing weapons. Grooms paused in brushing horses. Knights in long surcoats who stood in companionable clusters glanced up, and those at the chessboard stopped their play. Noel's instincts went on alert.

"I don't like this," he said softly.

Frederick's eyes were wide, but he kept his head high. His hand went to the hilt of his sword. "If they want trouble, I vow they will have it."

"Keep your head," said Noel harshly. He glanced back at the other knights and saw they were looking somber and watchful.

"D'Angelier," called a man in a blue surcoat embellished with brown chevrons, "you travel light this year. Is that your sorcerer with you?"

A sense of cold dismay crawled straight to Noel's bones. He shot a grim look in Frederick's direction and saw anger and worry mingled in the boy's expression. Noel swallowed. During the council of war in Sir Olin's chambers, they had argued over whether Frederick could handle this situation. Sir Olin and Noel had said yes, and Lord Theodore had said no. At the moment it looked like Theodore might be proven right.

"I keep no sorcerer for a pet, Mathieu Phrangopoulos," said Frederick. His voice rang out too loudly perhaps and held a hint of a quaver, but it was stronger than Noel expected. "I trust in God, rather than my horoscope."

Some of the onlookers chuckled, and the tension loosened noticeably. Noel realized Frederick referred to an inside joke at this knight's expense. It was gutsy of the kid. Noel smiled to himself.

"No," said Sir Mathieu, swaggering forward. He was a thin whippet of a man, bearded, with intense dark eyes. "Talk says that your father has fallen under a spell. He does not travel with you tonight, boy. Is Sir Olin indisposed?"

"He is well," retorted Frederick. "He arrives tomorrow with the rest of his train, and you may tell your brother so."

The knights laughed loudly at this, and one said, "The banty has fire. Hell's teeth, he ought to join the lists."

Frederick puffed up with visible pride. "And I will," he boasted, "once I am knighted. I'll—"

"Does Sir Olin's coming mean he will swear fealty to my brother?" asked Sir Mathieu.

Noel tensed again, furious at the man's insistence.

"My father is coming," said Frederick, cocky and insolent now. "He could have stayed home."

"But if he—"

"Politics are for Sir Magnin to discuss with my father," interrupted Frederick. "I have horses to feed and a camp to set up. Excuse me, sir."

He spurred his mount to a trot and Noel jounced along beside him. They held silence, not looking at each other, until they were out of earshot. Frederick wheeled into their campsite and jumped down. Only then did he crow merrily and slap Noel on the leg while Noel was still dismounting.

They looked at each other in the shadows and burst into laughter.

"I put him in his place, did I not?" said Frederick. "I would love to use him for a quintain. How he enjoys sneering at Father every chance he gets. Calls us country bumpkins and puts on his fine court airs. Oh, it felt good, Noel, to speak to him sharply and get away with it. Father will never stoop to reply to his barbs, but I say that—"

"He isn't the relative that we're trying to get on our side, is he?" asked Noel worriedly.

"Oh, no, not him. Sir Magnin has four sisters, and Peter Phrantzes married the eldest," said Frederick. "Did you see Sir Mathieu's face when I—"

"Yes, yes, Frederick," said Noel with a smile. "You did great. I'll leave you to this, all right? It's time I looked around."

"But you said we would explore the town together," said Frederick, his maturity falling from him in an instant. "I want to go to the fair."

Noel curbed his impatience with difficulty. "You'll see the fair. I won't be long."

He turned away, but Frederick caught his arm. "I do not think you should go off by yourself. Sir Mathieu can cause you mischief if your paths cross. Father said we should all stick together for safety."

Gently Noel took Frederick's hand from his sleeve. "Your father is wise. But I won't stray far. I'll be fine. And if I don't get back quick enough to suit you, start the fair without me."

"But, Noel—"

"I'll be all right."

With a smile, Noel moved into the darkness and made his way hastily behind a row of tents, avoiding the torchlight as much as possible. He found a shallow gully and dropped into it, threading his way through brush and stumping his toes on rocks unseen in the starlight. He winced, hating cloth shoes, and limped on until he felt far enough away from people.

Crouching in the bottom of the gully, he listened a moment to the crickets and the sound of his own breathing. Above him on the hill, the dark shape of the palace walls loomed against the night sky. Below him, torchlight twinkled and the lively sound of lutes twanging out dance music floated on the air.

"LOC, activate," he said.

His copper bracelet shimmered, and the real shape of the LOC appeared, its clear sides pulsing with the light circuitry operating inside.

"Acknowledged," it replied.

"LOC," he said, "scan internal diagnostics. Is return possible?"

"Specify."

"Voluntary return, dammit!" he said. "Come on. You know what I'm talking about. Chicago. Time Institute. Monday, May 14, 2503 A.D. You still have that destination code, don't you?"

"Negative."

His head felt cold and light as though someone had lopped it off and sent it spinning through the air. For a moment he simply sat there, then he blinked and was able to think again.

"Impossible!" he said sharply. "I've asked you that question before, and you have return time and destination codes. Scan safety-chain program and verify."

The LOC hummed while Noel wiped the perspiration from his face and put his hand on the back of his neck, tilting back his head to ease tension.

"Verified," said the LOC. "Time and destination codes for return in place."

"That's better," said Noel. "How about self-repairs?"

"Some repair possible."

The last time he'd asked this question, the LOC had said no repair was possible. Now, hope hit him like a skyrocket.

"Sufficient?" he asked eagerly.

"Unknown."

"Continue scan of safety-chain program. How much time remaining?"

"Running . . . program ends in twenty-two hours, fifty-two minutes—"

"Stop," said Noel, sweating. This was down to the wire. "Is there anyone on the other end? I wonder. Have the anarchists blown up the old TI?"

"I am not able to scan this material," said the LOC.

"I know. You can't get me back. You can't tell me how to fix you so we can get back. You can't even open a direct communications line to them because for all we know they don't even exist as history stands right now. So what good are you?"

"Rhetorical question," said the LOC.

"Yeah," said Noel bitterly. "What about it?"

"Rhetorical—"

"Stop!" He shoved his fingers through his hair several times until he regained control of his emotions. Stressing out wouldn't help. Besides, he needed to think how to ask his next series of questions without running the LOC straight into a malfunction warning. "Okay. Run hypothesis."

"Ready."

"If I succeed in restoring Theodore to power at any point within my time margin, will recall function? Can I afford to wait until the last minute with this?"

The LOC hummed to itself a long time. "Affirmative."

Noel grinned. "Continue hypothesis. Question. If I return, what will happen to Leon?"

The LOC did not reply.

"Will he die?" asked Noel sharply. "Will he cease to exist?"

"Unknown."

"Can he be brought through with me?"

"Possibility figures are seventy-eight percent."

Noel stared awhile into the night. He didn't like Leon, but he didn't want to be the cause of his duplicate's death either. However, judging from the LOC's scanty answers, Leon might just be forced to tag along in the return to the twenty-sixth century. Then the Time Institute could decide what was to be done with him.

All Noel had to do was make it through one more day, take care of his duplicate, and make certain Theodore won the joust. Right then he had no doubt of success. The pieces of his plan were all falling into place.

"Deactivate," he said and stood up to return to camp.

A figure detached itself from the shadows and leapt into the gully ahead of him, blocking his path.

Startled, Noel stumbled back and reached for his sword.

"I have an arrow trained on you," said familiar, husky tones. "Do not draw your weapon."

Noel swallowed and left his sword in its scabbard. "Elena," he said quickly. "This is—"

"Say nothing! There is a reward on your head. I want it."

Noel frowned. Sir Geoffrey must have been imagining things. Elena was no zombie. In fact, she sounded hornet mad.

"Elena," he said, "you don't really want to turn me in—"

He heard the dull twang of the bowstring a split second before the arrow hit him high in the left shoulder. It was either a remarkable display of skill in the darkness or a damned lucky shot. Either way, the impetus of the arrow fired at such close range drove him backward. He slammed into the side of the gully. The pain came then, hot and intense and deep. He gripped the shaft with his right hand and pulled himself upright although he had to lean against the bank for support.

His strength drained rapidly. If he was bleeding he couldn't tell. The very thought of tugging out the arrow made him sweat.

Elena ran to his side and turned him to face her. His knees buckled, and he slid down against the bank.

"Why?" His voice was a weak thread. He battled back the pain and shock, aware that he needed his wits about him.

She said nothing. There was brisk purpose in her hands as she felt along his chest and shoulders. She bumped the arrow with her wrist, and he felt as though all the cartilage in his shoulder was being twisted like spaghetti on a spoon.

"For God's sake!" he said, gasping. He caught her hand. "Don't pull it out yet."

She drew her hand from his and felt down his arm. Her hair, rough and smelling of grass and woodsmoke, swung against his face. She knelt before him, and her fingers found his left wrist.

He was going numb in his arm. Maybe that meant nerves were torn. Maybe that meant shock or blood loss. He didn't know or care. Right now, the absence of feeling was a relief.

She tugged at his arm. Thinking she wanted him to stand up, he pushed her weakly away.

"Let me rest," he said.

She tugged again, harder. Dimly he realized the bracelet was slipping on his wrist. She was trying to take his LOC.

"Hey!" he said sharply. He shoved her back. "Leave that alone."

She reached for it again, as silent and as determined as an android programmed to perform a task.

Leon, he thought.

The puzzle pieces fit together with a snap. Somehow Leon had planted the suggestion in her to steal the LOC. If he got the computer in his possession, there would be no going home for Noel.

"No!" he shouted.

Her fingers slid beneath the copper band. The light shock administered did not deter her. Noel drew back his right fist and socked her in the jaw. She toppled over and he nearly fell

with her. He pushed himself up, out of breath and shivery.
The fletched end of the arrow raked the ground, and the
corresponding agony made him groan. He had to get the thing
out, but not now. She might wake up at any moment, and in
this condition he was no match for her.

With effort, he made it to his feet and stumbled down-
hill toward camp. The stars overhead that had sparkled so
beautifully upon the velvet sky now spun and swooped at
him, making him dizzy. He staggered into a bush, and its
sturdy branches swayed beneath his weight but kept him from
falling.

He had to get to camp . . . had to hide . . . price on him . . .
bounty collectors . . . Leon searching . . .

Somehow he kept going. Sweat poured into his eyes. He
paused, swaying, to wipe it away.

The tent loomed ahead of him, the d'Angelier pennon hanging limply from its top. He remembered then that Frederick
had gone, but someone would be there to guard the horses and
possessions. A measure of hope sent him staggering forward.
His hand stretched out to touch the white expanse of canvas.

Someone tackled him from behind, pitching him forward
on his face. He barely had time to register that his attacker
was Elena before the ground drove the arrow clean through
his shoulder and snapped the shaft.

If he screamed he did not know it. Blinding agony convulsed
him, and he was helpless against it.

It took an eternity for the terrible pain to recede. He found
himself lying exhausted and limp. He was alone.

Elena had gone, and the sounds of a piping flute in the
distance floated shrilly above the laughter and noise of the
crowd. He heard the wheedling calls of peddlers. He heard
a woman's voice raised angrily after a cutpurse, calling on
people to stop the thief. He heard a groom crooning softly
to a horse, which rumbled and snorted in response. Help
was close, so close, yet he could not find the strength to
call out.

Possessed, Sir Geoffrey had said. Noel hadn't believed it.
He should have taken it as a warning. He shouldn't have let
his attraction to her distract him.

Easy to say now what he should or shouldn't have done.
Easy to say next time he would be more careful.

He blinked, conscious of the ground pressing into his cheek, and thought he'd better move a bit. Squirming about finally enabled him to roll over onto his right side. He rested, clutching his left elbow for support. There was blood now, the smell of it thick in his nostrils. He could feel it, wet and unpleasant, sticking his tunic to his skin.

Elena must have gone to alert the guards. After all, she had a reward to collect. But it seemed odd that she should have attacked him like a cougar stalking its prey, then left him here unfinished like this.

A sudden sense of foreboding filled him. Noel swept his hand down his left forearm. The bracelet was gone. Disguised as a cheap band of copper, it was a trinket of little worth to the local merchants. The idea of Elena selling it to a pawnbroker made him ill. He struggled to sit up, carried more on fear than strength. The LOC was all the lifeline he had left. He *had* to get it back.

"Slow down," he whispered aloud, sweat pouring off his face. The pain in his shoulder was brutal. His senses swam from the effort he was expending. "Think. You've got to think."

She wasn't going to sell the bracelet; she was taking it to Leon.

Come tomorrow night, Leon would wink back to the twenty-sixth century. He could take Noel's place, and no one would ever know. He could travel again in time if he chose. He could wreak havoc elsewhere in history if he failed to do so here. He would be gone, and Noel would be trapped here forever.

"No," said Noel, scooting himself along.

He reached one of the tall tent stakes and gripped it, groaning loudly with the effort of pulling himself to his feet. The ground swirled around him. His head felt as though it floated miles above his body. None of that mattered, however. He had to find Leon, and he had to do it now before Leon accessed the data banks and learned how to really cause harm. The isomorphic design of the controls mightn't stop him; after all, he was a duplicate.

Straightening his body took all the strength reserves Noel still possessed. He stared up the hill at the castle, its black crenellations outlined against the starry sky. An owl hooted nearby in the darkness, making a low mournful sound like an omen beneath the sounds of merriment and dancing from the town.

Noel told himself he could do it. He had to do it. But first he had to get his shoulder bound. "Cleope," he said, thinking of Lady Sophia's handmaid who had known about herbs and healing potions. "I'll find Cleope."

"Noel!" called Frederick from beyond the tents. "Where are you? Do come! I have found the most wondrous—there you are! Come and see the amusements offered. There is a knife juggler you must see, and a man who swallows flaming swords, and a . . . Noel? Is something wrong?"

He came closer, his footsteps hesitant, then quickening across the trampled grass. "Noel? Are you unwell?"

Noel realized that he'd started leaning over although he still clutched the waist-high tent stake for support. As long as he held on to it, he knew he could not fall. But having started leaning, he could not seem to stop. His chest hit the top of the stake like a pile driver, driving the breath from him. Then he slipped sideways and sank to the ground.

"Noel!" Frederick caught him and pulled him up against his knees. The boy's strong hands gripped him hard. "What's amiss with you? What's happened?"

"I—"

"Tobin! Armand! Fetch a torch, someone. Quickly!"

Others rushed to join them. The torchlight spread across Noel, blinding him as he squinted up into Frederick's face. He clutched the boy's arm and saw the bloody smears he was making on Frederick's sleeve.

"Deus juva me," whispered Frederick. He swallowed visibly, sorrow plain in his face. "You've been shot. Who—"

"Find it," whispered Noel. The torchlight was growing dimmer. He struggled to see. "Promise me you'll find it."

"Find what?" asked Frederick in bewilderment. *"Noel?"*

But the torchlight went completely out for Noel, and he could not answer.

CHAPTER 14

There was a lot of pain somewhere, and if he woke up he was going to feel it. Nevertheless, something compelled Noel to open his eyes. He saw nothing but dazzling brightness. Swiftly he shut his eyes again, but it was too late. A myriad of unpleasant sensations made themselves known, chief of which was a general state of sweaty, shivery weakness. He whimpered softly, shifting himself as though to escape the pain. Cool hands soothed him, and a soft melodic voice murmured in a language he could not understand.

He squinted against filtered sunlight, finding it less bright this time, and tried to sort things out. The hurt came entirely from his shoulder. He put up an exploratory hand and touched a smooth expanse of bandage. The aromatic scents of crushed herbs had an underlay of scorched flesh.

Cauterized? he wondered.

The cool hands caught his probing fingers and pulled them away. The voice murmured to him—gentle, female, and incomprehensible. He turned his head slightly to look at her and recognized those gentle features with pleased surprise.

"Cleope," he said.

As though his own voice unlocked a barrier, the world came into sharper focus, and he could understand her.

She smiled. "Noel, it is good to see you awake. We have been much worried about you."

He shook his head, too restless to listen. It was all wrong: his surroundings, the sunlight, her. It made no sense to him to be lying here on a cot under a pergola shaded by grape vines and roses. A walled garden about him gave the illusion of sanctuary. Birds sang from the delicate branches of blooming almond trees. Bees buzzed in the vibrant spill of pink bougainvillea. In a stone fountain warmed by the sun, water chuckled and burbled. The scent from pink and white flowers overflowing ancient stone urns nearby enchanted the air.

"Where—"

"Hush," she said. "You must not tire yourself. We are in the garden of Joseph the Moneylender." She paused, blushing. "My uncle."

"How did you—"

"Frederick d'Angelier sent word to me and I slipped away from the palace." She lifted his head and put a cup of water flavored with honey and lemon to his lips. Conscious of excessive thirst, he gulped it down and felt a little better. Cleope smiled and set the cup aside. "I would do anything for the man who rescued my mistress from that beast."

"Frederick," he said slowly, feeling tired yet certain he must sort it all out before he could rest.

"He is a good boy," she said. "Sir Magnin and that horrible Leon have men searching for you. They made all sorts of accusations, but Frederick was not frightened, and until they find you they have proof of nothing. We brought you here, where they are unlikely to search. They were very angry when they did not find you in Frederick's tent, but it availed them not."

Leon . . . men searching for him . . . Noel lifted his head with a jerk and tried to raise his left arm. The pain in his shoulder flared, and he sank back gasping.

"No, no," said Cleope worriedly. "Lie still, I beg you."

She wrung a cloth from a bowl of water scented with lavender and laid it across his brow. Its coolness felt marvelous on his hot forehead, but his distress was too great for him to care.

He pushed fretfully at the blanket. "It's gone. I've got to get it back."

"Lie still or you'll reopen the wound. Noel, no!"

She did her best to hold him down, but Noel gripped her arm and slowly pulled himself up to a sitting position. The garden spun crazily, and he thought he would fall off the cot. She held him tightly and called out for help.

"Lie down, please," she said. "You have lost blood. You are weak with fever."

"No." He pushed her away and lifted the blanket, only to realize he was naked beneath it. It was his turn to blush. "Uh, my clothes please."

"No, you cannot have your clothes," she said.

Frederick and two servants in livery emerged from the house and came down the shallow flagstone steps to join them.

"He's trying to get up," said Cleope. "Help me with him."

Frederick's curly hair was uncombed, and he looked as though he had not slept. He moved her aside and put his hand on Noel's uninjured shoulder. "You should rest," he said, "and give thanks to God you are not dead."

"I can't rest until I have my LOC back," said Noel angrily. He tried to shove Frederick's hand away. "Damnit, I must have my LOC!"

Frederick and Cleope exchanged glances. "And what do you want to lock away?" asked Frederick.

"Don't patronize me," snapped Noel. He rubbed his forehead fretfully, feeling as though his skull was going to roast. "You know very well that my bracelet is gone. She took it to Leon. You promised to help get it back."

Frederick and Cleope looked at each other again.

"The fever is affecting his mind," she said. "He needs to rest."

"My friend," said Frederick in concern, "it is impossible to find your trinket in this crowd. We can get you another one later—"

"There is no later!" cried Noel. "There is only today, and half of it is gone. If I don't get that bracelet away from Leon before dark, I am—"

He paused, breathing raggedly, too upset to go on. While he was trying to gather himself, they pushed him down on the cot and covered him. Cleope wiped his face with a damp cloth, and Frederick knelt beside her with a sigh.

"I don't know what to do," he said to her.

Closing his eyes, Noel fought off his exhaustion and listened.

"Have they not yet come?"

"No, and it's nigh until noon. The jousting is half-done, and I don't know what can have befallen them on the road. Turks, bandits, horses going lame . . . I think I should take the men and look for them. But Noel is in a bad way—"

"He will sleep soon," she said. "You do what you must. He is safe here."

"Yes, I suppose." Frederick rose to his feet with a faint scuffing of his cloth shoes upon the flagstones. "You," he said to one of the servants, "have my horse saddled. *Nom de Dieu,* but this is a bad business. Everything has gone wrong—"

"Master!" shouted a voice. "Master!"

Noel heard footsteps pattering across the stone paving and dragged open his eyes.

A man in d'Angelier livery ran to Frederick and bowed hastily. He was coated with road dust and breathing heavily.

"How the devil did you find me here?" demanded Frederick, plainly aghast. "Were you followed through the streets? Did you take care? God's wounds, if you have given us away—"

"Sir." Kneeling, the man gripped the hem of Frederick's tunic. "Tobin brought me from your tent to this abode. He twisted and turned us about through so many streets, I know not where I be now, but I beg you will listen to the message I bring."

"From my father? Speak it quickly."

The man rose to his feet and pressed close to Frederick's ear, murmuring too low for anyone else to hear. Frederick's face grew long with dismay and worry. Watching, Noel felt weariness seep through his bones. Something must have befallen Sir Olin and Theodore. So much for his plan to save the world. Now what was he to do?

Noel reached out and tugged a fold of Cleope's long saffron gown to get her attention. She turned at once, although her gaze lingered on Frederick.

"You must sleep," she said automatically. "All will be well."

"All isn't well, and it's getting worse." Noel propped himself up on his good elbow with a wince. "Frederick?"

But Frederick walked from the garden without looking back.

"Frederick, wait! What's—oh, hell." Noel gestured at Cleope. "Find out what's happened."

She gathered up her long skirts and scurried after Frederick. By the time she returned, Noel had managed to sit up and swing his legs over the edge of the cot. He rested, clutching his blanket to his waist, and cursed his weakness.

"What?" he demanded.

She was crying and twisting her sleeve into a pleat. "My lady is—" A sob burst from her and she buried her face in her hands.

Noel curbed his impatience and gently pulled her hands down. "Go on. Is she dead?"

"No." Cleope sniffed and wiped her eyes. "Injured. She was arguing with Lord Theodore and tried to gallop away from him. Her horse fell with her on the trail. She needs me now. I must go and tend her, but Frederick will not take me."

"You're needed here."

"She has bones broken. She could die!"

"Cleope," said Noel savagely, "there's more at stake here than a broken arm or leg. Is Theodore coming?"

"No. Frederick's messenger says they have turned back. Lord Theodore refuses to leave my lady's side. He is a good man, a true—"

"He's a romantic idiot," said Noel, then saw the shock on Cleope's face and relented. "All right. He's very noble, I'm sure. But he's needed here. He must challenge Sir Magnin and win today or—"

"Well, if a stupid joust is all you can think about at a time like this—"

"For God's sake, woman! I am trying to . . ." Noel found himself suddenly short of breath. He blinked and passed his hand across his face.

"Too much excitement," she said. "Now will you listen to reason and rest?"

"No," said Noel. "Where does Frederick think he is going? I need him here until we have finished this. Stop him, Cleope. Tell him to come back."

She looked doubtful. "Will you lie down until I return?"

He sent her a wan smile. "I promise."

"Then I shall go."

"One other thing."

"Yes?"

"You must make a potion for me. Something powerful that will give me energy and mask the pain."

She started to protest, but he gripped her hand.

"Please," he said. "It's important."

"It's foolish! My remedies are not for misuse."

"In times of emergency the rules change."

She frowned, horrified. "That is blasphemy. We must live according to the order we are taught by church and state."

"It's expediency. Look, we'll settle this in a few minutes. Just go after Frederick before he leaves. I can't do this without his help."

"What is it that you have in mind?" she asked suspiciously. "What is it that you plan to do?"

"I'll tell you when Frederick gets here."

She continued to frown at him while he adjusted the blanket and laid down. He was thirsty again. The sun hurt his eyes. He wanted to sleep for a hundred years. When she still stood rooted in place, however, he lifted his head.

"Cleope, go! Don't let him leave. Tell him anything. Tell him I am worse and calling for him. Do anything, say anything, but bring him back with you."

She took one step away and glanced back. Her brow was knotted with worry. "Whatever you are planning, it will get you killed."

She was right, but he wasn't going to let himself think about how crazy and desperate his plan was.

"That's my problem," he said impatiently. "Go!"

Shaking her head, Cleope hurried from the garden and vanished from sight into the house.

CHAPTER 15

If chain mail was this heavy, Noel wondered how men could endure wearing the suits of massive plate armor that would come into vogue within the next few decades. The clinging drape of the finely linked chains irritated him. He found the shirt too long and the leggings too short. The latter were held up by a pair of primitive garters that made him feel he might lose them at any moment. When Frederick pulled the mail mittens over his hands, Noel felt completely helpless, like a four-year-old bundled into a snowsuit.

"How can I hold a weapon without my fingers free?" he asked.

Frederick knelt to fasten the steel greaves to his shins and did not answer.

The argument was long since over, and although Noel had won it, Frederick still disapproved.

"It's wrong," he muttered, fastening the other greave. His words were muffled against Noel's leg as he fitted on a pair of knee cops.

"What's wrong?"

"You know."

A sullen Frederick was less than desirable company. Noel was having enough trouble with his own flagging courage without having to boost Frederick's morale.

"Stop sulking," said Noel. "We've settled this already."

"You should not compete. You are not a knight, and it is wrong to pretend. Deceit is the first step toward damnation. Even if you win, it will invalidate the—"

"I can't worry about that now," said Noel. He reached for the collar.

Frederick sprang up. "The breastplate first. Just wait for me to do it."

He buckled on the front and back halves of the steel corselet. Noel felt pressure on his wounded shoulder and sucked in his breath sharply.

"Too tight?" asked Frederick.

"Yes."

"I told you this would not work. The plate has to be snug or a lance can catch it and rip it from your body. Why will you not let me—"

"No," said Noel. "You can't participate—"

"I know more about fighting than you!" said Frederick hotly. "I shall probably be knighted by Michaelmas."

"Fine. In the meantime, no glory for you. Don't argue, Frederick. It's not to be, and that's final. I can't explain."

Frederick hesitated, then lifted the collar bearing Theodore's coat of arms—hastily painted by the armorer at Sir Olin's castle. Everything was borrowed piecemeal since Theodore's own resplendent armor had been lost in the initial ambush. Noel didn't like his colors of yellow and black. He felt like a bumblebee once he put on the long surcoat. The ends flapping about his ankles made him feel ridiculous. Frederick snapped the helmet to the chain on the breastplate and knelt to buckle spurs on Noel's feet.

Next on went the mail coif. It covered Noel's chin to the lips and the edges scratched his cheeks. He wondered how the others could stand to wear these things all the time. His head itched and while he was rubbing it through the links, Frederick buckled on his sword.

Noel practiced grabbing the hilt a few times in his mittens. They were clumsy all right. With these things on he might well drop his sword.

"How do I look?" he asked. "You have three choices for an answer: class A dork, class B dork, or the pride of Camelot."

"I understand you not, but verily you look frightened." Frederick's gaze met his earnestly. "Are you certain you will not have a priest's blessing? To go into combat unshriven is tempting fate."

Exasperating though it might be, the boy's concern was

genuine and well intentioned. Noel smiled and clapped him on the shoulder. "No, thank you."

"Noel?"

"Yes?"

"Father says that when everything goes amiss it is time to pause and reevaluate the situation. He says if God is against you, then stop and either abandon your purpose or go at it differently."

Noel wished he could follow that advice. Even if he got very lucky and didn't drop his sword, his borrowed war-horse didn't run away with him, and he found he had a natural aptitude for lances, he hadn't much of a prayer against Sir Magnin's skill and experience.

"Sir Olin is a wise man," Noel said. "If I'm defeated by circumstances, that's one thing. But if I quit now, before I've done all that I can, then I've defeated myself. I can't."

Frederick nodded. "No one can doubt your courage."

"Just my sanity, right?" Noel grinned.

Frederick smiled back. "I do not wish to unman you by saying this, but you are truly mad."

Noel pretended the hollowness inside him was nothing to worry about. "Time to go."

"Noel?"

This time he let his impatience show as he glanced back. "Yes?"

"I sent word to Father. He should know about this."

Noel shook his head. "You think he'll come? There's no point now. By the time they get here, it will be over one way or the other. Come on. I'm not going to miss this."

Before he went outside, Noel put on the helmet and lowered his visor. It cut off most of his vision and some of his hearing. It was incredibly hot and once he had a good dose of sunshine warming it, he would be a prime candidate for roasted skull.

Whatever drug Cleope had given him was working. Its taste was so foul, he almost couldn't swallow it, but now he felt pleasantly numb. If the sky tended to become a weird shade of pink at the edges and if sometimes his arms and legs seemed to float away . . . well, so what? He would pay the consequences later. Right now, the trip was worth the ticket.

The ruse of passing himself off as Theodore simply by putting on armor that bore the man's ensign seemed too simplistic to work. No one in Noel's own time would swallow it, but while men and women here might scheme and connive, they still apparently took coats of arms and insignia at face value. Frederick was not yet entirely over his shock at this duplicity. Noel decided if Leon could show these folks how to break a few rules, he might as well do the same. Besides, Theodore had started it by having Noel take his place once already.

Swathed in a cloak to conceal himself from the watchful eyes of guards patrolling everywhere, a tense, silent Noel rode a nondescript palfrey along the streets to the tent enclosure. Noel opened his cloak to show the emblems on his surcoat, and the guard waved them through with scarcely a glance.

Indeed, there were armored knights and squires milling everywhere in such confusion no one had time to be suspicious. Most were comparing wounds or complaining that the tournament field and tents should have been closer together. It was an awkward arrangement, mostly for the squires who had to dash back and forth for mislaid gauntlets or forgotten weapons.

At the d'Angelier tents, Frederick and the other squires set to work transferring Noel from the gentle palfrey to a massive war destrier dappled gray with a black mane and tail. The animal's head was nearly as long as Noel's torso; his shaggy feet were the size of dinner plates. Noel stared up at the creature's back with trepidation and barely stopped himself from asking for a stepladder.

"Percheron?" he asked, drymouthed.

"Yes, indeed." Frederick patted the horse's shoulder with visible pride. "Bloodlines all the way back to Normandy. He is a steady old campaigner. He knows every trick of the jousting field. Leave him his head once you start down the tiltyard. Do not attempt to rein him short."

Noel watched the brute prance around like a yearling colt while his bardings were put on. He might be huge, but that didn't prevent him from being frisky. Although horses were extinct in Noel's century, the Time Institute had brought a few specimens back for training purposes. Noel knew that Percherons were considered the most spirited of the big draft breeds.

It took two men to lift the heavy chanfron and buckle it on the horse's head. Constructed of wood and leather, it made the

animal fret and snap. Smooth mail and plate covered his chest
and shoulders, and his rump was draped with a massive leather
crupper at least two inches thick. Feeling as though the horse
was better protected than he, Noel wondered if it could even
move, much less run with so much weight to carry.

Once up in the saddle, Noel had to close his eyes a moment
against a wave of unexpected weakness. He wasn't sure how
long Cleope's opium mixture was going to last, especially
under exertion.

Handling the reins, Noel quickly discovered his mount had
a mouth of iron and the temperament to match. It was like
trying to ride a moving mountain.

Frederick climbed into his own saddle and another squire
handed him a bound bundle of lances. Another moved ahead
of Noel and unfurled a gonfalon of black and gold silk. The
wind made the colors swirl. Noel cast off his cloak and wished
himself luck.

As they rode through the town in their own miniature procession, people paused to look, then to point. Word flashed
ahead, and by the time he rode past the round Byzantine
church with its red tile roof and bell tower, and reached the
stone bridge spanning the river, spectators had begun to gather
beside the road. Many of them cheered, and Noel felt like a
complete impostor as he lifted his hand in return.

"Jesu mea," muttered Frederick as the cheering grew loud-
er, swelling ahead of them in a wave. "Do not open your visor
for any reason. I vow this will goad Sir Magnin like tossing
water on a hornet."

"Good," said Noel. "That's what we want."

He saw the field ahead on the flat plain. People thronged
the stands. Gonfalons waved in a myriad of colors. Sweating
horses stood tied to their saddles out of the way. Knights yet
to compete roamed restlessly on horseback, their visors up,
colorful pennons fluttering from their lances. Others stood
about, flirting with ladies in the stands. A boy and girl in
servant's homespun were rolling in the hay beneath the stands,
half-concealed by the cloths hanging over the support posts.
Food sellers hawked their wares from wooden trays slung
around their necks. The smell of seasoned goat meat in the
hot afternoon air made Noel queasy. Broken lances had been
thrown in careless piles. Five corpses wrapped in blankets lay

stacked for burial later. Noel averted his eyes quickly and tried not to listen to the buzzing flies.

Two combatants were in the tiltyard now, careening toward each other at full gallop, their lances blunted for the contest. They came together with a crunching smack that made Noel flinch. The crowd screamed in frenzy. One man in pale blue went flying over the hindquarters of his horse. He landed on his feet, staggered a few steps to catch his balance, and bowed in rueful acknowledgment of defeat.

Other onlookers, already losing interest, craned to see Noel as he edged his horse onto the field. A few recognized his ensign. Some rose to their feet. The noise receded for a few shocked seconds, then swelled.

One of the four judges in crimson gestured at a herald, who came trotting over to Noel on horseback.

"Your name, sir knight."

"I wish to make challenge," said Noel.

"We do no challenges today. This is a joust of celebration and good spirit, intended to honor our new governor."

"I am Theodore of Albania," said Noel loudly. "Rightly appointed governor of Mistra by Andronicus, your liege and sovereign emperor. I have come to challenge Magnin Phrangopoulos and lay claim to what is mine."

The herald's face turned as pale as his linen. "My lord prince," he gasped. "What—"

"I have brought challenge," said Noel. He gestured and a grim-faced Frederick brought forward a gauntlet stitched and embroidered with Theodore's coat of arms on one side, the two-headed eagle of Byzantium on the other. "Take my glove to Sir Magnin."

The herald swallowed and although Frederick held out the glove, the man did not take it. "My lord, I dare not—"

"What is this?" demanded one of the judges, riding up. He scowled beneath his crimson cap. "You are delaying the tournament, sir. Take your place or stand aside for others."

The herald turned in his distinctive tabard and murmured quickly to the judge. The man also turned pale. He glanced at Noel and coughed.

"My lord, we have no—"

"Stand aside," said Noel.

The two men swung the horses from his path. Taking the

gauntlet, Noel spurred his destrier hard. Startled, the old horse lumbered into a gallop and picked up speed as they crossed the field. Reining sharply before the canopied section of the stand where Sir Magnin's court sat transfixed with amazement, Noel flung the gauntlet with more force than aim. By sheer luck, it hit Sir Magnin in the face.

He slapped it away and jerked to his feet. Decked out in cloth of gold and saffron-colored hose, a feathered cap cocked on his long black hair, Sir Magnin wore a heavy gold chain studded with thumb-sized emeralds across his chest. His handsome face blazed scarlet, and his eyes held murder. "What is the meaning of this outrage?" he shouted. "You pathetic whelp, how dare you challenge me—"

Noel bowed in the saddle. "I challenge you to a fight to see who will run this province in the name of the emperor."

Leon, who had been sitting quietly to one side, looking gray-faced and ill, jumped at the sound of Noel's voice. He tugged at Sir Magnin's sleeve, only to be brushed off like a fly.

"The name of the emperor no longer matters here," said Sir Magnin.

"It matters to many," said Noel.

A flicker in Sir Magnin's black eyes told Noel he was right. Sir Magnin's position here was still shaky. Noel pressed the point.

"Is this grand tournament an attempt to create allies for yourself? Do you think you can feed men and throw them some entertainment and expect them to commit treason for you? Do you expect them to break their oaths of fealty to the emperor?"

"Enough!" shouted Sir Magnin.

"You are a dastardly coward without honor, a man who stabs in the back, a man who must wait until darkness to attack his enemy. Can't you face me man to man, in the open, for all to see?"

"By God, I shall," said Sir Magnin forcefully. "I vow you'll regret those charges when I ram them down your throat."

Noel barely listened. His attention was on Leon, searching for the LOC. But other than a huge silver cross slung around his neck, Leon wore no other visible jewelry. Disappointment surged through Noel. Where had Leon hidden it? It was all

Noel could do to keep himself from jumping off his horse and shaking the answer from his double.

"I'll teach you what honor is," Sir Magnin went on. "I'll show you who is—"

"On the field, sir," said Noel.

"This instant." Sir Magnin pushed his councillors aside. "Stand back. Stop gibbering among yourselves, and send for my squires and my horse! Move!"

"Wait, excellency," said Leon. "He is not—"

Sir Magnin's hand shoved him hard, and Leon went sprawling into the laps of several onlookers. "Out of my way, you mewling wretch! I've heard enough drivel about witchcraft and portents. Where are my arms?"

Ignored by Sir Magnin, who strode off the stands, still shouting orders, Leon picked himself up and shot Noel a look of pure malice before merging with the excited crowd. Noel forgot all his good intentions and swung himself from the saddle, intending to go after him.

Frederick, however, appeared as though from nowhere and caught Noel before his foot touched the ground.

"*Nom de Dieu,* what are you doing?" he demanded. "Running away, now that you've baited him like a gadfly on the nose of a bull? He will kill you sure."

Noel kicked, trying to free his ankle from Frederick's grasp. The destrier sidled, snorting, and Noel had to climb back into the saddle. "He's getting away," said Noel in pure frustration. "While I'm stuck with this damned joust, he has plenty of time to leave town."

"Soft," said Frederick, glancing over his shoulder to make sure no one overhead them. "You have begun this. You cannot stop it now. I shall go after this thieving twin of yours—"

Gratitude surged through Noel, making him feel light-headed. He bent over, although it made him dizzy, and gripped Frederick's shoulder. "Then do it! After him now, before he gets away. You've got to get my bracelet back."

"Yes, yes. I do not understand its importance, but I shall do my best."

Noel's gaze bored into his through the visor. He had to make Frederick see how vital it was. But how? The inability to explain frustrated him. He gestured. "Go then. Just go!"

Frederick gripped his stirrup and gazed up at him with open

worry. "God strengthen you in this contest. Do not fail us now. We have risked all on this gamble."

"I know," said Noel impatiently.

Frederick stepped away and gestured to the other squire, blond-headed and middle-aged, his weathered face set with stoic resignation. "See to his needs, Tobin."

"Aye, Master Frederick." Tobin spat on the ground and led Noel's mount to the far end of the field. "Ain't right to send the boy off alone into that crowd," he commented when they were apart from anyone who could overhear. "Magnin's brutes know whose side the d'Angeliers are on. They be spoiling for a chance to catch us in the wrong."

"Frederick can take care of himself," said Noel. He flipped up his visor and wiped his face, ignoring Tobin's alarmed protest. Snapping down the visor, Noel said, "Some water, please."

"The hell you'll drink any," said Tobin in outrage. "Lady Cleope said you were to eat and drink nothing. It will dilute the—"

"And what do you know about that?"

"Master Frederick gave me full instructions."

Noel glared at him, but the man looked stubborn. "The potion is holding fine—"

"Hush, sir, I pray you!" Tobin glanced about fearfully. "Let us have less talk of potions if you please. Do you want the lady burned at the stake?"

"No," said Noel, chastened.

"I should think not. Lady of mercy, do watch what you say. And nothing to drink."

"I'm thirsty," said Noel.

"Suck on your own spit, then."

A fanfare of trumpets kept Noel from retorting. He saw Sir Magnin coming onto the field on a jet-black charger, a white saddlecloth embellished with scarlet falcon heads flowing to the horse's knees. The cloth was whipped aside to reveal heavily embossed bardings, including a fanciful chanfron fitted with a mock unicorn spike. Sir Magnin himself also wore white and red, the same falcon heads represented upon his surcoat and shield. A red pennon fluttered from his lance. Long plumage flowed from his helmet, and sunlight glittered upon his steel breastplate and knee cobs.

The herald rode into the center of the field, and the red-cloaked judges took their places at each corner.

"Challenge has been made and accepted for the right to rule this province," bellowed the herald. His voice carried plainly through the sudden silence. "This will be a full passage of arms, with the lance, the ax, and the dagger." He hesitated a moment, and Noel saw Sir Magnin speak to him. "This contest is to the death. God's hand be upon you both."

A murmur went through the crowd. Noel swallowed hard and blinked fresh perspiration from his eyes. Adrenaline coursed through him like racing oil. He had to admit he was scared. He didn't want to die with a pole run through his guts. Trojan had shown him how to hold a lance one day when they were horsing around on the training grounds. In return Noel had taught him how to drive a chariot. He wished he were driving a chariot now, in a circus, with the crowds cheering for blood. That, at least, was familiar.

The herald went on with a fresh speech, outlining rules of combat and chivalry. Perhaps chivalry also demanded that Noel and Sir Magnin meet halfway and shake hands, but they didn't. Even across the field he could feel Sir Magnin's rage blazing at him.

He knew he had to keep Sir Magnin's fury hot to the point of recklessness, to the point of mistakes. That was his only chance against the man's superior skill.

Tobin handed him a lance. The yellow and black pennon flapped across Noel's helmet, momentarily blinding him until Noel jerked it free. He fumbled to get a grip behind the vamplate, cursing the mail mittens, and managed to jab his horse's side with the butt end. The destrier shied, nearly stepping on Tobin, and Noel almost dropped the lance altogether in an effort to maintain control.

Some onlookers laughed; others jeered loudly. Tobin calmed the destrier; Noel's face flamed inside his helmet. He felt like an idiot. He was certain he looked like one.

On the field Sir Magnin rubbed it in. With his lance held straight up, he cantered across the field, then put his horse through several stylish dressage maneuvers. The crowd cheered.

"Show-off," muttered Noel. But having Sir Magnin over-confident was almost as good as having him angry.

Noel deliberately fumbled more with his lance and nearly impaled Tobin in the process.

The man angrily slapped it away. "Watch your point!"

More people laughed. "Drunkard's courage. Look at him!" called one.

Noel started the destrier forward, but Tobin caught the reins.

"Settle deeper in the saddle, but keep your feet loose in the stirrups. Else, you'll be dragged when you go off."

"Who said I'm going off?" retorted Noel.

Tobin's cynical eyes never wavered. "See his breastplate? It's got a lance rest to fit the grapper to. It makes the whole breastplate take the shock, and not just his arm. You brace the end against your side; that'll give you firmer balance, see?"

Noel nodded, and Tobin sprang away. The destrier lunged forward with his armored nose outstretched eagerly. He swung around the end of the tiltyard so sharply Noel nearly tumbled from the saddle. He was having trouble compensating for the weight and length of the thirteen-foot lance. It was constructed of ash; the wood was not heavy, but balancing it was difficult. The crowd jeered him again, hooting insults freely.

"Keep your temper," muttered Noel to himself.

The destrier pranced in place, snorting and pushing at the bit. Noel tucked the reins beneath his thigh and at the herald's shout of "Ready" he lowered his lance diagonally across the saddlebow.

He was maneuvering the lance with his right arm since his left shoulder was stiff and bound too tightly to permit much range of motion. The weight of the shield, however, dragged heavily upon his left arm. Although he felt no pain, sticky wetness at his shoulder told him the wound had reopened. He disregarded the squire's advice to jam the blunt end of the grip against his body.

"Do that against a stronger man on a faster horse and you'll be flipped head over heels quicker than you can blink," Trojan had said. "Hold it loose. Let the saddle support it if necessary. Keep your elbow flexed. Before the fifteenth century it was all skill, not brute force."

The herald dropped his arm and Noel's horse sprang forward. There was no more time to think. He knew only the fear and excitement coursing in his veins. He heard only the thunder of the horses' hooves. He saw only the blur of color and motion as they hurtled at each other. He wanted to do something Trojan called the Bleinheim twist. It involved slipping the lance point through any slight opening between shield and saddle, staying low to catch your opponent's thigh. If you hit the precise spot correctly, the impetus and a slight twist of the lance would flip your opponent from the saddle every time.

Using the computerized quintain dummy on the training grounds, Trojan had a ninety percent score. Noel had managed it only once. After he cracked his collarbone by getting hit with a blunted practice lance, he'd quit jousting with Trojan.

These lances, however, weren't blunted. They were deadly sharp and if he didn't hold his shield higher, Sir Magnin's red-and-white-striped lance was going to spit him like a shish kebab.

They came together faster than he anticipated. The crashing impact of Sir Magnin's lance upon his shield was like being struck by a battering ram. Pain flared in Noel's shoulder with a fierceness that wrung a cry from him.

His own lance, held low and on his horse's withers rather than atop the saddle pommel, hit the inner edge of Sir Magnin's shield and skidded in toward the man's groin. The point imbedded itself in the saddle and bowed with a twang of stressed wood. It should have snapped, but it didn't, and when the point ripped free of the leather it snapped Sir Magnin into the air.

A roar went up from the crowd, and Noel's heart leapt, but Sir Magnin caught his saddle pommel and clung dangerously over the right side of his galloping horse until he could drag himself back into the saddle. He had dropped his lance, and his plumed helmet was askew, but he reined in his horse and wheeled around.

"Hold!" shouted the herald.

Noel's horse had already swept to the end of the tiltyard. It turned around smartly, ready without instruction for another pass. Noel sat there, noise and yells around him, and panted heavily within his helmet. Sweat ran off him in a river. His shoulder throbbed with agony as though a hot iron had been pressed to it. He gripped his lance in a daze, disappointed that he'd failed to unseat the knight and uncertain what came next.

To his dismay the judges allowed Sir Magnin another lance. Boos came from the crowd. Men stood on their seats, shouting with anger. Tobin handed Noel a fresh lance.

"This one is fine," said Noel.

"It could be cracked. You stressed it mortal hard."

Noel's lips tugged into a bitter smile. "Not hard enough."

"No, sir. Not hard enough. But it was a shrewd aim you took. I thought you had him split for sure." Tobin's eyes met Noel's. "You can't hold back when it's to the death. Go at him for the finish."

He sounded like a football coach on the sidelines. Noel nodded, and pulled himself together.

Tobin took away the old lance, and while Sir Magnin reentered the lists Noel's destrier pawed the ground. Noel felt the world blurring around him and struggled to keep his concentration. What he needed was a decisive unseating, but Tobin was right: he didn't want to actually kill Sir Magnin. He knew that put him at a disadvantage, but he couldn't help it.

He failed to notice the herald's signal and only the destrier's lurch into a gallop brought Noel's attention back to the matter at hand. Something had gone wrong with his depth-of-field vision. His lance looked twenty feet long. It wavered dangerously. He knew his shield was too low, but he could not raise it without arousing sickening agony in his shoulder. Sir Magnin crouched forward, coming at him like a hornet.

The crashing impact stunned him. His point hit Sir Magnin's shield square in the center and snapped. Sir Magnin's lance rammed him backward, out and over the saddle with a wrenching twist of his spine. Noel hit the ground with a thud.

He lay in the churned dust, wheezing for breath. His shield covered him like a broken wing. His steel helmet felt like a lead weight holding him down. Only the sound of approaching hoofbeats roused him. He struggled to lift himself too late to avoid Sir Magnin's lance.

It caught the edge of his shield and flipped it. The leather straps snapped, jerking Noel's arm mercilessly. The world went gray with a sickening wave of agony. Gasping, he could do little more than roll away from those deadly, dancing hooves. He groped for his sword, although the dim part of his brain still functioning told him he hadn't a prayer against a man on horseback, especially without his shield.

"Secondary weapons!" shouted the herald.

Sir Magnin wheeled away and handed over his lance in exchange for a ball and chain. He swung it a few times, making the heavy, spiked ball whistle wickedly through the air.

Noel pushed himself to his knees, but by then Sir Magnin was cantering toward him. Noel dragged out his sword and tried to lift it. The point sank to the dust. He planted it in the ground and started to use it to climb to his feet, but Sir Magnin was too close, bearing down on him like thunder.

Noel seized the long hilt of his sword with both hands and swung it up like a bat, pivoting on his knees as he did so. The spiked ball struck the flat of his blade with such a clang Noel feared the impact had snapped his weapon. But the steel held although sparks flew from its length.

Unbalanced, Sir Magnin turned his black horse so sharply the animal stumbled. The ball whistled mere inches over Noel's head as he ducked. Sir Magnin flipped it to wrap the chain around Noel's sword. He yanked hard, but Noel had been expecting such a trick. He did not resist; instead, he went with Sir Magnin's tug, using the impetus to gain his feet.

A cheer rose from the crowd, and it heartened Noel. He could see Sir Magnin's black eyes glaring at him through the visor.

"Fool!" said the knight. "You cannot beat me now. Why not surrender and end this farce?"

Noel bit back a groan. "Now? When I've got you right where I want you—"

Sir Magnin yanked his sword from his hands and sent it flying. The sun flashed on the blade as it spun end over end through the air. Noel heard the groan of the crowd.

Sir Magnin laughed.

It was a smug, malicious sound—the sound of a bully who can afford to play with his victim. Noel's temper flared. He rushed at Sir Magnin's horse and kicked it hard between its hind legs. With a scream, the animal reared. Noel seized Sir Magnin's foot and twisted it within the stirrup.

Cursing, Sir Magnin kicked at Noel but he was hampered by the stirrup and his horse's rearing. His spur rowel raked his horse's side, and the mount threw itself sideways in a twisting, bucking leap that sent Sir Magnin flying to the ground.

He landed badly, half on top of his shield, with his weapon arm twisted painfully beneath him. Noel dragged himself forward, knowing his time of advantage was short. Weaponless, save for his dagger, he drew it and struck.

Sir Magnin must have sensed the attack, for at the last second he rolled, bringing his shield up and over him. The dagger raked its hard surface harmlessly. Sir Magnin gathered his feet under him and launched himself at Noel, striking him with the shield in a short, savage punch that sent Noel reeling back.

Sir Magnin followed, his right arm dangling uselessly. Noel could hear the agonized wheeze of his breathing from inside his helmet. The fancy plumes were dirt-caked now and torn; his surcoat looked the same. He struck Noel again with the shield, this time knocking him down.

Tossing away the shield, Sir Magnin stamped upon Noel's wrist to hold his dagger useless and drew his own knife.

"Now," he said, panting heavily. "By means of force and lawful passage of arms, by night and by day, in secret and in open, I have shown my worth over you. I am ruler of this province, and I shall remain so as long as there is strength in my arms. Send your last prayer to God's mercy, Lord Theodore, for I have none for you."

He drew back his arm to strike the mortal blow. Noel braced himself.

"Wait!"

The hoarse cry was so raw with desperation it actually made Sir Magnin hesitate. Leon came running across the field, stumbling and staggering, his face drained of all color, his eyes wild.

"Wait, my good lord. I pray you, wait."

Sir Magnin drew off his helmet and flung it upon the ground. His mail-coifed head whipped back as Noel made a feeble move.

"I wait for no one," he said arrogantly. "I have won the right to dispatch this man. His life is forfeit to me."

Leon stumbled and skidded on his knees the final short distance to Noel. He held up beseeching hands, while Noel could only lie there on his back, struck incredulous at this unexpected intercession.

A squire came up with Sir Magnin's sword. He exchanged his dagger for it, wielding the broadsword awkwardly in his left hand. His eyes were dark with pain and battle lust. They held not one scrap of mercy.

As he swung up the sword, Leon snatched the helmet from Noel's head.

"Look at him!" he cried. "This is not Theodore of Albania, but an impostor. The contest is invalid."

Sir Magnin never swung. He stared openmouthed at Noel, and for once he had nothing to say. Others came up, circling them, and Sir Magnin's foot came off Noel's wrist. He backed away in sudden distaste, looking almost fearful.

"What magic is this, that a lowly varlet without name or training could fight me with such valor and skill?" he whispered hoarsely. "What ensorcellment has been cast here?"

Lord Harlan, the thin old councillor with the black hood tied beneath his bony chin, pointed an accusing finger. "It is said that twins are the sons of Satan. Burn them both before their evil falls over us all."

Noel managed to reach up and grab Leon's tunic in his fist. "The bracelet," he gasped. "You—"

"Let it be done," said Sir Magnin. "Burn them."

His voice was harsh and final. Guards shouldered their way through the crowd to surround Noel and Leon, still crouched together. Without a glance back, Sir Magnin left the tournament field.

CHAPTER 16

Sir Geoffrey, his thin face set grimly, took charge of the guards who conducted Noel and Leon back to the dungeons. Although he was weak with exhaustion and had to be supported by Leon to even walk, Noel looked around in search of Frederick. He could not find the boy's face among the crowd, which hissed and made signs warding off the evil eye.

Others ran ahead, gathering firewood, sticks, and dung—anything that would burn. By the time Noel and Leon made their slow, painful way to the town square, the bonfire was ready for them.

"Let us light it!" implored the crowd. "Sir Geoffrey, rid us of these evil ones now."

An old woman crept up and spat upon Leon. He flinched and wiped off the spittle. Noel stared at him, wondering what had made him change.

"The bracelet," he said beneath the noise of the crowd. "What have you done with it? Where is the LOC?"

Leon glared at him, still wild-eyed and frantic. "It doesn't work, any more than mine works. It's no good to us."

"It's isomorphic," said Noel grimly. "It works for me."

"Mine doesn't work." Leon was almost sobbing. "They're going to kill us. We have to—"

"Where is it? Damn you—"

The guards shook them. "Shut up. Attempt to weave a spell on us and we'll cut out your—"

"Hush there!" called Sir Geoffrey. "You men, line the prisoners by the fountain. Bind them. Sir Magnin is coming back

192

from the palace to witness this. We shall await his pleasure."

The crowd shoved a priest forward. The man's cassock was rumpled as though he had been manhandled. He clutched his rosary beads, and sweat shone upon his brow. His reluctance to approach Noel and Leon was obvious.

The guards did as Sir Geoffrey ordered. With his hands bound behind him, Noel hunched over to ease the torment in his shoulder.

"It's your fault this is happening to us," said Leon savagely beneath his breath. "You caused this. You stirred them up with your boasts and your challenges."

Noel looked at him in distaste. "Why didn't you let him kill me? You hypnotized Elena so she would shoot me, didn't you? Why not let Sir Magnin finish the job?"

"Don't you know?"

"No," said Noel blankly.

Leon glared at him in plain hatred. "Because I feel your pain. Because if you die, I shall die. Try as I might, I cannot be rid of you."

Noel blinked, and found himself with nothing to say. It made sense. They were more than twins. Leon, however repulsive and twisted he might be, was somehow a part of Noel. The reverse must also be true. It was a disquieting thought.

He frowned. "I was hurt before. If you're telling the truth, you felt that."

"Of course I did."

"Then why program Elena like a little killer droid to get me?"

Leon shut his eyes a moment. "I thought if I had your LOC it would protect me. But it doesn't. Nothing does. Why can't I be free? That's all I want, to be free of you."

"You must return the bracelet," said Noel. The expectant rustle of the crowd wore on his nerves. It was all he could do to keep his voice low and calm. The varlets still stacking wood on the bonfire were going at the job with an eagerness he could not admire.

The tournament was over. Were the people already so hungry for the next amusement they had to stage a public execution? He stifled his black thoughts about their lack of gratitude. The citizens of Mistra did not understand what he had tried to do for them, would never understand, even if he could explain.

"It's almost the end of the time loop," said Noel. He squinted at Mt. Taygetus, where the sun had already sunk, casting the craggy peak into dark silhouette against a golden blaze of coral and pink. "I am implanted with a command to keep the LOC on me at all times. It's a feature that keeps a traveler from going rogue and staying in the past. That way history is protected—"

"I *know* what it is," snapped Leon.

"Then you know that by nightfall, one of us will go back." Noel stared into those silver-gray eyes so like his own, yet unlike them. "One of us has to."

"Neither of us is going. It doesn't work."

"It does! Unless you've tampered with it—"

"I didn't. But you failed today, remember? The LOC won't send you back because there's nothing to go back to."

Noel felt sick. "And you're proud of that, aren't you? You *fool!*"

They glared hotly at each other while more townspeople crowded into the square and came out onto balconies on the buildings surrounding the space.

"He's coming anon," said someone eagerly. "Sir Magnin is coming."

Trumpets sounded from the palace gates higher up the hill. Noel turned his head to watch as the procession rode down the narrow, winding road, glimpsed in flashes through the trees and bushes.

The priest lifted his hand and started a nervous drone, *"In nomine patris . . ."*

"Give it back," said Noel urgently. "You must give it back."

Leon hunched his shoulders. "It will do you no good to have it now. We're going to be cooked. It doesn't matter who has it."

"It *does* matter," insisted Noel. "It—"

The blare of a horn, an insistent warning, cut across his sentence. A messenger galloped over the bridge and past the church, coming into the square just as Sir Magnin's slow-moving party reached it. People scattered.

"Sir Magnin!" shouted the man breathlessly. "An armed party of horsemen approaches from the southeast."

Noel held his breath, certain the Turkish invasion force had arrived at last. All his efforts had been for nothing. He could not stop the tragedy that would happen. Leon's meddling with history was about to have disastrous results.

Sir Magnin—changed back into his resplendent cloth-of-gold tunic and feathered cap, his broken arm bound in a sling, and his handsome face drawn into a tight, pain-filled mask—spoke briefly to the messenger in a voice too low to be overheard.

Sir Geoffrey spurred his horse away and dispatched someone to summon the garrison force. "Man the walls! Close the city gates!" he shouted.

People scattered, screaming and shoving in a mad rush for safety. But the guards around Noel and Leon remained in place, and the priest, gathering his courage momentarily, called out, "Appease God, good people, and burn these sons of the devil."

Sir Magnin nodded, his black eyes hooded and unreadable.

Noel shot Leon an exasperated look. "Can't you hypnotize these guards and—"

"It's not hypnosis," said Leon angrily. "I push upon their minds with—"

"Telepathy, then. Whatever," said Noel. "Don't be so damned pedantic. Just *do* it."

Leon closed his eyes a moment, then opened them with a gasp. "I can't." His voice was shrill with fear. "I *can't!*"

"Concentrate. You can't focus if you're—"

"Shut up," said a guard, shoving them forward. "Climb on the wood."

They hadn't even bothered to erect a pole for their victims to be tied to. Noel struggled up the shifting, unstable stack of wood and branches, wondering if they expected him to sit there tamely like a nineteenth-century widow in India and be burned on the pyre.

The priest darted forward and snatched the silver cross from around Leon's neck. "Blasphemer."

Leon said nothing. His face was chalky, and great drops of sweat rolled off his forehead.

Cleope appeared on the fringes of the remaining crowd. She was crying. She called out something, but Noel couldn't hear her over the noise.

A roar went up in the distance. He heard the sounds of fighting, and hope lifted him.

"Light the wood," said Sir Magnin.

Noel's gaze whipped around. He met those implacable black eyes for a long moment, then Sir Magnin's lips curved in a faint, cruel smile.

"I would have helped him achieve everything," said Leon almost in a sob. "My knowledge could have handed him the known world. He could have carved out an empire with me at his side. Why wouldn't he listen to me?"

"Prophets are never heeded," said Noel. "Shut up about it."

"At least you've lived for—"

"And that makes this better?" broke in Noel derisively.

"You might be grateful for my help."

"Yeah, instead of my head cut off I get burned to death. Big difference," said Noel. "You know this is going to be horrible. We'll smell ourselves burning—"

"Shut up," said Leon.

A torch was thrown at the base of the bonfire. The dry sticks caught fire almost at once. Flames and smoke burst upward. Noel struggled to his knees in spite of his attempt to appear calm. His heart was thudding hard against his rib cage. He looked at the crossbows the guards held trained on them and wondered if an arrow wouldn't be the quickest way to go. It had to be better than this.

He crawled over the top of the woodpile, moving away from the flames. Leon followed in spite of the angry shouts hurled at them by the crowd.

An arrow whizzed past Noel's ear, missing him by inches. He froze involuntarily, but the heat was escalating. He couldn't breathe. The urgent need for survival clawed at his throat, threatening to conquer his powers of reason.

He leaned over and shouted in Leon's ear, "We have to jump off together—"

"No! It will make us a bigger target. Jump in opposite directions."

Horses and riders came galloping into the square, closely pursued by their attackers. At once all became confusion, with horses trampling, women screaming, people running in all directions, swords clanging upon armor and shields. Through the hazy orange of the flames, Noel could see the pennons of d'Angelier and Byzantium flying boldly.

"Come on!" he shouted to Leon. "Jump!"

"We can't," said Leon. "It's too late. The fire has ringed us. God, I'm burning!"

Noel kicked him. "Jump, damn you!"

Eyes shut and head ducked to protect himself as much as possible from the flames, Noel leapt through them and felt the horrifying heat consume him. He landed on the ground and fell, rolling himself over and over to extinguish the fire in his clothing. The stench of singed wool and hair stung his nostrils. Coughing and half-blinded, he staggered out of the way of a plunging horse and saw Sir Magnin rein his mount around to flee.

Men in the d'Angelier colors of brown and crimson hemmed him in, and Sir Magnin reluctantly faced a rider in black mail and a surcoat of resplendent purple. By now the fighting was nearly over. Wounded men lay upon the cobblestones, and blood stained the water in the fountain. Riderless horses darted here and there in a panic.

Lord Theodore took off his helmet and the fading sunlight struck glints of red from his chestnut hair. Ablaze with triumph, his blue eyes swept the scene, then returned to Sir Magnin.

For a moment nothing was uttered between them, then Lord Theodore spoke: "Where is my seal of office?"

Sir Magnin's face twisted with defeat and bitterness, but he replied clearly enough, "It lies in my chamber within the palace."

Lord Theodore turned to one of his men. "Go straight and fetch it."

"Yes, my lord."

The man rode away at a gallop.

Lord Theodore returned his attention to Sir Magnin. "Your rule is over. Mistra is once again within the empire. Frederick, strike that flag and see that the imperial eagle rises in its place."

Frederick stepped forward, bloody over one eye, but alight with eagerness. "Yes, my lord." He grinned at Noel as he ran to do Theodore's bidding.

"These men here, my lord," said a knight. "They are bound up and about to be burned. What is to be done with them?"

"They are witches," said Sir Magnin. "Be careful of them."

Lord Theodore raised his hand swiftly. "Cut them loose."

"But, my lord—"

"Cut them loose! They are not witches, but rather my agents sent here to cause what mayhem and confusion they could."

Lord Theodore's gaze met Noel's as the ropes were cut away. He nodded, and although nothing more was said, Noel knew he had the man's thanks.

As soon as he was freed, Leon tried to dart away, but Noel caught him by the sleeve. "Not so fast. We have a bracelet to discuss."

They moved from the square, and people parted to let them pass. Behind him, Noel heard the orders being given to disperse the townspeople, to round up the survivors of Sir Magnin's force, to take care of the myriad details necessary in a change of power.

"And me?" said Sir Magnin's deep voice. "Am I executed in the morning?"

"Your life depends upon the will of the emperor," said Lord Theodore.

Noel glanced back. He had many questions. In whose keeping had they left the injured Lady Sophia? Had Frederick's message caused them to ride on with their fighting force? Would Theodore remember not to surrender to the Turks when they came up the river in a few days? Would the Milengi tribe be punished more than it had already suffered at Sir Magnin's hands? Would the rebellious part of the province swear fealty to Theodore?

His questions would never be answered completely. He could only consult the history texts to learn what had become of these people.

"We've got to find a hiding place," he said to Leon, shoving him along the steep streets. "Quickly. It's growing twilight."

Leon shifted irritably in his grip. "Let me go. I don't care what becomes of you—"

"You've proven that's a lie," said Noel grimly. "I'm not going to miss my only chance to get back because of you. Hurry!"

He quickened his pace, peering into doorways or down steps leading to shops lower than the street, searching for somewhere private. The keening wail of a grief-stricken woman rose upon the air, joined by others. There would be no merriment tonight in the streets of Mistra.

He saw a girl huddled in the crossroads of two streets. Her tangled auburn hair identified her. Startled, Noel dropped his hold on Leon's arm and went to her.

"Elena," he said.

He touched her shoulder, only then realizing she was weeping. She straightened on her knees to glance up at him, and he saw Sir Geoffrey lying dead there with her. The young knight's blood had stained her gown where she knelt. Her wild, vital face looked aged, and Noel regretted the loss of that untamed innocence that had marked her before. Her eyes were old too, and he did not think they would lighten again.

"I thought it was Sir Magnin you loved," he said, unable to put into words what really needed to be said.

"He never saw me," she whispered. "I know now that Sir Geoffrey always did. But it is too late."

He gave in to the impulse to touch her head, to dig his fingers gently through the thick texture of her hair. She wept against his leg.

"I killed you. God forgive me now, and you forgive me too, ghost of Noel. I did not want to kill you."

The lost note in her voice made tears sting his eyes. He looked at Leon, standing a short, wary distance away. "Make her whole again," Noel said urgently, anger filtering through his voice. "You did this to her. Put her back the way she was."

Leon shook his head. "I can't. I don't know how."

"Try."

"I *have* tried." Leon threw out his hands in a gesture of defeat. "Things don't always work for me. Don't you understand? I can't—"

"Then for God's sake stop meddling," said Noel, and his voice cut. "Leave people alone. They aren't toys."

He looked down at the girl and stroked her rough hair. She reached up blindly in her grief, and he saw the copper bracelet shining upon her wrist.

He gasped and snatched it from her, holding it up to examine it, afraid it might not be his LOC. But the metal warmed beneath the touch of his fingers.

"LOC," he said, relief and gladness filling his voice. "LOC, activate!"

The device hummed softly and shimmered into its true, transparent form. The glow from its internal circuits shone dimly upon his face and hands as the shadows deepened around him.

Elena looked up at him with a gasp and scuttled back. "Have mercy upon me!"

"It's all right," he said soothingly, unable to hold back his smile. He fitted the LOC around his left wrist, wincing at the sore stiffness along his entire arm. An entire catalog of bruises and aches were making themselves felt, but he didn't care. He was going home.

Glancing about to make sure no chance passersby were watching, he said softly, "LOC, scan data retrieval. Find Theodore of Mistra."

"Acknowledged," said the LOC.

Elena crossed herself, but he touched her shoulder for reassurance. Leon came wistfully closer.

"Theodore of Mistra," said the LOC tonelessly. "Governor of Peloponnese for five years, succeeded by—"

"Stop," said Noel. "Cross file. Lady Sophia."

"Lady Sophia weds Theodore. Bears three children, two sons and a—"

"Stop," said Noel. "Cross file. The Emir of Aydin—"

"Malfunction," said the LOC. "Override."

"Cancel data retrieval," said Noel quickly. His relief drained away. He stared anxiously at the LOC. "What is it? What's malfunctioning?"

"Override. Override. Time course ending. Prepare."

Emotion caught Noel in the throat. He looked at Leon, waiting for something, although he didn't know what. Finally he held out his hand.

"Leave me," said Leon, making it a plea. "I saved your life. Don't make me go back."

Noel lowered his hand, realizing the gesture had been misunderstood. "Very well," he said, although his better judgment warned him he was making a mistake. "But you must not tamper with events."

"How can I avoid it?" said Leon. "I can't dither over every move and decision, wondering how it will affect others."

"I don't think you can stay," said Noel, frowning. "I think whatever brought us here will take you back as well."

"Then I'll die!" said Leon in anguish. "I can only live here. Let me go. *Please*."

Noel hesitated, knowing only seconds were left. "I don't have control over this. I don't know what will happen."

"Take off the LOC then, and we'll both stay. I'll cause you no more trouble. I swear it."

"You don't belong here," said Noel. "And you know I have to go back. I don't belong here either."

Leon's face twisted. "Then go to hell!" he said and ran.

Noel started after him. "Leon! Come back! You—"

But his feet were dissolving. He felt the cool touch of recession as the time stream opened around him. He stood still, watching Leon run down the street and vanish in the twilight. A part of him could not help but hope Leon managed to stay and carve out his own fate somehow; however, he knew that Leon would only cause more trouble. How to fix the problem of Leon would be for the Time Institute to solve.

Elena rose to her feet, her eyes wide with fear and astonishment. She stretched out her hands to Noel, and although he tried to clasp them her flesh passed through his. "Good-bye, ghost," she called.

"Good-bye, Elena," he said.

He did not know whether she heard his farewell. He hoped so. He hoped she would have the good sense to keep quiet about her vision and not be labeled a madwoman for the rest of her life.

"Good-bye," he whispered.

Then he was sucked away into the time vortex.

EPILOGUE

Noel materialized with a blinding flash of lightning, squinted in an effort to clear his vision, and opened his mouth.

Water gushed in, making him cough and sputter. It tasted horrible, like mud and God knew what else, but it cleared his wits enough for him to realize that he was thrashing about in water running swifter than thought between two narrow dirt banks. Sweeping along with him were tree branches, tumbleweeds, snakes, and a dead antelope.

This was *not* the white, sterile, safe confines of Laboratory 14, where he should be.

Where the hell was he?